Where the Blacktop Ends

S.L. McPherson

ACKNOWLEDGMENTS

Cover design by Kristen Cox

My editing team for helping me with this story.

This is a work of fiction. Names, characters, places and incidents are a product of the authors imagination or are used fictitiously and any resemblance to actual persons, living or dead, business establishments, events or locales is entirely coincidental.

ISBN:
ISBN-9781719906906

DEDICATION

To the people who have encouraged me to write this story.
You know who you are. May all your dreams come true
for you too

WHERE THE BLACKTOP ENDS

CHAPTER ONE

A new day was just beginning. The sky was changing from black to gray. As Hank rolled over in bed his thoughts drifted to the dream that he had again. *When will I ever quit dreaming of her?* He put himself on auto pilot as he staggered into the bathroom. After a quick shower and shave he got dressed for the day. Dressed in his blue jeans and cambric shirt he walked down the hall to the kitchen to make a pot of coffee.

Ben was pulling up in his pickup truck as I filled my cup with coffee. Ben helps me run my ranch, the Rocking R Ranch. He is more like an older brother to me than a ranch hand. He smiled as he walked in the back door as he does every morning. Ben walked over to the coffee maker, poured himself a cup of coffee before he sat down next to me at the kitchen table. We discussed what chores needed to be done. It was my turn to go into town to pick up some supplies. Ben went to the barn to work as I headed to my pickup truck.

The Rocking R Ranch is a fifteen - minute drive from town. The ranch is considered one of the larger ranches in the area. It is bordered on the north side by state land. The east side the Smith property, on the west side is another small ranch, the Double T, owned by Trevor Thomas. The Rocking R Ranch supports itself from the horses and cattle that Hank sold.

After parking the truck in the feed store parking lot, I walked inside the store to place my order. Jerry stood behind the counter. I gave my order to him and told him that I would be back in a few minutes. I needed to go to the grocery store to pick up a few things. Jerry said he would have my order ready by the time I got back.

Since the town of Cedar Creek isn't very big it did not take me long to drive down the street to the grocery store. With my list in my hand I entered the store. I got a shopping cart and walked to where the coffee was. After picking up a few more things I headed to the one and only checkout line. Amy was working, as soon as she saw me she said, "Hi Hank, how are you doing today?"

As I placed my items on the counter I replied "I

am doing just fine Amy. How are the boys doing? "

"They are growing like weeds. They can't wait for school to let out for the summer."

"I guess school will be out in a few months. Those boys of yours got summer jobs yet? "

"Josh does, but Jake doesn't yet."

"Is Jake good with horses? "

Amy laughed and said, "That boy thinks he was born to ride. He wants to have his own horse but that is something I can't afford."

"I will keep that in mind. I could use an extra hand with the mustangs. I will be rounding them up and moving them to the ranch soon. I will see if he is interested in helping me out."

After leaving the grocery store I returned to the feed store. When I approached the counter to see if my order was ready I heard Jerry talking to someone in the back of the store. I walked out on the loading dock to see if my order was ready. Sam spotted me and told me to back up my truck he was just about done with my order. It only took him about five minutes to finish loading my truck with the supplies. I stood and talked with him for a few minutes. If you want to know what is going on in town, you go to the feed store or the Post Office. Sam was married to

Maggie who works at the Post Office. Between the two of them, the town didn't need a newspaper.

As I was returning back to the ranch I happened to see a car driving down the driveway of the old Smith place. The Smith place has been vacant for a few years. Joe Smith owned the place before he died. I wonder what is going on there? Maybe someone bought the place. It was rundown with no one living there. Whomever bought the place will have to put some money into it to make it decent and livable. The Smith place was a lot smaller than the Rocking R Ranch but, someone could do something with it. If it does come up for sale maybe I will check it out. Maybe, the new owner, will be willing to sell the place just to get it off their hands.

I turned the truck on to the gravel drive that led to the house and barn. I stopped the truck close to the back door. I unloaded the things from the grocery store and then drove over to the barn to unload the supplies from the feed store. As soon as I finished I went looking for Ben. I found him in the inside arena working with one of the horses. I leaned against the railing while he worked with Star. He was putting her through some exercises.

Star was coming along slowly. She was pretty beaten up when she first came to the ranch. She is a wild mustang hat was separated from the herd. She was weak and the coyotes had her down on the ground when Ben and I found her. She was in really bad shape. With some medicine and some care, she fought her way back. Star trusted Ben and I but she wouldn't let us put a saddle on her yet. She is dark brown with a white diamond marking on her forehead. She is getting stronger every day . She will make someone a good horse, but she still has a long way to go.

After watching them for a few minutes I decided it was time for me to get some chores done. I walked to the other side of the arena to the other barn. I turned on an old radio that was there on a shelf. Some country song came on while I put the horses out to the side corral so that I could clean out some stalls. I was deep in thought about the dream I had last night of the beautiful woman. She had been in my dreams several times now. Before I knew it all the stalls were cleaned out.

In a couple of weeks, we would be getting another horse. The horse had been injured in an accident and the owner did not want to get rid it. I received a phone call from the owner a couple of days ago and the owner is willing to do whatever it takes. The horse belongs to his daughter. He wants his daughter to be able to ride the horse again. I told him to bring the horse and the medical records.

It is spring and the weather is so unpredictable.

This time of year, there is a lot of things to be done around the ranch. Ranching has changed so much over the years. The breeding of the animals was becoming a science to get the best of the best, but working with the animal was still done one on one. There were still fences that needed to be mended and stock that needed to be moved. Some of the areas could be reached by truck, but some places you had to travel on horseback.

Hank preferred to ride a horse most of the time. He enjoyed being outside in the fresh air. He loved working with the animals. He loved taking care of the animals, watching the sick or injured horses get well again. He enjoyed the sight of new calves and colts being born.

The birthing barn had to be prepared for the heifers to give birth and one of the mares was going to be due soon. Ben and I were working from dawn till after dark. The days were not long enough to get all the work done.

I think it's time to give Amy a call and set up a meeting with her and Jake. There were rumors that Jake had been giving his mother a hard time. It had to be hard for Amy Watson to raise two teenage boys by herself. She could use some help, but she is the type of person who would not let anyone know. If Jake and his mother agreed, he would be working on weekends until school is out. During the summer months, he would work full time.

A week later I made arrangements to meet with Amy and Jake. Jake is sixteen years old. He is slim built with light brown hair and brown eyes. His height was just a couple inches shorter than mine. He was quiet while I talked to him and his mother. I explained the rules that I had laid out for him. He had to attend school and keep out of trouble. He also had to have passing grades. He was going to work long hours and I would pay him a decent wage. He would arrive on Fridays after school. I would take him home on Sunday evenings. If things worked out then he would work more hours during the summer. Jake said he would give it a try and would arrive at the ranch on Friday after school.

CHAPTER 2

Ella Smith and her niece Beth pulled up in front of a rundown ranch house with a barn. *What in the world was I thinking? I sold everything I had to move here.* Beth pulled the earphones out of her ears and looked at Ella and said, "You have got to be kidding me! You moved me half way across the country for this."

The ranch had belonged to Ella's late Uncle Joe. He had passed away a few years ago. An attorney by the name of Mr. Johnson contacted her to see if she was interested in the property. She had ended a relationship several months ago, so she decided it was time to start her life over in a new place.

The house was an old ranch house. The shutters that were around the windows were in need of repair and paint. You couldn't see through the windows they had so much dirt on them. Ella looked at Beth and said "Maybe the inside isn't so bad." When Ella opened the screen door, the top hinge fell away from the door frame.

Ella got the key out of her pocket that Mr. Johnson gave her. After she unlocked the door, she walked into what appeared to be the living room. The dust was thick on everything. After taking a look around it looked like there was a couch and a chair with a small table that sat by a fireplace in the living room. Someone had covered them with something. It was hard to tell with all the dust.

They walked into the kitchen next. It looked like the kitchen had not been updated since the house had been built. There was an old refrigerator that was left wide open. It had a small freezer in the top. The stove looked to be older than Ella herself. A small table with four chairs sat in the middle of the room. The cupboards were long one wall. It looked like they had not been painted in years. The floor was covered with so much dust you couldn't tell what color it was. What was she thinking? The whole house needed a coat of paint inside and out.

Beth walked down the hallway and found two bedrooms , a bathroom, and a small room that had a washing machine and dryer in it. She came back to the kitchen and asked Ella, "Are we really going to stay here?"

"With some work, we can make this place livable. Let's unload the car and see what we have to work with here, then we can go into town and get some food and cleaning supplies."

Before unloading the car, Ella made sure that the electricity was turned on and the water worked. When she turned on the faucet in the kitchen the water came out a brown color from sitting in the pipes for so long, but after a couple of minutes the water turned clear. It was going to take them a while to clean this place up. They went into town to buy some cleaning supplies and some groceries.

It took most of the day to clean the kitchen. They needed a place where they could cook and eat. Ella left Beth to finish up and she went to work on the bathroom. There she found a shower stall, a toilet and a vanity sink. What she wouldn't do for a long soak in a tub since there was no tub she would have to settle for a long hot shower to relieve the aches in her back and arms from doing so much cleaning.

On Monday, she had to take Beth to school to get her registered. On Wednesday she had her appointment with Dr. Stevenson for a job. Dr. Stevenson was the area veterinarian. She needed and wanted the job of being his assistant. Her phone conversations and emails that she had with him had told her she had the job if she wanted it. The pay would be enough **for her** and Beth to live on. That was the biggest reason she moved here, plus it was time for her and Beth to start over again and put the past behind them.

Monday morning, she drove Beth into town to the high school. The school was small compared to the school that Beth had been attending. After finding a parking spot they walked into the high school to get Beth registered. They met with a guidance counselor and Beth was given her class schedule. They took a tour of the school so that Beth would have an idea of where to find her classes. The school bus would pick her up in the morning.

The next morning Beth was dressed to go to school. She had her blonde hair that was just past her shoulder pulled into a ponytail. She was a little over five feet tall and had a slender build. But, looking at her you could see that she had already lived a life well more than her sixteen years. After breakfast, she picked up her iPod and her backpack and went to wait for the bus. *I hope that I meet someone that can drive so that I don't have to ride this stupid bus. Don't most country kids drive? I will have to find out where the nearest shopping mall is.*

While Beth was at school Ella decided to take a look at what was out in the barn. As she opened the barn door she heard it creak with age. She could see the dust dancing in the sun light that came through the door. The first thing that she saw was an old

11

pickup truck parked on the left side of the barn. The right side of the barn had a couple of stalls. There were a few bales of hay by the stalls and along the back wall. The barn was not in that bad of shape that she could see. It looked like it was in better shape than the house.

The corral beside the barn had to have a lot of work done if you were to keep anything in it. It looked like a lot of the post and rails needed to be replaced. Since they didn't have anything to put in the corral it would be one of the last things to be fixed around here.

She returned to the house and started making a list of things that needed to be fixed in the house . After looking at the list she decided to start with the most important things first. She needed to find a newer refrigerator, the one they had made a sound like it was dying a slow death. She just prayed it would last until she could get another one. She would ask Dr. Stevenson if he knew where she could get one

She drove into Cedar Creek and found the clinic where she would be working. She parked her car and walked inside the clinic door. She was met by a man in his thirties about six feet tall with light brown hair that had natural blonde hi- lights. He was dressed in a plaid shirt that covered his broad shoulders. The blue jeans he wore hugged his hips but, at the same time where loose fitting around his legs. He wore a pair of work boots that were well worn. He had a pleasant smile and asked if he could help her.

She put a smile on her face as she introduced herself to him. She explained that she wanted to meet him. To let him know that she was here and ready to start work tomorrow.

They talked while he showed her around the clinic. The clinic was bigger than it looked from the outside. He gave her a key to the front door so that she could open up the clinic if he was not there because of an emergency. Ella told him she would see him in the morning.

While she was in town she decided to walk around to see what stores the town had for hopping. Since there were not very many stores it did not take her long to walk down the main street. She walked into a shop that was called "The Sweet Shop". It was a small ice cream shop that had several tables with a few booths. It had a long freezer case that had tubs of ice cream in them.

The girl behind the counter that waited on her was in her mid- twenties. She had beautiful red hair in a ponytail. She had a very nice smile that lit up her whole face. Ella ordered a scoop of rocky road ice cream. She sat at one of the tables to eat her ice cream. She was looking out the front window and noticed that not a lot of people were walking the streets.

I know this is a small town but how do people stay in business? She talked to the girl with the red hair whose name was Brenda. She asked her how the town got tourists to come here since there were not any major attractions in the area?

Brenda told her that the town put on a couple of events during the summer. She told her that during the winter months it was very hard to keep a business open. A lot of shops had what they called winter hours. They were only open for a few days during the week, and closed earlier in the afternoons. Every year more and more shops close down. Some people started working out of their homes because they couldn't keep a shop and raise a family too.

When Beth got home rom school Ella went over the list that she made with her. They decided what color to paint each of the rooms. She also promised to see about getting a computer so that Beth could keep in touch with her old friends, and she could do some research on it.

Ella asked Beth how her first day of school went. Beth didn't say much. She just said it went ok. She asked her if she made any new friends yet and she said "No, I am not anything like these people here so why would I want any of them to be my friend." Beth left the room before she could say anything more. Beth went to her room and closed the door. Ella didn't see her again until dinner time.

During dinner Ella told Beth that she went into town and met her new boss. Beth didn't say one word so they ate in silence. Ella was thinking, *I hope that I didn't make the biggest mistake of my life by moving here. The town was dying a slow death. People were moving away because of no jobs. Beth keeps withdrawing more and more.*

CHAPTER 3

Hank laid in bed thinking about the dream that he had. He had another dream about her. The woman in his dreams was becoming a more frequent visitor. She was very pretty with long blonde hair and blue eyes. He knew that the time was getting close to their time when they would meet. He did not know how they would meet or when, but he knew the time was getting closer because his dreams of her were getting closer together.

When Ben arrived for coffee they decided to go check n the herd of mustangs that were not are from the ranch. The mustangs were in a canyon where there was some drinking water for them. He got his permit from BLM stating he could get his usual twelve horses. It was quicker for them to go on horseback than to go by truck. They went to the barn, he saddled Danny Boy as Ben saddled Brownie. They left the barn and headed northwest. After riding for about an hour they stopped on top of the ridge. When they looked down they saw he herd of wild mustangs. The mustangs were grazing n the canyon below. "They always take my breath away every time I see them" said Hank.

The herd was over thirty horses in size. They discussed which ones in the herd would e best to take. The big black stallion that led the herd had sired a son last year. Hank. was hoping that he would be able to get him this year. He was going to be as beautiful as his father. He was all black ust like his father. By the size of him he was about nine months old. Hank wanted the colt for himself.

Ben and Hank rode in silence on the way back to the ranch. Ben finally broke the silence and asked Hank if something was bothering him. Being a man of few words, he asked him why he would ask him that. "You just seem to be extra quiet today and you have acted like you have got something on your mind. I was just wondering if it was something you wanted to talk about."

"I have just got a couple of things bouncing around in my head. When I get a plan together I will let you know. *"How could I tell him that a blue eyed vixen had been taunting me at night. She is so beautiful that she has stirred up some things that have not been affected in a long time.*

Now, she was beginning to take over my mind while I am awake. How could someone do that when you haven't even met them yet? She is going to be a woman to watch out for.

When they returned to the ranch they rode up to the barn so that they could dismount and take care of the horses. After Hank had taken care of Danny Boy he took Star to the arena to work with her. Ben let a couple of horses out in the paddock so that he could clean some stalls. They had a lot of work to get done since they were gone for half of the day.

Before Hank knew it Friday had arrived. Jake would be coming after school and spending his first weekend. After Jake got off the bus he saw Hank in the paddock by the barn working one of the horses. He put his backpack on the back porch and walked over to the fence. He leaned against it to watch Hank with the horse. He watched Hank as he led the horse around the paddock at a slow walk and then worked the horse to a faster pace.

After the horse went through the routine of exercises Hank walked over to the fence and said to Jake "I am glad to see that you made it ok. After I take care of this horse, you and I will go inside. I will show you around the house and get you settled in."

Jake followed him into the barn. The barn was large and Jake noticed from the breezeway where he stood there had to be at least fourteen stalls. A man came walking toward them from the far end of the

breezeway. Hank made the introductions. Ben had told Hank that he had finished up and was going to head home. Hank told him that Mr. Davis was having his horse delivered tomorrow morning instead of next week.

After brushing down the horse Hank walked out of the stall. He went to get some feed to put in the feed bucket. He checked to make sure that there was fresh water in the other bucket in the stall. When he was satisfied with everything he walked out of the stall and closed the stall door.

He turned and said to Jake, "Let's get you settled in."

They entered the house through the back door and stepped into the kitchen. Hank took off his Stetson and hung it on a hook by the back door. Then he walked over to the sink to wash his hands . He stepped aside to make room so that Jake could wash his hands also. Jake got the silent communication and washed his hands.

Jake followed Hank as they walked down the hallway until they came to some stairs that led to the upstairs. When they reached the top of the stairs Hank opened the first door on the right. He turned to Jake and said, "This is your room while you work for me." Jake walked into the room and set his back pack down. "I'll meet you downstairs in the kitchen in twenty minutes."

Jake stood there looking around the room thinking, *I have my own room and I do not have to share it with anyone. This was better than room that he shared with his brother Josh.*

The bedroom had a large bed with a night stand next to it. It had a small desk with a chair in the corner near a window. He walked to the wall that had two doors together and slowly opened one of the doors. To his surprise behind the doors was the biggest walk in closet that he had ever seen in his life. Never in his life time would he ever fill a closet like that. Farther down the wall a door was partially opened, looking inside he noticed he even had his own private bath which included a shower, toilet and a double sink.

The rooms were decorated in shades of brown with a masculine touch. He liked it a lot, but he also knew it was temporary, just like so many things in his life. He better not get attached to it. He better get moving if he was to meet Hank in the kitchen.

In the kitchen, he found Hank with his head in the refrigerator looking for something for them to eat. To his surprise, Maria had left him some covered dishes with written instructions on the lids. He made a small sound that sounded like a chuckle. Hank had mentioned to her that he had Jake coming for the weekend. She had made them dinner. Hank took the notes off of the top of the dishes and turned the oven on and put the dishes in the oven.

Maria was his housekeeper. She was in her fifties and only worked Monday, Wednesday and Fridays. She cleaned and cooked on the days she was there. She did the grocery shopping every Monday. When she was there she was like a mother hen. She was always looking out for Hank and telling him things that he should do, like getting himself a woman and having a family.

Hank turned around to look at Jake and said, "You don't talk much, do you?"

Jake looked at him and said "Sometimes, when I have got something to say."

"Well I hope you start talking soon, because I would like to get to know you a little bit better since we are going to be sharing the same living space. One of the first things you will learn about me is that I do not judge people. The second thing you need to know is I demand you to respect me and listen to what I say at all times. You will also respect my property and all the animals that are on my property. If I catch you hurting any of my animals I will personally take you behind one of my barns and whip your ass so you will know how it feels. Did I make myself clear?"

"Yes sir."

He did not doubt that Hank would really whip his ass.

Hank set the table then the two of them sat down to eat. "Okay, your turn to talk. Tell me about yourself. What grade are you in and what are your plans for the future?"

Jake told him that he was in the eleventh grade and was majoring in agriculture. Someday he would like to get a place of his own and raise a few horses. They talked about horses for a little awhile. When he was asked about going to college he shook his head no. He could never afford to go to college.

After supper, they cleaned off the table and put the dishes in the dishwasher. Hank gave him the tour of the house. This was the biggest house he had ever been in. A person could get lost in this house if he wasn't careful. He showed him what he called a sitting room where he entertained guests. There was a large room that served as a formal dining room. The study was next where Hank worked and kept his records. There was also a game room with a large TV and a pool table. The last room was Hank's bedroom.

There was a stairway that went upstairs in the

front of the house by the front door. The other stairway the one that he used earlier that led from the kitchen area. Upstairs there had to be at least four bedrooms.

After the tour Hank turned to Jake and told him that he had some phone calls to make and he would see him in the morning. Jake went up the back stairway to his room. He quietly shut the bedroom door behind him. He turned the light on by the bed then laid down on the bed looking up at the ceiling. *I hope that I don't screw this up. I know that it is just temporary. Mom sure could use the extra money. This is also a dream job for me just being around horses.*

Ben arrived for his morning coffee right on time. Hank and Jake were already in the kitchen having breakfast. Hank was explaining to Jake about some of the horses that were there on the ranch. Some of the horses were boarders, some were there for rehabilitation and treatment. There are a few here for training and the rest of them I own.

The ranch also has twenty head of cattle that have to be taken care of. The herd gets bigger every year with the calves being born. Right now, I have six first time heifers giving birth soon. We will have to get the birthing barn ready for them. We have to separate them from the rest of the herd, and will have to move them to a pasture close to the barn.

Mr. Davis will be here sometime this morning. He will be calling me by mid -morning to let me know when he will be here. I already have a call into Doc Stevenson to come look the horse over. While he is here, he will be checking on the heifers and checking on Sandy the mare that will be giving birth to her first colt. He would also be checking on the two horses that were there for rehabilitation.

Hank asked Jake "Are you ready to get to work?"

"Yes sir, I'm ready." replied Jake.

After cleaning up the kitchen, the three of them headed out to the barn. Hank had Jake and Ben saddle up a couple of horses so they could move the heifers to the pasture closer to the barn. He let a couple of the horses out of their stalls and put them in the paddock next to the barn so that he could clean out their stalls.

As Ben and Jake rode out to get the herd of heifers, Ben told Jake a little bit about the Rocking R Ranch. "Hank's grandfather started the ranch with just a couple of head of cattle and a couple of horses. Hank's grandfather was part Indian and knew a lot about horses. Hank's father didn't run the ranch the way it should have been run. He was just about ready to lose the ranch when he got sick and died. Hank was away at college at the time and had to come home to run the ranch. It took him a couple of years to pay off his father's debts. He has been improving the ranch every year with the money he makes from selling the cattle and the mustangs.

Hank is making a name for himself by working with the horses that he has here for rehabilitation, treatment and training. He keeps getting more phones calls. I don't know how people are finding out about him, but he has done some really good work. The owners have been very pleased with the results.

There is a lot of hard work in running the Rocking R Ranch. If you stick around long enough you will learn a lot. The days will be long and hard on your body. If you have any questions don't be afraid to ask. Hank is a good person to work for and he will treat you right. "

Ben and Jake rounded up the heifers and drove them back to the pasture next to the barn. When they arrived, Hank was in the barn finishing up the stalls. He still had the second barn to go and needed to exercise the horses. It was past noon and he was ready to get some lunch.

Hank walked over to the paddock where the heifers were. He told Ben and Jake that Mr. Davis should be here in about an hour. He was going to the house to have some lunch. He told them to meet him there as soon as they could.

As soon as Hank hung up his coat and hat his cell phone rang. "This is Hank." It was Doc Stevenson telling him that he would be there in about an hour to check on the new arrival and do his rounds . "See you in a little bit."

After he washed his hands in the sink. He went to the refrigerator pulled opened the door, looked inside for something to eat. He wasn't a cook so he would have to settle on a couple of sandwiches. He left the stuff out for Ben and Jake to make their sandwiches. They came in the back door about ten minutes later.

Jake hung up his coat then headed to the nearest bathroom. Hank chuckled to himself as he watched Jake run down the hall. Ben hung up his coat and hat then walked to the kitchen sink to wash his hands. As he was making his sandwich Hank asked him how Jake was working out with him. He told him that he did well.

Jake returned to the kitchen to make himself a couple of sandwiches. After Jake joined them at the table , they discussed what chores were left to be done out in the barns. Hank's cell phone rang. After he answered the call he advised them that Mr. Davis would be there in thirty minutes.

Thirty minutes later a truck pulled in with a horse trailer attached. A short round guy climbed out of the truck. There was a young woman in the truck who didn't get out. *I will bet that is his daughter.* Hank extended his hand to shake Mr. Davis' hand. "I am Hank Robinson glad to meet you."

"I have brought Lady Jane's medical records for you. Her vets name and phone numbers are written down in case you have any questions about her care. The vet gave her a sedative for the ride over here. I better get her unloaded before the sedative wears off."

Mr. Davis walked to the back of the horse trailer and pulled out the ramp. He unlatched the doors and went into the trailer. A few minutes later he had Lady Jane standing next to the trailer.

Lady Jane was a palomino with a noticeable large gash on her right hind quarter. She also had scratches with some smaller gashes on her right front shoulder. Hank pulled out his cell phone and called Ben to come out of the barn. He wanted Ben to walk the horse around the paddock so that he could see how she walked and to help with the sedative wearing off. He also wanted her to get adjusted to her new surroundings.

Hank told Mr. Davis that he would call him with weekly reports on Lady Jane's progress. Mr. Davis handed him a check. He told him that it was a down payment on Lady Jane's care. The amount was what they had agreed on. Mr. Davis told him goodbye, got into his truck and drove away.

When Doc Stevenson and Ella arrived, Hank was watching Lady Jane in the paddock. As Doc and Ella walked over to the paddock, Doc was telling Ella that he was going to talk to Hank first before they did the rounds on the ranch. Hank turned around to see who he was talking to when he saw her. He just stood there and watched them as they walked to the fence. He couldn't say anything. It was like his mind and mouth didn't work. *It was her, the woman that has been invading his sleep at night and his thoughts during the day. He finally met her. She was more beautiful in real life. She stood about five feet four and had blonde hair. She had blue eyes and slim built with a beautiful set of legs.* Doc was asking him a question about the horse and was waiting for Hank to answer him. He realized that he had only heard part of the question. Hank handed him Lady Jane's medical records so that he could look at them. As Doc looked over the medical records he introduced Ella Smith to Hank. He explained that she was his new assistant and also Hank's new neighbor.

"According to the medical records her sedative will be wearing off in about twenty minutes. Let's take a good look at her while we can." Hank motioned for Ben to bring her over to them. Ben got a better grip on the lead rope so that they could get a good look at her. The large gash on her hind quarter was about seven inches long and about four inches in width. The depth of the gash was deeper in some places. There was some muscle loss and there would be some scarring. Doc ran his hands down her leg and said that everything looked ok and she should heal alright physically.

Doc, Ella and Hank walked into the barn so that Doc could check on Moondance. Moondance had a bad infection from a cut on her front right leg. Doc could not believe how fast her leg had healed. Hank asked Doc to check on Sandy to make sure everything was going ok with her pregnancy since she was due in about two weeks.

At supper that night Hank asked Jake how his day went. He told him that he liked working there. He was trying to do a good job. He could not believe how fast the day went by. It was already dark outside by the time they cleaned the kitchen. Hank told him that he would see him in the morning,

Jake went to his room and closed the door. After he took a shower, as he laid down on the bed he was thinking *I hope that I can work here all summer. I really like it here.* He closed his eyes and fell asleep.

Downstairs Hank was in his room thinking about Ella Smith. *She is so beautiful. I cannot believe I acted like some high school kid and didn't say a word. I was speechless. She utterly took my breath away. She had her hair in a bun at the back of her head. I wonder how long her hair is. Her eyes are as blue as the sky on a summer day. She was slender with long beautiful legs under a pair of jeans that she wore. I am really going to have to be careful around her.*

CHAPTER 4

By the time Ella got home it was dinner time. Beth had made dinner for them. Beth was really becoming a good cook. Ella never knew what she would be having for dinner .The rule was that whoever cooked didn't have to clean up the kitchen . When Ella was home she cooked and when she was running late Beth cooked.

Ella told Beth that she had met their neighbor today. She told Beth that he was a man of few words. He did not talk much. *But he sure did know how to wear a pair of jeans. He had broad shoulders and a slim waist. His jeans covered a pair of muscular legs and he had a nice butt. He also had a smile that could stop a woman in her tracks. Real nice eye candy to look at. Mental note to self - BEWARE OF MAN. LOOK BUT DO NOT TOUCH. Don't need another man to break your heart!*

She told her the Rocking R Ranch was larger than theirs, and it looked like there were several horses there. There were some cattle there also. She didn't know how many men worked there.

Since Ella did not have to work tomorrow she asked Beth if she would like to go shopping with her. Beth asked her if she found out where he nearest mall was. She told her that she did not know where the mall was. "Actually, I thought we would go and buy a couple of gallons of paint so that we could start painting the walls in here."

Beth replied "That doesn't sound like a lot of fun, but since it will get me out of this house I will go with you. Do you think we could do some other shopping while we are out? I have a list of things that I would like to get."

"We will see how much the paint is going to cost first. Then we will see if we can pick up a couple things on your list."

"What did you find out about getting us a refrigerator? Did you ask Dr. Stevenson where we could find one?

"Yes, I did ask him where we could find one. He knew of someone who was getting rid of one and told me he would let me know in a couple of days. If not, he said there was a place in town that sold **second** hand furniture. We might be able to find one there. We can also check out the furniture while we are there to see what we can get."

Beth went to her room leaving Ella alone in the kitchen. Her thoughts wandered to her neighbor Hank Robinson as she cleaned up the kitchen. *His hair is almost black in color. His blue eyes were so light in color that they almost looked gray. His skin coloring indicated that he worked outside and that he was part Indian. The high cheekbones and a slightly crooked nose worked to make him even more handsome.* He didn't say anything to her all the time she and Doc where there. *That is just fine with me!*

Hank and Jake worked on getting the birthing barn ready for the heifers and Sandy. They worked all morning on it. That afternoon they rode out to check the fence line on the east side of the ranch. Jake was riding Black Jack to give him some exercise. This was the first time someone had put a saddle on him since he got burned. Jake asked Hank "Why does Black Jack have his own corral with a half- built barn on it. It has a top and sides but no front or back on it?"

"Black Jack was in a barn when it caught on fire. He was hit with a burning beam which is why he has all the scars on his body and legs. He survived the fire and was brought here. I will coach him back into a barn again. But, right now he won't go inside a building. We'll give him some time and he will come around."

After supper Hank took Jake home Before Jake got out of the truck he handed him some money for his pay. He also gave him some extra money and told him to get himself a pair of boots and a couple changes of clothes that he could leave at the ranch. He would have Maria wash his clothes. He didn't want Amy to have to wash his work clothes as they would get real dirty from time to time.

He told him that he did a good job. Next weekend if the weather held out they would go round up the mustangs. He wanted to get them before they decided to move out of the canyon. There was a lot of work to be done on the ranch in the next few weeks. Jake couldn't wait until next Friday.

Before Hank went to bed he went out to the barn to check on Lady Jane one more time. When he reached the barn door he could hear one of the horses making a sound like it was frightened. Hank walked to Lady Jane's stall. She was pawing at the floor and was acting kind of strange. When he opened the stall door she backed away to the far side of the stall. He started talking to her in a comforting voice trying to calm her and let her know that she was safe. He ran his hands down the side of her neck. He was asking her what was upsetting her when he heard a voice behind him.

"She is not accustomed to spirits. I am something that she sees but does not understand."

"Great Grandfather it has been a while since you have been to visit me. I have missed you. You normally visit me in my dreams."

"Lady Jane will need one of your special poultices to help with her healing and with her pain. Have you noticed how she keeps the weight off her right hind leg?"

"I will make one and put it on her. Have you noticed how Black Jack is coming along? He has healed nicely. The poultice you told me to make for him worked well."

"You are doing a good job with these horses. They trust you. You get to know them and their needs. You make them well again."

"You have taught me well Great Grandfather. I try to make them well, but I do not know what happens to them after they leave here. They have to trust their owners again. Maybe I should check up on a couple of them just for peace of mind."

"They are all doing well. You are making a name for yourself. They are saying you are one of the great healers with horses."

"I still have dreams for the ranch. The money that I get from treating the horses helps me to improve the ranch. I love getting to know the horses and working with them."

"Just remember some things are not what they seem."

Great Grandfather left me to think about what he had said . Lady Jane calmed down after the poultice was applied to the wound on her hind quarter. I talked to her for a while to reassure her that she would be alright.

The next couple of days went by fast. We got the heifers into the birthing barn. Doc and Ella had come to the ranch to check on them again. Doc had said that the calves would be born within the next week. They would be back in a couple of days to check on them, if anything should happen to call him.

By Thursday night the first calf was ready to be born. A call was made to Doc and he told Hank that he was busy at another farm. He would call Ella and have her come over to check on things. She arrived at Hank's about twenty minutes later.

Ella went into the stall where the heifer was in

labor to check on the contractions and to see her progress. She asked Hank if he had a birthing tub with supplies in it. He looked at Ella and went to grab the tub and put it in the stall with her. "How much longer do you think it is going to be before she gives birth?"

"Her contractions are steady and strong; it won't be too much longer."

"I am going to go to the house and fix some coffee. Would you like a cup while we wait?"

"Yes, that would be nice. I take my coffee with a touch of cream."

Hank left to get the coffee. While he was gone she checked on a couple of the other heifers that were in the barn. There were two more heifers in labor. The heifers were all bred at the same time so they should all give birth in the next couple of days. It looked like Doc or her were going to be spending a lot of time here checking on everything and giving shots to the new calves.

When Hank returned with the mugs of coffee he found Ella in the same stall as when he left. She walked over to him and took the coffee that he handed her. Hank noticed that she had her hair up in one of those bun things that women wear. She was wearing jeans and had a long sleeve top on with a scrub top over it. As she turned away from him she told him that two more heifers were in labor. The birthing barn would have new calves filling it in the next couple of days.

"Ella, will you be here on Saturday?" asked Hank

She took a quick look over her shoulder and told him "I will be here with Doc. Why?" She looked at Hank. "Look cowboy, if you are thinking about asking me out, save your breath. I don't date."

"No, that is not why I wanted to know, but thanks for the information. I am going to round up the mustangs on Saturday morning and I just wanted to make sure that someone was going to be here with the heifers if need be. We should be back by late morning or early afternoon."

"I can plan to check on them Saturday morning if you like."

"Yes, I would like that. Now, if you will excuse me, I have some work to get done and I will check back with you in a little while."

He turned and walked out of the birthing barn. As he was walking to the barn to check on Lady Jane, he was thinking *I would love to let her hair down to see how long it is. I bet it would feel like silk running through my fingers.*

Lady Jane was very quiet in her stall tonight. The

other horses acknowledged him and begged for attention as he walked by their stalls. He talked to them all just like they were people. Hank walked into Lady Jane's stall. He talked to her as he ran his hand down her neck and back to her right hind quarter to look at the gash there. It was looking better since she arrived here. "I 'll put another bandage with medicine on tonight. It will help you heal girl. It will also take some of the pain away. You will be as good as new before we know it. I don' t know what kind of accident you were in, but I am sure it wasn't all your fault. I am going to call your vet to see what he can tell me."

Hank took care of Lady Jane. She seemed a little more relaxed when he walked out of her stall. When he reached the barn doors he turned and said, "Good night everyone," as he turned off the lights. He then went to check on Black Jack.

When he returned to the birthing barn to see how things were going, he found Ella in the stall with the heifer. She was talking to the heifer telling her it was time. She checked her one more time and said, "I can see the legs coming, that's it girl you are doing good." In the next ten minutes, the calf was born and the mother was doing her thing with her newborn. She cut the cord and put a clamp on the newborn.

She didn't hear Hank come into the barn." You are good with animals. I can see why you chose the profession that you are in."

"Yes, I do love animals, and it is a job that has a lot of rewards to it. I hear that you are really good with horses. Doc speaks very highly of you."

"I have worked with Doc for quite a few years. He wants to know how I heal the horses so fast. Talking about horses, do you like to ride? I would like to take you for a ride sometime."

"I do like to ride and I have not had a chance to ride for a couple of years. I would like to go for a ride with you sometime."

Her cell phone rang. "Yes, I will be done here in a few minutes. I have to check on a couple of heifers and then I will come home to eat."

He told her that he would clean out the stall and put fresh straw down. She took off her protective outfit and put them in the birthing tub with the gloves that she wore. She checked on the two heifers, they were progressing nicely. She told Hank that she would check in with him in a couple of hours. He watched her exit the barn. *She really knows how to wear a pair of jeans. I think the woman would look good in anything. She is just so beautiful. I wonder how long her hair is.*

Hank was just returning to the birthing barn when his cell phone rang. It was Ella checking in to see how the heifers were doing. "I'm on my way to the barn now to check on them, give me a few minutes and I will call you back and let you know."

A few minutes later he called her back and told her what he thought. She told him what to look for and she told him she would be there in an hour. *This is going to be a long night but it will be worth it just to see her. She is so beautiful.*

The night was so quiet that he heard Ella pull up in her car an hour later. He had already put the birthing tubs in the stalls. He heard her walk toward him. He could feel how close she was to him. He could also smell her. He loved her smell, it was sweet and fresh smelling. She must have taken a shower while she was gone.

She walked into one of the stalls to check on the first heifer. When she finished examining it she would then check on the other one. Hank just stood there watching her. He never said a word to her. He couldn't because his senses were working overtime, taking in everything about her. The way she moved her body, the way she tilted her head and the expressions on her face as she worked.

To break the silence she asked him, "How many head of cattle do you have? How does your cattle operation work?"

"I have twenty head right now. I will sell at least six to ten head this year depending on my buyers I'm am in search of a good seed bull to breed better cattle. I'm also doing research on I what to feed them to make them leaner and healthier for people to eat. In a couple of years, I hope to double the size of my herd."

"How many men do you have to help you here on your ranch?"

"Ben and I do most of the work. I have just hired a part time young man named Jake to help me on weekends and I will work him all summer. I will also hire a couple of young men to help me this summer. "

"How young are these men and where do you find them?"

"Actually, they are in their late teens, and they are having problems at home or they just want to have experience with horses. I hear about them from people that I know. Working here gives them the self confidence that they need. It also teaches them to work in a group and by themselves. I don't allow them to drink, smoke, or do drugs. They leave here a different person. I want to think a better person.

Everyone benefits from them being here."

"How do the mustangs fit into all of this?"

"I get a permit every year to get the mustangs. I will bring in the buyers to buy them. They will take them and train them. Some will stay here to be trained. The ones that don't get sold will stay here and I will keep them. So far, I am lucky if I get to keep one. I do have my eye on one this year that I want to keep."

"It sounds like you have a nice operation going on here. You do good things here, not just with the animals, but with people too."

"This ranch is a work in progress. I still have a long way to go. It belongs to me and I love what I do here and that helps."

He stayed out in the barn with her and two calves were born around midnight. She checked on the heifers one more time before she went home. He cleaned out the stalls and then went to the house to get some sleep. Morning would be here soon.

When the new day was beginning, Hank was thinking *I would love to touch that woman's hair just to run my fingers through it. She sure is beautiful, and she must have someone waiting for her at home. I didn't notice a wedding ring; maybe she just has a boyfriend. What a lucky man.*

CHAPTER 5

On Saturday morning Hank and Jake were in the kitchen waiting for Ben to arrive. Hank was drinking a cup of coffee and talking to Jake about how they were going to get the mustangs. They would be going on horseback and driving them to the east pasture. He handed Jake a cell phone. "You need to carry this all the time. I want you to be able to get in touch with me at any time. I am here for you, so do not be afraid to call me. I have my number already programmed into the phone. The phone will work pretty much all over this ranch.

"We will get the horses fed and put in the paddock next to the barn since it is going to be a nice day. We will get as many chores done as we can before we have to leave. "

Ben arrived by mid -morning. Right behind him was another truck with a horse trailer attached. Hank and Jake walked out of the barn to meet the guys. After the four men saddled up they headed northeast to the canyon.

As they sat on top of the ridge looking down on the horses they decided on a plan to get the horses that they wanted. As soon as the black stallion saw them he let out a loud whining noise as he rose up on his hind legs. He started to move his herd. The guys had to move fast before the stallion got them out of the canyon. They rode down into the canyon.

Hank and Ben tried to separate the herd while Jake and Johnny tried to keep the horses from leaving the canyon by circling them back toward the canyon. The black stallion let out a screaming sound calling to his mares to follow him. It took them awhile to get the herd that they wanted. Hank made sure that he got the stallion's colt . He also got another colt. They headed the horses toward home.

When Ella pulled up in her car, she could see that there wasn't anyone around. Beth decided to come with her since she had never seen wild mustangs before. Ella went into the birthing barn and checked on all the animals. Beth stood by the paddock where some of the horses were to watch them. Doc was due later in the day to check on the new calves and give them shots. He would also be making his rounds to the other animals.

She had walked out of the birthing barn to see what Beth was doing when she heard the horses coming. The horses were running in to the east pasture trying to find a place to run. Along with the horses were the four men trying to move the mustangs into the pasture. She said to Beth "Isn't that a beautiful sight."

Beth wondered if she was talking about the men or the horses. Beth did manage to say, "Yes." They watched as the men rode closer while the mustangs were trying to figure out what was going to happen next. Within ten minutes, the horses started to settle down. Beth and Ella walked closer to the pasture so that they could get a better look at the horses. Beth noticed that there were two young colts with the herd. They stood and watched the horses for a little while.

Hank was thinking what a beautiful sight as he rode in. He saw Ella standing there waiting and watching them ride in. He would like someone like that waiting for him all the time. She took his breath away and his heart started racing every time he saw her. The more he saw her, the more his body was wanting her. She had no idea what she was doing to him, and he couldn't let her know.

Beth had recognized Jake from school and noticed him riding the bus on Fridays. She wondered where he was going and why he was only on the bus on Fridays. He was cute, but he was also a loner just like her. He kept to himself and didn't talk to anyone. She had overheard a couple of girls talking about him one day that he had gotten into some kind of trouble at school and now no one would talk to him because of his reputation. She wondered what he did to get the reputation.

They were both in the same grade at school. Jake had his school locker just down the hall from hers. She saw him there a couple of times. They only had one more year of school left. He has never spoke to her or even looked at her. She didn't talk to anyone. She was just fine being by herself. She had nothing in common with any of the girls at school and didn't want to get wrapped up in any of their drama.

She asked Ella how much longer they were going to be there she was getting hungry and thirsty. She knew that Ella was waiting on Doc to arrive. When she looked at Ella she saw her looking at a certain cowboy and then she would look away like she didn't want to get caught looking at him. Ella told her they would be there for a while.

Hank rode up on his horse near Ella. He brought his fingers to the brim of his Stetson and nodded before he dismounted. Ella introduced him to her niece Beth. Beth looked at Hank and said, "Hi." He told the girls that they could go into the house and help themselves to anything they could find in the kitchen. They would be done with the horses in a few minutes.

They headed to the house while Hank mounted his horse to return to helping with the horses. When they walked into the kitchen Beth couldn't believe her eyes. It was the most state of the art kitchen she ever saw. It was a cook's dream kitchen. It had all modern appliances and room to move around in. She opened up the big refrigerator to see what was inside. She pulled out two bottles water for them to drink.

Ten minutes later Hank walked in the back door. He saw Beth and Ella sitting at the kitchen table drinking their water. Ella asked him where the bathroom was, he told her down the hall on your left. He walked over to the kitchen sink to wash his hands. Then he looked into the refrigerator to see what there was to eat. He asked Beth how she liked it here and she said it was ok she guessed. He asked her if she was hungry and she told him no.

Ben and Jake walked into the kitchen. They both looked at Hank and stopped talking as soon as they saw Beth sitting at the kitchen table. This is the first time that Jake really got a look at her. He had seen her on the school bus on Fridays. Hank introduced her to Ben and Jake.

Ella returned to the kitchen and then Beth went to

the bathroom. She couldn't get out of the chair fast
enough to escape the look that Jake was giving her.
He was looking at her like she had two heads. He had
never spoken to her, and this was the first time she
heard his voice. *He has a very nice voice. I wonder what he
did to get his reputation at school.*

Ella went outside to wait for Doc to come. When
Beth returned to the kitchen and didn't see Ella, she
asked where she was. Hank told her that she was
outside waiting for Doc. She grabbed her bottle of
water off the kitchen table and walked out the back
door.

Doc drove into the barn yard a couple minutes
later. Ella spoke with Doc and asked him if he needed
her help. They walked to the birthing barn with Beth
following behind them. She got the shots ready for
Doc to give to the calves. He checked them all over
and the new moms too.

They were just about done when Hank came in
the barn as he was talking on his cell phone. He was
talking to Maria. "Take all the time you need. I'll
figure out something for the buyers. No, I am not
going to starve to death before you get back." There
was a small silence, then he said, "Keep in touch and
let me know how things go, and don't worry about
me." a

Hank closed his eyes and took a deep breath. He

continued walking to where Ella, Beth and Doc were. He asked Doc, "Do you know of a good cook and a caterer?" He told them that Maria, his housekeeper and cook, just called him and was called away for a family emergency. She didn't know how long she would be gone because her father was ill. He had buyers coming in two weeks to look over the mustangs and the cattle. He planned a little shindig for the buyers while they were here. He needed someone to cook and serve the food.

"I can help you with that." Beth had spoken the words and then everyone looked at her.

Hank said "Are you sure you can handle something like this? This is a pretty big shindig, but if you can do it I will let you . It would be doing me a big favor and I will pay you for your time."

"How many people are you talking about?'

"I have two dozen buyers coming to look at the cattle, and about the same amount coming to look at the mustangs. They start arriving at one o'clock in the afternoon. It will last until about six or seven o'clock in the evening. Maria usually served snack stuff from two o'clock until about five o'clock then she serves the real food."

Beth already had ideas going on in her head. "What kind of people are you trying to impress, cowboys or business people?"

"I guess you could say that all kind of people attend this thing. If you have questions about the kind of food to serve I will give you Maria's phone number, so you can talk with her. She has done this for the last couple of years for me, with the help of her daughter. You can call her daughter Mary, I'm sure that she will be glad to help you and answer any questions."

"Ok, I will do it."

He left the barn so that he could write down the phone numbers that she would need. A couple minutes later, Beth walked outside and walked to the big corral where the mustangs were. She slowly walked up to the fence. She didn't want to scare any of the horses. She was watching the colts. She could tell that they were scared because they stuck close to their mother's.

Jake saw her looking at the horses and walked up slowly behind her. He was so quiet that she didn't hear him. "Do you like horses?"

"I think they are beautiful creatures". The words came out a little bit shaky. He made her so nervous. *I love the way he talks.*

"Do you ride horses?"

"No, I don't know how to ride a horse. I've always

lived in the city. This is the first time that I have lived in the country."

Slowly he walked to stand beside her. "If you would like to learn to ride horses I will be glad to teach you."

"I would like that."

He turned his head so that he could get a good look at her and said, "I have chores to do so I will see you around."

Beth didn't realize that she was so nervous until he walked away. *I can't believe that he spoke to me. He is so good looking that I am surprised that he doesn't have a girlfriend. I don't have time to think about him now. I just got my first job.*

Beth contacted Maria and her daughter, Mary. She found out where Maria kept the recipes that she had used for the last couple of years. She was anxious to see them. After dinner a few days later, she asked Ella to take her over to Hanks house. She had fixed extra food for dinner so that she could take a plate over to Hank. She really wanted to impress him with her cooking.

When Beth and Ella arrived at his house it took him a few minutes to answer the door. He had just finished taking a shower. He was getting ready to go into town to get something to eat. He answered the door in his jeans, socks, and a tee shirt. His hair was still wet from his shower and it looked like he had towel dried it.

Beth explained to him that she wanted to take a look at the recipes that Maria had told her about. She handed him a plate and told him she also brought him dinner. Ella followed her into the house. He walked over to the table to set the plate down. He asked Ella to join him at the table while Beth got what she needed.

Ella slowly walked to the table and sat down at the opposite end of the table. Hank offered to get her something to drink while he got a cup of coffee. She cupped her hands together and placed them on top of the table. She kept looking around the kitchen. She didn't want to keep staring at him.

Beth walked over to the table with a notebook that Maria kept her notes in. She told Hank that she contacted Mary. She had agreed to help her with the food for his buyers. She had some ideas of her own that she wanted to try along with Maria's.

He told her that he would buy any supplies she would need. She was welcome to use any of the food that was in the freezer. "Make whatever you want, I'm sure it will be ok."

"I will go over the menu with you as soon as I have it made. It should only take me a couple of days to put it together. I will be talking it over with Mary too."

"If you're not busy on Saturday, I will be able to meet with you in the late afternoon. I have Lady Jane's owner coming in the morning to check on her. I can cook some steaks or something if you like and you and Ella can have dinner with Jake and I."

She looked at Ella with a questioning look as she didn't know what to say. Ella finally replied "Let's see what Saturday brings. I am on call this Saturday."

He watched them walk to Ella's car. *e noticed that Ella wore her hair down for the first time in a single braid down her back. The braid was more than half way down her back. I would really like to undue that braid and run my fingers through her hair. Every time I see her, she is more beautiful than the last.*

He returned to the kitchen to eat his dinner. Later that evening he sent a text message to Ella.

Tell Beth that I enjoyed my dinner very much. Hope to see you Saturday. Have a good night and sweet dreams.

She read the message. *He is one dangerous cowboy. He has got to know how good looking he is with that dark hair that reaches to his collar. The blue eyes that make you want to look into them and just melt. I get a flutter in my stomach every time I see him. What am I going to do about Saturday?*

CHAPTER 6

Saturday morning, Ella went to the clinic to do her morning routine and check on the animals. Someone had dropped off a litter of puppies earlier in the week. There were only two of them left. She decided that she would take one and see if Hank would take the other one. Everyone needs a dog, especially those who live in the country, right?

When the chores were done, she loaded up the car with puppy food, food dishes, along with a couple of leashes. She put the puppies in a carrier. On her way home, she was wondering what they should name them. Beth is going to be surprised. She never brought home any of the animals before.

Beth was in the kitchen when she arrived at home. She put the carrier on the porch, and then started to unload the car. Beth heard the puppies barking. They were telling Ella that they wanted out to play and to see their new home.

"What did you bring home?" asked Beth.

"Just a couple of puppies. One for us, and I hope that Hank will take the other one. It is worth a try. If not, we are going to have two dogs."

Ella let the puppies out of the carrier and carried them to the yard. After a few minutes of sniffing around they started to play with each other. Beth just stood there on the porch and watched them for a few minutes and started laughing. This is the first time in a very long time that she heard Beth laugh.

After they all went inside Beth asked Ella "What time are we going to go over to Hank's? I made a salad to take with us."

"Let me take a quick shower and then I will text Hank and find out what time."

Ella walked toward her bedroom to get ready for her shower. When she returned to the kitchen she told Beth that she received a text from Hank. They could go over at any time.

When they arrived at the Rocking R Ranch, Hank was walking Star toward the barn with a saddle on. He stopped and told the girls to make themselves at home. He was almost done and would be there in about ten minutes.

Beth took the salad, and her notes into the kitchen. Ella took the puppies out of the carrier so that they could get used to the area. It did not take them long to start playing again. Ella walked to the barn where Hank was taking care of Star. The puppies followed her to the barn. When Star saw the puppies she started getting restless.

"Whoa girl, what has gotten into you?" he said to Star. "Let me get this saddle off of you. You are alright."

Then he heard a little whine from one of the little puppies. Without even looking at her he asked her "Do I hear a puppy? Do you have a puppy with you?"

"Yes, I have two puppies with me."

He removed the saddle and the blanket from Star's back. He put them on the stall door. He kept talking to Star trying to reassure her that she was just fine.

"Ok, now I know what is wrong with Star. How old are the puppies?"

"About ten weeks old."

"This is what I want you to do. I want you to pick up one of the puppies and put it by your face. Star needs to know that the puppy won't hurt you. Let her see how small the puppy is."

Ella picked up one of the puppies and did as she was told to do. The puppy started licking her face, which made her giggle.

He had started rubbing down Star and told her the stall was her area, and no dogs were allowed in her stall. Star saw Ella holding the puppy and sensed that there was no danger from something so small.

Ella asked Hank if there was anything she could do to help him. He told her no. He was just about done. He took the saddle and blanket to the tack room. Then he grabbed some water for Star's stall.

He pulled out his cell phone and called Jake to see what he was doing. He was with Black Jack. He told him that Ella and Beth had arrived. He told Hank that he would be done in about five minutes.

Hank and Ella walked to the house with the little puppies following behind them . He asked Ella where Beth was and she told him that she went into the kitchen to put the salad away. That was about fifteen minutes ago.

When they walked into the kitchen Beth was putting something in the oven. Hank walked over to the sink to wash his hands. Beth said to him "I hope you don't mind I made some brownies for dessert. I will put the potatoes in the oven in a few minutes."

"I will go take a quick shower. Jake should be here any minute. You can tell him that he will have time to take a shower before dinner."

During supper, Ella asked him why Star was at the ranch. He told her that when he and Ben found her, she was on the ground with the coyotes attacking her. That is why she acted up in the barn with the puppies.

"Animals are a lot like humans. The physical scars will heal first and the emotional scars take longer. They have to learn to trust again."

She started chewing on her bottom lip then said, "I guess you wouldn't be interested in keeping one of the puppies then."

He sat there thinking for a minute, and then said to Jake, "What do you think about having another little animal around?"

"Hey, I'm only here on the weekends. But, they sure are cute! You're the boss, it is up to you."

"I have puppy food and dishes in my car if you say yes. They already have their shots and are ready to go."

He sat there for a couple more minutes and then turned to her and said, "It will be good for Star's training so I will keep one. She has to get over her fear of being around dogs."

After supper, Beth went over the menu that she chose to prepare for the buyers. She told Hank that they could put ice in a big barrel or a tub and keep bottles of water in them. She could also put out some coffee and ice tea for them to drink.

He told Beth that everything looked good to him. I just have one question to ask, "How did you get interested in cooking?"

"When I came to live with Ella, she was working long hours at the clinic. When she got home sometimes it was very late. She would be too tired to cook. I started watching cooking shows on TV and learned a lot about cooking. I looked on the internet for some recipes and tried some of the simple dishes. I got to the point where I liked creating new foods for us to try. I can make simple desserts, but I haven't done too much cake decorating yet."

"I love cake and cookies. I will help eat any practice cake that you make." He told her as he winked at her.

"This week I am going o bake some cookies for the buyers. I will make sure that I save you some."

"Make me up a list and I will pick up everything for you when I go into town this week."

After the girls left, Hank walked into the house and found a rug for the puppy to sleep on. He told the puppy as he laid him on the rug. "Welcome, to your new home. I have to think of a name for you so that I won't be calling you something stupid like Dog."

He walked down the hall to his den .He sat down at his desk. Then turned on his computer. He wanted to look at some reports before he went to bed. As he sat there looking at a blank screen he started thinking about Ella. *She is so beautiful. When she wears her hair down she looks like an angel. I bet her hair will feel like silk running through my fingers. She also looks good in a pair of blue jeans with those long legs. I wonder why she doesn't date. Some guy must have really done her wrong.*

He decided that he wasn't going to get any work done. He couldn't think of anything but Ella. When he stood up from his chair, a groan escaped from his lips. He walked into his bathroom. He took a cold shower hoping that he wouldn't think of her anymore that night.

After he got out of the shower he walked into his bedroom, he heard his Great Grandfather say, "That Ella sure is a pretty woman. Ever since you met her you seem to be taking a lot of cold showers."

"I am sure that you didn't come to see me just to tell me that. And yes, she is very pretty."

"You are right. I came to tell you that Lady Jane's owner just found out that she has to walk with a cane the rest of her life due to the injury to her leg. The woman's name is Nancy. She is going to tell you she wants to sell Lady Jane because she will never be able to ride her again."

"I wondered what was going on, because when Mr. Davis came today he really didn't seem too interested in Lady Jane's progress. He just wanted to know if someone could ride her. I told him to give her a couple more weeks and she would be ready to ride. "

"Mr. Davis is just concerned with his daughter. He doesn't care about Lady Jane. He is the one telling her to sell the horse."

"But, Nancy will still be able to ride again . I will have her come here in a couple of weeks. I will talk to her. She doesn't need to give up riding. I just need to figure out how I'm going to get her to ride Lady Jane again. "

"Have her come out when Billy is here."

"That is a great idea."

Great Grandfather left and Hank was still standing there in his underwear. *I wish that man would let me know when he is coming to visit so that I could at least get dressed. He just pops in here whenever he feels like* **it.**

The next morning, he texted Ella.

Hank: "I hope you slept well last night. Wyatt had a hard time sleeping without his brother. He woke me up several times last night barking and whimpering."

Ella: **"I slept well. Toby slept with a stuffed teddy bear."**

Hank: "Do you have an extra teddy bear?"

CHAPTER 7

The next week flew by so fast. There was so much to do before the buyers came. Thursday afternoon Hank got a call from Doc Stevenson. Doc wanted to know if he had room for one more horse. Someone had abandoned a paint mare. A neighbor called Doc because they had not see anyone around for about three weeks. Doc gave him the address and told him he would meet him there in half an hour.

When he met up with Doc to get the mare, Doc had found out that the owner of the horse was in the Army. The horse was to be taken care of by a cousin. The cousin got laid off from work a month ago and no one has seen him since. He put the horse in the corral and left. No one was living in the house on the property.

The neighbor told Doc that the horse's name was Baby. He got the name and address of the owner. He will write to the owner to tell him what happened to her. You could tell that no one had been feeding her. Her ribs were showing and she needed some clean water to drink.

Hank loaded her into the horse trailer. He was ready to take her home. When he got her to the ranch he got a good look at her. He found a small stone under a shoe which was hurting her when she walked. She needed new shoes put on. She had been neglected for quite a while. Hank wondered how long her owner had been gone.

He got her settled into a stall with some feed and water. She needed to be brushed as she had mud attached to her hair. He told her that he would be back later to check on her.

Hank still had to put the colts in a separate pasture because they were not for sale. He wanted to put them in the same pasture as Sandy and her new colt. He still needed to get his paper work ready for the sale.

Later that night, Hank with Wyatt on his leash, went to the barn to check on Lady Jane and Baby. They had been going to the barn every night since Wyatt's arrival. He wanted Wyatt to get acquainted with the horses and the horses with him. He tied

Wyatt's leash by Star's stall and went into Baby's stall. Wyatt laid down on the floor waiting for Hank to come and get him. Hank heard Star do a little snicker and looked over the stall wall and saw her looking for Wyatt. As soon as Star saw where he was, she was trying to lean over her stall door to get a closer look at him. She was getting accustomed to Wyatt's presence.

Hank gave Baby some more feed and water. He brushed her down. Which gave him the chance to check her out more while grooming her. She just needs some food and with some loving care she should be ok. She won't be neglected anymore.

When he got finished with Baby he walked over to Star's stall. He talked to her for minute. He rubbed her between her ears. She likes that a lot. She kept nudging him with her muzzle telling him that she wanted a special treat. He took one out of his shirt pocket to give to her. She has come a long way since he got her. She is now saddle trained and ready to ride.

He grabbed Wyatt's leash and headed for the door. He still had to check on Black Jack before they headed for the house.

Ella was at home in her bedroom cleaning. She pulled open a drawer in a dresser that was in her room when she found a bundle of letters tied together with a piece of string. She was going to throw the letters away but as she flipped through the letters she noticed that they were letters from a woman to Uncle Joe while he was in the Army.

She went through the letters and noticed that they were in date order. She sat down on the bed wondering why Joe kept the letters all these years. She opened the first letter and she read.

Dear Joe,

I know why you left town and joined the Army. I heard that you had a fight with your parents. I knew that you were tired of your parents fighting and your father drinking all the time. I hope that you will find peace since you are no longer living with them.

I also know how sweet you are on Lily but she has started seeing someone while you have been gone. I know that you can't do anything being so far away. I just hope that you make it home safe.

Always,

Annalise

She folded the letter and put it back into the envelope. She pulled out the next letter and read.

Dear Joe,

I write this letter with a sad heart. They arrested your father for beating your Mom. She is in the hospital in pretty bad shape. Your father got drunk again and they started fighting as usual. One of the neighbors heard them and called the police. I don't know what will happen to him, but they are not letting him out of jail.

I miss you coming here and visiting us. I will be fine. I have seen Lily around town with her new boyfriend. He drives a car and works in a factory over in Shiloh Bend. Just thought you would want to know.

Please take care of yourself and pray for your Mom.

Always,

Annalise

Ella returned the letter to the envelope. This was a part of Uncle Joe's life and her father's that she never knew about. Her father never talked about his parents and now she knew why. Her father moved away after he got out of school. He called his brother about twice a year. They were not close because she never heard her father talk about Joe. He never came to visit when her parents were alive.

Ella opened up the next letter hoping to find out what happened to her grandparents. The next letter was dated six months later.

Dear Joe,

I'm sorry that I haven't written to you sooner. It has been a bad winter here. I'm so glad that spring is just around the corner. Your father is still in jail. It looks like he will be there for a while. Your Mom has been in and out of the hospital. I have heard that she has cancer. Has she written to you at all? She has been working when she is well enough at Longwell's Nursery. I don't know how she does it.

I have also heard that Lily will be getting married this summer. I'm sorry Joe I know how you felt about her. You will have to find yourself someone new if you haven't already. A nice guy like you shouldn't have a problem with that.

It is time for me to go to work. I will try to keep you informed on your parents and pray for your Mom. Take care and hope to see you when you come home on leave.

Always,

Annalise

She finished reading the rest of the letters that Annalise had written to Uncle Joe. She found out that her grandmother did die from cancer about a year later. It was time she found out where the cemetery is where her grandmother and Uncle Joe are buried. She would talk to Hank to see what he could tell her about Uncle Joe. Maybe he could also tell her what happened to her grandfather.

She was also going to see if she could find Annalise. She was a friend of her Uncle Joe's. She must have been a neighbor or someone he went to school with. She had so many questions to ask her. This was a small town and everyone knows everyone so she can't be hard to find. Annalise is not a common name so someone has to know her.

I think it is time for me to learn about my family. It doesn't sound like my father and Joe had a good childhood. At least now, I understand my father more than when I was growing up.

CHAPTER 8

Hank was still drinking his coffee and talking to Jake when Ella and Beth arrived. Ben's truck was right behind them. Chad and Derrick would be there around ten o'clock to help with the horses. There were still a lot of things to do before the buyers started coming.

Beth and Ella started making breakfast as soon as they arrived. The smell of food cooking reminded Hank of how hungry he really was. Beth told him to give her about ten minutes and breakfast would be ready.

Hank could feel Ella's presence in the kitchen. She was driving him crazy. She had her hair pinned up and she was wearing a pair of jeans that fit her just right in all the right places. She was wearing a light blue tee-shirt. When she brought the plates of food to the table he could smell her scent when she leaned next to him to put his plate down. It took all his inner strength to concentrate on eating his breakfast and planning the things that needed to be done.

As soon as the men left the house, Beth and Ella got busy around the house. Ella went through the house to do a quick inspection to see if anything needed to be cleaned. Since Maria had been gone she knew no one was doing any cleaning. She cleaned up the living room and the dining room. She could hear Beth talking to someone in the kitchen, Mary had arrived.

She entered the kitchen and saw Beth talking to a tall, dark haired, woman in her early twenties. She was very beautiful and very voluptuous in all the right places. After Beth made the introductions, she went back to her cleaning.

She had opened the door at the end of the hallway and realized it was Hank's bedroom. She slowly walked in breathing in his scent. She loved the smell of him. She made his bed then walked into his bathroom to see if it needed to be cleaned.

She picked up a towel that was on the floor by the vanity sink. She raised the towel to her face so that she could smell his scent better. She was so engrossed in her thoughts that she didn't hear Hank come into his bedroom.

"Ella, what are you doing in my bathroom?" Hank's voice came out a little rougher than he wanted. He didn't want to scare her.

She quickly lowered the towel from her face and said, "I was just cleaning up the bathroom for you. I didn't think you would mind." She was so embarrassed that she couldn't turn around to face him.

"It isn't necessary but, thank you." He backed away from the doorway and left the room after his eyes took her image in from her hair to the shoes she wore on her feet.

He walked into the den to check on some paperwork. The groan that escaped rom his lips as soon as he was alone came from the bottom of his gut. His body was letting him know how much he wanted her. He needed a few minutes to get his thoughts together and his body to calm down after seeing her.

The rest of the morning flew by so fast getting ready for the buyers. As soon as Chad and Derrick arrived, he had them working on setting up tables for the food. They found a tub to hold the bottles of water.

They went into the kitchen to see if there was anything more that they could do. Beth asked them to fill up the tub with ice and put the bottled water in it so that they could start getting cold. Chad starting flirting with her by winking at her. He told her he would do anything for her. She just ignored him hoping he would get the hint.

Ella managed to get away to take a quick shower. She put on a pair of black jeans with a black long sleeve shirt that had an Indian mosaic design on the shoulders and across the back. She swept her hair up into a hair clip leaving a few tendrils of hair loose that curled on each side of her face. She applied some mascara and eye make up to make her eyes stand out more. She then applied some lip gloss. With one last final look in the mirror she decided that she was ready.

By noon the pickup trucks, and trucks hauling empty trailers started arriving. Hank acknowledged everyone when they arrived. There had to be at least thirty trucks parked out there. He was pleased to see so many people turn out for the sale. They were going to do the cattle first then the mustangs.

Many of the buyers knew each other from previous sales and other events. The list of buyers got larger with each passing year. Buyers were contacting Hank to be put on the list. His reputation was getting around by word of mouth.

Beth was pleased with the food. She hoped that Hank was also pleased. Ella and Mary took care of the serving the food, while she stayed in the kitchen. She had no idea what was going on outside as she was busy in the kitchen preparing the food and trying to clean up the kitchen when she had time. She was praying that she would not run out of food.

It was six thirty when the last truck left. When Hank walked in the back door he found the women talking in the kitchen. Ella was giving Beth some business cards from people that were interested in her catering an event for them. Beth couldn't believe it.

Hank walked into his office and returned to the kitchen with two envelopes in his hand with Mary's and Beth's name on them. He handed them the envelopes. Mary thanked him. She told everyone goodbye before she left to go home. Beth folded hers and stuck it in her pocket. She asked him if he needed something to eat before she left. She told him that she put some of the leftovers in the fridge for him.

A few minutes later, the back door opened again, in came Jake with Wyatt on his leash. Wyatt was so happy to see Ella. He was at her feet jumping on her and then turning around in circles. He started barking at her until she bent over and spoke to him. "I am glad to see you too, Wyatt. Toby misses you too. I will have to arrange a play date for the two of you."

Jake walked over to the sink to washed his hands. He then took a bottle of water out of the fridge. He walked up beside Beth and told her that the food was really good. She smiled at him before she told him thanks.

Hank asked the girls, "Do you have to hurry home or can you stay for a few minutes more?"

They decided that they could wait for a few minutes. He walked into the living room. He started a fire in the fireplace then turned on a couple of lights. The girls sat on the couch while him and Jake sat in the chairs . He was telling them about how the sale was such a success. He was going to use the money to purchase more cattle. He was hoping to double the size of his herd.

Jake looked at him then asked him, "Have you thought about changing some of the grasses that you are feeding them to make them leaner and more prize cattle?"

"I have thought about it, but haven't had much time to look into it. Do you have some ideas that we could discuss later? Right now, I just want to sit down and relax."

Hank left the room and returned a few minutes later with two guitars. He handed one to Jake. He kept one for himself. He sat down in the chair then started playing some chords. Jake picked up on the song that he was playing. The two of them played a couple of songs. The girls didn't speak, they just sat there enjoying the music.

Hank enjoyed watching the fire light play against Ella's face. She was so beautiful. He could just sit and look at her for hours.

Jake was looking at Beth and was trying to figure out what was going on in that pretty head of hers. The more he was around her the more he was beginning to like her. She wasn't like any of the other girls that he knew. She was more real. She didn't put on a show for anyone. He also knew that she was a city girl and she would probably be moving back to a city someplace when she got through school. Maybe they could just be friends. He would like that, but would she?

Later that night when Ella was getting ready for bed, she heard Beth scream from her bedroom. She ran from her room to Beth's room to see what was wrong. She threw open the bedroom door. She saw Beth jumping up and down, then she saw her sit on the bed with tears streaming down her face . Ella said "What's wrong?"

"Oh my God I don't believe it!" She handed Ella the check. The amount on the check was $400.00. There was a note in with the check that stated he wanted her to save the date of the second Saturday in October for him for his fall harvest cookout.

She said to Beth "This is great, why are you crying?"

"I never thought he was going to pay me so much! Not only that, but he wants me to do another event for him. He wrote me a note to save the date."

"I'm so happy for you. Isn't this what you wanted?"

"Yes, it is. I just never dreamed that this would be such a success. If these other people are interested too and I do a good job for them, who knows where this is going to go."

"Just don't get ahead of yourself. You know you have to take baby steps first to build anything right. You did a good job today. I'm proud of you. I will help in any way I can."

Ella gave Beth a hug then returned to her bedroom. Before she closed her eyes to go to sleep, she thought of Hank. *He was one dangerous cowboy. She was starting to like him, REALLY like him.*

When Hank walked into his bathroom that night,

his thoughts drifted to earlier that day when he found Ella in his bathroom. *He found her smelling the towel that he had used that morning. He noticed in the mirror the way her body was reacting to his scent. What he really wanted to do was to pull the clip out of her hair so he could run his fingers through it. He wanted to kiss her. He wanted to wrap his arms around her so that he could feel her in his arms. He had to get out of there before he touched her. He didn't know how much longer he could hold on before something happened between them. She had to make the first move.*

CHAPTER 9

Two weeks had gone by and Hank had not seen Ella. He needed to see her soon. He was trying to think of an excuse to get her to come to the ranch when he saw her car coming up the driveway. Ella, Beth and Toby got out of the car.

Hank was talking to Stella Williams about her horse. Stella had taken her horse out for a ride and had just returned. He cut his conversation short so that he could go talk to Ella and Beth.

He walked to where Ella stood and put his hand on her upper arm. Ella explained to him that Beth was here for a riding lesson with Jake. They brought Toby along so that he could play with Wyatt. Before she could ask where Wyatt was he was at her side jumping on her for some attention. After Ella paid attention to him he was content to play with Toby.

Hank told Beth that Jake was in the barn the last time he saw him. She said "Thanks, I'll find him."

She walked to the barn, and found Jake getting a horse out of a stall. When he noticed her he said "Hi! I am glad that you decided to come today."

"I hope you still have time to give me a riding lesson. I had to wait for Ella to get home."

"Sure, I have the time. You could have called me and I would have come to get you."

"I don't have your phone number."

"What is your phone number?"

Jake took out his cell phone, and stored her number in it before he dialed. Beth's phone rang in her back pocket. "Now you have my number."

After he saddled the horse that he picked out for her to ride, he led the horse to the corral next to the barn. He asked her if she needed help getting on the horse. After a couple of failed attempts, he came to her side and helped her get into the saddle. Beth sat there with both hands on the saddle horn, wiggling her butt trying to get comfortable.

He explained to her that he would leave the lead rope attached and walk the horse around the corral until she got accustomed to the feel of the horse. He was going to take his time with her as he wanted her to enjoy riding as much as he did. He would teach her everything he knew.

After the riding lesson, he showed her how to take care of the horse. He showed her how to remove the saddle and brush the horse down. He told her how important it was to take care of him. While she was brushing the horse, she told him that she had contacted some of the buyers that came there for the sale. There were interested in knowing if she had some dates open for her to cater for them. She told him that she never expected anything like this to happen to her. He told her he was not surprised because the food was really good. He was happy for her.

She also told him about the old truck in the barn. She didn't know anything about trucks, but was hoping he did. She was wondering if he could get it running. If so, she had plans for that truck. Right now, she knew it was just a dream. He told her he would be happy to take a look at it.

He had told her about the conversation that he had with Hank about the grass he suggested for him to get to feed the cattle. Some of it had to get planted soon so that the cattle could eat it over the summer.

He also told her he knew that Hank was getting

ready to go to some cattle auctions. He was going to buy some cattle to replace what he sold, plus more. Hank had asked him to go with him to the auctions. She could tell that he was excited about it.

Before he realized it, they had left the barn and walked to the corral that had the colts in it. Beth liked watching the colts. They stood there looking at the horses when her phone rang. It was Ella wanting to know if she wanted to stay for supper. She told her yes, she would be right there. She would make them supper.

Hank was glad that they were going to stay for supper, so was Jake, because Hank was not a good cook. Hank suggested that they just have something simple like hamburgers. Beth said that would be fine. She went into the kitchen and looked into the cupboards and started getting out pots and pans. She made a macaroni salad and some green beans with dill sauce she had pulled out the hamburgers that were frozen and started to thaw them out so she could season them.

When Hank returned to the kitchen from taking his shower, she asked him if he wanted to cook the hamburgers outside on the grill or inside. He told her he would cook them outside on the grill. I'll go light the grill then come back for the hamburgers. While he cooked the hamburgers, Beth was busy setting the table when Jake walked into the kitchen. He asked her if she needed any help. She told him she had everything under control.

When they sat down to eat, the dogs had settled on a rug that Wyatt used when he was in the house. Everyone was so hungry that no one said anything for a few minutes. Hank was the first one to talk. He asked Beth if she would be interested in cooking for him on weekends until Maria got back. He talked to Maria and she didn't know when she would be back. He said that he needed to find someone to clean the house for him. If they heard, or knew of someone to let him know. Jake said that he would ask his mom to see if she might know of someone. Beth told him that she would be glad to do it until he found someone.

When they were finished with supper, Beth and Ella were clearing the table of the dishes when the dogs started whining and digging at the back door. Hank heard Black Jack making all kinds of noise out in his corral. He opened up the back door and Jake was right behind him. He had his cell phone out and was calling the fire department. There was a fire in a field behind Ella's house. He told Ella and Beth to stay put. They both ran to the barn and grabbed some shovels and threw them into the back of the truck. Hank cut across the field to Ella's house.

The fire was a slow burning fire because it looked like it was just burning the grass on top. There was a lot of smoke. What was burning was dead grass and weeds. It had been years since anything had been planted in this field. Hank and Jake started on the side closest to the house with the shovels trying to put the fire out. They weren't making any headway, the fire trucks needed to get here soon.

The fire was still far enough from the house that they didn't have to worry about it. The fire trucks arrived, the firemen went to work and had the fire put out before it spread too far. Hank stood there talking to the Fire Chief asking him some questions when Ella appeared at his side. He told them that he would look around in the morning to see what started the fire. He asked Ella if she had a place where they could spend the night just to be on the safe side until he could determine the cause of the fire.

Hank told the Chief that they could stay at his place, he had plenty of room. He would see them tomorrow at Hank's. Hank told Ella for her and Beth to grab what they would need for the night. He and Jake waited outside the house while they got what they needed.

When they returned to the ranch Jake told Hank that he wanted to check on Black Jack before he went into the house. "That's a good idea, just let me know how he's doing."

Hank went into the house with Beth and Ella. He told them that they could use any bedroom upstairs.

He told them what room Jake was using. They took their bags upstairs. They took two rooms at the other end of the hall from Jake's room.

Hank took another shower to get the smoke smell off of him. He walked back into the kitchen to get something to drink when Jake walked in the back door. "How's Black Jack?"

"He's doing ok, now. I couldn't get close to him until I took off my shirt and washed off some of the smoke smell with the hose."

"Go take a hot shower before you catch a cold from using that cold water out there."

"Yes Sir."

"Thanks for all your help out there tonight."

"No problem."

Jake went upstairs to take his shower. As soon as Jake left the room, Ella appeared in the kitchen. She had her hair loose and was wearing pajamas. She walked over to Hank and stopped in front of him and said, "I want to thank you for everything you did. I don't know what I would have done without your help. Could I ask you to do one more thing for me, actually two things?"

He looked at her wondering what she could be wanting. His body was already starting to respond from being close to her. "What would you like? I try to please all my guests."

"Would you please hold me for just a minute and then get me two aspirin for my headache?"

Hank wrapped his arms around her and couldn't stop himself from touching her hair. It felt like silk, just like he knew it would. *Cool it buddy, just play it as cool as you can!* He held her for a minute until he could feel her relax in his arms. He pulled back just enough to put a kiss on her forehead. As much as he wanted to stand there and hold her all night, he needed to step away from her. He went to the cupboard to get a glass and then pulled open a drawer to get her a couple of aspirin. He filled the glass with water from the sink then walked toward her.

He handed them to her. When she took the aspirin, he was admiring her long neck. *Oh, how I would love to leave a trail of kisses down the side of that neck of hers.* When she was finished with the water she handed him the glass. Then she got closer, wrapped her arms around his neck, and pulled his face to hers, and kissed him like no other woman had ever kissed him before. He responded with kissing her back.

When they broke apart she said to him, "Thanks again." She walked out of the kitchen while she still could walk.

He said to her retreating back, "My pleasure!"

*That woman even looks nice in pajamas. I love her hair. Man, does she know how to kiss. Good thing I don't have any socks **on**, she would have blown them right off. I think I've got it bad for her. God help me!*

While Jake was in the shower he started thinking about Beth. She wasn't at all what he thought she would be like. He actually enjoyed spending time with her. When Jake walked out of the shower he noticed a text message on his phone. It was from Beth.

Beth: "Thanks for the riding lesson. I had fun. Can't wait for my next lesson."

Jake: "I will make time for you tomorrow afternoon."

CHAPTER 10

When Hank woke up, he heard he rain coming down. They needed the rain. The sun was to come out in the afternoon. He had a busy day today. He was looking forward to starting his day by seeing Ella this morning.

He walked into the kitchen and realized that a pot of coffee had already been made. Beside the coffee pot was a clean cup. He looked around and didn't see or hear anyone. He poured himself some coffee. He heard Jake come down the stairs. He grabbed a cup and poured himself a cup of coffee. They were discussing today's schedule when Beth came in the kitchen. She looked at Hank and said with her eyes half closed, "Do I have time to take a shower before I make your breakfast? I forgot how early you guys get up on weekends."

"Jake and I will go feed and water the horses. That will take us about forty- five minutes to an hour. We can come back in for breakfast then. Will that work for you?"

"Yes, I will have your breakfast ready in an hour. Maybe Ella will be back by then and can eat breakfast with us. She sent me a text message saying that she got an emergency call from Doc. She went to go help him. She left about five o'clock. "

"Did she say what the emergency was?"

"No." She turned around and walked toward the stairs to go take a shower and get dressed.

Hank noticed that Jake didn't say one word when Beth was in the room. He just sat there and drank his coffee and never took his eyes off of her.

They went to the barn to start the chores. When they returned to the house for breakfast, Hank noticed that Ella hadn't returned yet. He was getting a little worried. He knew he would feel better after he saw her and they talked to the Fire Chief today.

Beth had breakfast ready. She made pancakes, bacon and eggs. She also brewed a fresh pot of coffee. She placed a glass of milk on the table for Jake to drink and gave him a look that said you better drink that.

They were just about done eating breakfast when they heard a knock on the back door. Hank pushed his chair back so that he could go answer the door. When he opened the door, the Fire Chief was there. He invited him in and offered him a cup of coffee. He said, "I came to ask Ella a few questions. Is she here?"

"No, she's not here."

"She must still be with Doc. There was accident on the interstate early this morning. A guy was taking a truck load of chickens to market. A doe ran out in front of him. He tried to miss her but hit her pretty good in the back legs. The truck went in a ditch and landed on its side. The cages that held the chickens broke open. The chickens scattered everywhere. The doe was pregnant. Doc did a cesarean section on her to save the fawns. She was pregnant with twins.

The last I heard about an hour ago they were still trying to gather up all the chickens. The driver was taken to the hospital. I haven't heard what kind of injuries he has.

Well, I'll come back when Ella is here. Sorry to interrupt your breakfast."

The Fire Chief walked out the back door. Hank sat there with thoughts going through his head. If the Fire Chief wanted to talk Ella, then they found something suspicious. He would wait until the Fire Chief talked with Ella, then he would do his own investigation.

When Ella returned to the ranch, it was almost lunch time. She walked in the back door soaking wet from being in the rain all morning. She needed a hot shower. When the smell of something cooking registered in her mind it reminded her that she hadn't eaten anything today.

Beth heard her come in the back door. Wyatt and Toby also heard her come in. They were right there to greet her. She bent down and petted each of them. She then turned her attention to Beth. "What are you cooking that smells so good?"

"I have stew cooking in the crock pot. I have started doing some cleaning for you. It gave me something to do while I was waiting for you. The Fire Chief was here looking for you earlier, he wants to ask you some questions."

"I need to get something to eat and take a shower. I need to put some dry clothes on."

Beth told her to go upstairs and she would bring her something to eat. She fixed her a sandwich then took it to her room. She left it on the dresser so that Ella would see it when she got out the shower.

Beth went back downstairs to make lunch for

Hank and Jake. She was rolling out pie dough when they came in from the barn to eat. She told them that she would make them some sandwiches for lunch and they could eat some salad. She finished making the pie and put it in the oven to bake.

They had just sat down to eat when Ella walked in the kitchen. She told them that she called the Fire Chief. He told her he would be there shortly to talk to her. She got a bottle of water then sat down at the table next to Beth.

As soon as he saw her he had to remind himself to breathe. He could smell her scent from her shower as soon as she sat down. "Sounds like you have had a busy morning. The Fire Chief told us about the accident this morning when he was here looking for you." Hank was trying to act as normal as possible.

"Yeah, the doe died just after Doc and I got there. He said the fawns still had a chance but he had to do the cesarean section right now, so he did. He handed me the fawns as soon they were born so I could clean them up. The chickens were running all over the place. The police officers were trying to keep them out of the road so they wouldn't get hit. I never knew that chickens could make so much noise."

"What is going to happen to the fawns?" asked Beth.

"Doc contacted the Wild Life and Conservations guy to see if they could find the fawns a doe that would be able to nurse them. Hopefully they have one somewhere. If they can't help him, then he will contact the zoo to see if they will take them."

The rain finally stopped when Hank walked back out to the barn. Billy and his father were due to arrive soon. Nancy Davis and her father were also coming. He hoped his plan would work. Billy was a special needs child that loved to ride his horse. Billy was born with MS, who was confined to a wheelchair. When they put him on his horse, they had straps on his saddle to help keep him on the saddle, and his legs in the stirrups. They used a ramp for the wheelchair to get up close to the side of the horse. Lizzy was trained to stand still while they put Billy in the saddle, and she was led away from the ramp.

Hank had just put the ramp n the indoor arena when Billy and his father arrived. He stood and talked to Billy for a few minutes before he went to get Lizzy. He returned a few minutes later with the horse saddled. He walked Lizzy next to the ramp. He told her to stay as he let go of the reins.

"You ready to be a cowboy, Billy?"

"Yeah" Billy replied with a big smile on his face.

Hank and Billy's father lifted him up on Lizzy's back.

They strapped him in the saddle. Then strapped his legs in the stirrups. He had his riding helmet on.

Billy said, "Hat, I need my hat!"

Billy's father found his cowboy hat and put it on top of Billy's head over his helmet.

"Otay, I ready!"

Hank moved Lizzy away from the ramp, then handed Billy the reins. He told Billy "You walk Lizzy real slow around the arena two times. She has to get warmed up. You understand what I'm saying Billy?"

"Yeah"

While Billy was walking Lizzy around the arena Hank moved two barrels around in the arena. He placed a barrel at each end of the arena.

"This time around you walk Lizzy around the barrels, okay Billy."

Billy did as he was told. "You are doing a good job cowboy."

He worked with Billy for thirty minutes before he saw Nancy and Mr. Davis walk into the arena area. He told them to have a seat on the bench and he would be with them in a few minutes.

"Do the barrels one more time. This time do it a little bit faster than last time."

He watched Billy ride around the barrels. "Good job Billy! Now cool Lizzy down and walk her slowly around the arena two times."

Hank walked over to the side of the arena where the bench was located to talk to Nancy and Mr. Davis. He shook hands with Mr. Davis and said hello to Nancy. He noticed that Nancy had laid her cane down by her feet.

"Excuse me for a couple minutes, I need to help Billy dismount."

"Billy, bring Lizzy up to the ramp please."

Billy's father was standing on the ramp waiting for him. When Billy got Lizzy up to the ramp, Lizzy stopped. Billy handed the reins to Hank. Hank let the reins fall so that he could undue Billy's straps. "It's time to dismount cowboy."

"Otay."

They slid him off the horse and got him settled into his wheelchair. He moved his wheelchair next to Lizzy. Billy placed his hands on each side of Lizzy's head, then bent over, and kissed her. "You are the best horse ever Lizzy. I love you."

Hank bent down in front of the wheelchair. He

removed the riding helmet from Billy's head. Then he placed his cowboy hat on his head with a little tap. He told him that he did real good job today, and he would see him next week.

"Otay, cowboy."

He then walked back to Nancy and Mr. Davis. He looked straight at Nancy and said "Are you ready to ride Lady Jane?"

Before she could answer him, he had his cell phone out. He called Jake and told him to bring Lady Jane to the arena. A few minutes later Jake walked Lady Jane into the arena. He walked back into the arena to get the reins from Jack. He asked him to take care of Lizzy for him who was still standing still at the ramp.

While they were waiting on Lady Jane, he explained to Nancy that no one has ridden Lady Jane since she has been there. Her cuts and bruises are all healed. She needs to bond with you. She belongs to you, and she trusts you. She needs to see you, and know that you are not the same as before. She needs to know that you walk with a cane. It is not something that you are going to use to hurt her.

Nancy bend down to pick up her cane. She stood up, then she slowly walked into the arena with her cane. Before she could say a word, he handed her the reins. He walked to the side of the arena to where Mr. Davis sat watching his daughter. He watched her stand there holding the reins in one hand and her cane in the other. She just stood there. He could see different emotions on her face like she was having a hard time making a decision. She finally started walking around the arena with Lady Jane walking behind her. He let them walk around the arena for about ten minutes.

Hank went and got a saddle and a saddle blanket. He told her to bring Lady Jane over to the ramp. He put the blanket and then the saddle on Lady Jane. "Can you get up on the saddle by yourself, or do you need some help?"

"I think I can balance on my left leg while I slide my right leg over the top of the saddle."

"Let me turn her around so that you can mount her on the other side. I will stand on the other side just in case you need help."

She slid on the saddle with no problem. Hank adjusted the stirrups for her feet. "You ready Nancy?"

"As ready as I will ever be."

She rode Lady Jane around the arena for about thirty minutes. When she was ready to dismount, she rode up to the ramp and dismounted without any help. She walked over to Hank and asked if he would build her a ramp. She also wanted to know how long it would take to train Lady Jane to use the ramp.

He told her to bring the horse trailer next weekend so that she could take Lady Jane home.

"Really!"

"Really!" replied Hank.

CHAPTER 11

Later that afternoon, Jake saddled a horse for Beth. He called her on his cell phone and told her where to meet him. When she found Jake, he had Black Jack and another horse saddled. Her name was Dolly. He helped her get on Dolly and handed her the reins. He turned to her and said, "Let's go for a little ride."

"Okay, but don't go too fast."

They walked the horses through the pasture until they came to a creek before she finally broke the silence. "Can I ask you a question?"

"Sure, you can ask me anything."

"What did you do that was so bad at school that no one will talk to you?"

"I got into a couple of fights."

"What were the fights over?"

"The first fight was over a girl. I liked her a lot. I found out that she was seeing someone behind my back. She got pregnant and he tried to blame it on me. I found out who the guy was. I confronted him at his locker at school. I knew I didn't get her pregnant because I wasn't that close to her. Our argument ended up in a fight. I broke his nose and he walked around for over a week with a black eye. "

"What happened to the girl when the truth came out?"

"Her father got his job to transfer him to another area, so they moved away. After that, I don't know what happened to her. I heard that she gave the baby up for adoption."

"What about the guy?"

"He still goes to our school. He plays a lot of sports. He will graduate this year. We don't speak to each other and try to stay out of each other's way."

"What else happened?"

"A few weeks later one of his buddies started some stuff with me. He came up ehind me in the hall while I was at my locker. He told me I wasn't going to be anything but a loser, just like my father. Well, that just pissed me off. I turned around, and pushed him up against the locker. I knocked him out with one punch. I got suspended from school for a week."

"Why do people do stuff like that? It is so stupid." replied Beth.

"So, now I don't talk to anyone because I don't want to get dragged into their drama. I just want to finish school and get on with my life. If I get into another fight, I'm out of school for good."

"That's not fair when you didn't start the fight."

"I might not have started the fights, but I 'm the one that threw the first punch."

For the rest of the ride, they rode in silence. When they returned to the barn, Jake dismounted first. He moved next to Dolly's head so that she could hand him the reins. Beth slid off the saddle and almost into his arms. She was so embarrassed that her cheeks turned pink.

"I'll take care of Dolly for you so that you can get back to the house."

"Okay, thanks for taking me riding. It was nice."

"Your riding has improved a lot."

He stood there for a few seconds and watched her walk toward the house. *Now that she knows about me, she will probably stay away from me. That's all right because I came here to work and learn about horses. I don't need anything else in my life right now, especially a girl.*

As Beth walked back to the house she was thinking how some things were just so unfair in life. Now that she talked to Jake, she knew why he was such a loner. She did not blame him for his actions. *I love to hear him talk. I hope he proves everyone wrong and does make something of himself.*

She walked into the kitchen, washed her hands. She then started making biscuits to go with the stew that was cooking . When Ella walked into the kitchen to talk to her. Beth noticed that she had a puzzled look on her face. "What did the Fire Chief have to say about the fire?"

"He asked me a couple of questions. He wanted to know if you or I smoked cigarettes. I told him no. Then he asked if we had made any enemies since we have moved here. I told him no again. He was going to look around one more time. He thinks the fire started from a lit cigarette. I haven't walked out in that field since we got here, have you?"

"No, I stay pretty much in the house since I'm here by myself most of the time waiting for you to get home. I did take a look in the barn, but that is all."

"Have you seen anyone out in that field walking around or anything?"

"Now, that is a stupid question. You know I would be on the phone calling you if I did."

"I am not sure how I feel about this whole thing. I just want to believe that it was just an accident."

Beth told Ella that dinner would be ready in about ten minutes. Ella left the room to finish cleaning the living room. She noticed that there were no family pictures in the room. She didn't see pictures in any of the rooms, except the den where she saw a couple of pictures. *Why aren't there any pictures of him with any of the horses that he has owned over the years? As good looking as he is, why isn't he married? He has this big house and he is the only one that lives in it.*

During supper Hank asked Ella what the Fire Chief had to say about the fire. She told him about the questions that he asked her. She told him what she told the Fire Chief. "I just think it was an accident."

"We'll be going home s soon as we clean up the

kitchen for you. We have things that need to be done at home. "

"If you don't feel safe going home, you can always stay here." replied Hank.

"Thanks, but we really need to go home."

CHAPTER 12

When Hank took Jake home that night Jake talked to him about buying a couple head of cattle when they went to the auction. He wanted to know how much he would charge him to have them graze at the Rock R Ranch. He wanted to start out small just like Hank did. He wanted to help provide for his mom, and he knew that would help. He has been saving up his money so that he could buy a truck and a horse. *That is if he kept working for Hank.*

Hank told him that next Saturday they would go to an auction. They would see what they could get. He was looking for some calves because he wanted to double his herd this year. They would work out something if Jake bought a couple calves.

When Hank returned to the ranch he had to check on the horses one more time before he could call it a night. He checked on Baby and gave her some extra feed. After he left the barn he walked to Black Jack's corral. As soon as he reached the fence Black Jack saw him and walked over to see him. He reached over the fence so that he could run his hand down the side of his neck. He said to Black Jack, "Are you starting to like Jake? I know he really likes you. I think you are good for each other."

He stroked his hand up and down the side of Black Jack's neck a few more times. Black Jack moved his head up and down a couple of times in reply to his words. A little chuckle escaped out of his mouth. "Good night, Black Jack."

Wyatt was waiting for him in the kitchen when he entered the house. He let Wyatt out and stood out there with him. Taking in a quick look of the property, he saw how much he has done to the place since he has been there. There was so much more that he wanted to do.

He walked into his den. He sat down at his desk and turned on his computer. Images of Ella popped up on his screen. He took some time to do some research on the grasses that he and Jake had discussed. Jake might be on to something. The field would need to be plowed and the grass planted soon. He would call Jerry tomorrow. Jerry owned the feed store in town. He would find out the cost of the grass seed and how soon he could get it.

He turned off the computer. He then headed to his room where his thoughts had changed to Ella. *She has the most beautiful blonde hair. I can't wait to touch it again. A man could get lost, looking in those blue eyes of hers.*

Now that I have had a taste of her I want more. I will have to watch and see what she does next. The kiss that we shared was not something I will forget. With a groan Hank headed for the shower.

Ella was glad to be home. She needed to put some distance between her and Hank. She needed time to think. *When he held me in his arms last night in his kitchen, he made me feel so safe. I have never felt so safe before. It felt so right. When I kissed him I never thought that he would deepen the kiss as he did. If the kiss lasted any longer I wouldn't have been able to stand. He is a magnificent kisser. I could have let him hold me and kiss me for hours.*

How am I going to keep our relationship professional when he is so good looking and so sexy? I have to keep focused on getting Beth through school and keeping a roof over our heads. I will have to make sure that we are not alone too much.

She rolled over in her bed trying to find a comfortable

position and prayed that sleep would come soon.

CHAPTER 13

Hank went over to Ella's property to see what he could find. He found several different paths behind her house. It looked like someone has been watching the house or her. The person or persons that have been watching the house used a different path that led in a different direction every time they were there. The recent rain washed away any foot prints. He wandered over to the far side of the property and was surprised at what he found.

He decided that he wasn't going to share this information with anyone just yet. He wanted to know who was behind it. He was going to set up a few cameras around the property to see what he could find out. He knew the law enforcement would not spend the time to investigate things so, he will do his own.

A few days later, he had been in the barn working when he found Ella standing at the stall door of Baby's stall. She had her forehead resting against Baby's forehead. The sight of her took his breath away. He took a picture of them to remember the beauty that he saw. He slowly walked up behind her.

"What are you doing here?" he asked

She was so startled that when she turned around, she stood just inches from him. She slowly tilted her head to look at his face. She ran her tongue over her bottom lip.

In a voice that was so soft he said "I hope that you are not working right now because I am going to kiss you."

He brushed his lips against hers before he deepened the kiss. A soft moan escaped from her. She brought her hands to his chest and rested them there. She could feel his heartbeat under her hand. She could feel his hardness against her softness. She heard a moan come from him as he ended the kiss. He still held her in his arms.

She was waiting for the dizziness to stop. Her legs had gone weak. She was glad that he was still holding her up. In a voice that sounded almost normal she said "Doc gave me some papers to give to you. I wanted to drop them off on my way home."

He took a step back from her. She was driving him crazy. He had to put some space between them or he was going to kiss her again.

"Doc called me earlier today to tell me about Baby's owner. He was killed in action overseas. He told me he was going to do the paperwork so that I could sell Baby if I wanted. She now belongs to me. She has a ways to go before I can even think about selling her."

"I feel so bad for her, but I know that you will take good care of her."

"It seems that Baby likes you. She trusts you. You know that you can visit her anytime you want."

They turned and walked out of the barn to her car so that she could get the paperwork for Baby. She handed him the papers. He asked her, "Do you have plans for Saturday?"

"I have this weekend off from the clinic unless there is a big emergency where Doc will need me . I was planning on coming over here with Beth. While she cooked meals for you, I was going to do some cleaning for you."

"I was wondering if you and Beth would be interested in going to an auction on Saturday afternoon. Jake and I are going to a cattle auction. I'm going to see if there is anything worth buying. I was just wondering if you and Beth would like to go. "

"Let me talk it over with Beth and I will let you know."

Before she could turn away rom him, he pulled her closer to him. "Please tell me to stop, because I can't help myself." He lowered his lips to hers. It started out as a gentle kiss until she parted her lips then he deepened the kiss. He was waiting to see if she would push him away, but she didn't. A small moan escaped from her lips. He was about to lose his mind. She was making him want her more. He broke the kiss and looked into her eyes. He could see her eyes starting to darken in color with desire.

With his voice just above a whisper, he said "I'll see you on Saturday."

He watched her get into her car and drive down the driveway. He walked back to the barn to get some more work done.

Well Buddy, that was stupid to kiss her like that. Not once, but twice. You are going to scare her off if you don't watch out. But, her mouth is so kissable. I so want to put my fingers in her hair again.

Ella drove the car up to the front of the house. She turned the motor off and sat in her car staring out the windshield. *That man sure does know how to kiss. Those kisses were amazing. I would have turned into putty if he kissed me any longer. I have to get it together before I walk into the house and Beth sees me. Saturday is only a couple days away.*

When she walked into he house she found Beth in the kitchen. She could smell meatloaf cooking. "Supper smells so good and I am starving." She told her that she had stopped over at Hank's to give him some papers. She told her about the conversation that they had about going to the auction.

Beth told her if they went over early in the morning, she could get a lot done before they left to go to the auction. What she didn't get done on Saturday, she could finish on Sunday if that was okay with her. She had never been to an auction before, so this was something new for her to see.

After dinner, Ella took Toby outside for a few minutes. Toby walked around the yard a few times before he finally walked back to her. She just realized that Beth was beginning to change since she started working for Hank. She didn't seem to be so withdrawn and hiding in her bedroom. She couldn't believe that she was willing to go to a cattle auction. Is this the same girl that would hang out at a mall all day shopping?

Before she went inside, she took a walk around the house to make sure everything looked alright. She looked out over the field behind the house. She didn't see anything. She had been checking every night since the fire.

CHAPTER 14

Ella and Beth arrived at Hank's house just after breakfast. Hank and Jake were already out in the barn doing the chores when they arrived. Ella got busy cleaning the upstairs. Beth started cooking in the kitchen. When Hank came into the house around eleven o'clock he told Beth that they would be in at noon for lunch. They needed to leave for the auction no later than one o'clock.

When Hank came back to the house around noon, he walked down the hall to his bedroom to take a quick shower before lunch since they would be leaving soon. He closed his bedroom door. He had stripped off his shirt. He was in the process of undoing his belt buckle when Ella came out of his bathroom.

She took in the sight of him from head to toe.

Starting with his broad chest and tight abs. Her eyes moved down to his hips and muscular thighs. Damn, he was so sexy. Her senses were already working in overdrive from smelling his scent. She could never get enough of it.

"Do you like what you see Ella?" he asked in a raspy sexy voice. He stood where he was because he knew if he walked closer to her he would want to kiss that kissable mouth and run his fingers through her beautiful hair.

"I will finish your bathroom later. I lost track of time." she walked past him to leave the room.

He walked into the bathroom to finish undressing before he stepped into the shower. He heard her close the door behind her. *So much for trying to play it on the cool side.*

When he returned to the kitchen about fifteen minutes later, he noticed that Jake came in. As he was heading for the back stairs. He got himself a cup of coffee while he talked to Beth. Jake returned to the kitchen about ten minutes later with damp hair and he was buttoning up his shirt when he walked in. He grabbed his lunch from the counter. He ate it without saying a word.

When Ella came into the kitchen, Hank took her in from head to toe just as she had done earlier to him. She had her blonde hair pulled back into a ponytail. She had a long sleeve t-shirt on that she had tucked into her jeans with boots on her feet. Damn, she was beautiful. "As soon as everyone is ready, we will leave. The auction is about twenty minutes away."

When they arrived at the auction, they headed toward where the cattle were being penned. They were just finishing auctioning off the horses when Hank told them they better get a seat in the arena area. Hank bought a couple of Angus cows that were about a year old. Jake bought two Angus cows and a young bull.

When they went to go pay for the cattle that they just bought, they left the girls by themselves. Ella went to the lady's bathroom. Beth stood outside in the hallway waiting for her when a young man walked up to her. He was wearing a cowboy shirt, chaps over his black jeans. His black cowboy hat was pushed back on his head. He said, "Hey beautiful, you aren't from around here because I would remember a beautiful face like yours. If you like I can show you around this place or maybe get you something to drink."

The next thing she knew, Jake had walked up beside her. He placed his hand on her back and kissed the side of her face and said "Are you ready, Baby?"

"I see that you have someone to show you around.

Maybe sometime I will see you again." The young man raised two fingers to the brim of his cowboy hat. He then turned around to walk back the way he came.

Jake moved his hand from her back to her arm because she turned toward him so that she could see his face. *Did he just call me baby? I will have to ask him what that was all about.*

When Jake saw Ella approaching them he dropped his hand from her arm. He also stepped back a step so that he wasn't so close to her. He told her that he was going to the men's room and then they were going to load up the cattle.

As they rode back to the ranch, Hank talked about the rodeo season that was just beginning in the area. He asked Beth if she had ever gone to a rodeo before. She told him no. He replied, " I hope that you get the experience to go, they are a lot of fun."

"Are you going to sign up for any of the events this year, Jake?"

"I haven't decided yet. I have been thinking about entering a couple of events."

"Tomorrow I will see what you can do to see if I can give you some pointers. "

"Sounds good to me."

When they arrived at the ranch, Ella and Beth

went into the house. Hank pulled the trailer to the pasture next to the birthing barn. Jake jumped out to open the gate so that Hank could back the truck in. As soon as the truck was backed in, they unloaded the cattle from the trailer.

When Hank entered the kitchen, Beth was stirring something on top of the stove that smelled so delicious. She told him that supper would be ready in a few minutes. He took out his cell phone to let Jake know about supper. He asked her where Ella was before he started down the hall toward his bedroom.

If she is in my bedroom or my bathroom, I am not going to be able to control myself.

He found her in his den dusting. She had an I-pod in her pocket with the earphones in her ears. She was dancing away to the music that she was listening to. She didn't hear him come to the doorway. He stood there watching her for a minute before she realized someone was watching her. As soon as she saw him she stopped dancing. Their eyes connected across the room. His eyes never left hers as he told her that supper was ready. He finally broke the spell by looking away from her. She followed him to the kitchen enjoying looking at his hot butt.

After dinner, the girls cleaned the kitchen. Before they went home Beth told Hank that she would be back tomorrow for a little while. She needed to make more meals for him so that he would have enough for the week. He told her that would be fine.

Beth didn't see Jake before she left. She wanted to ask him about what happened at the auction earlier today. When she was alone in her bedroom, she decided to text him.

Beth: Would you please tell me why you made that guy at the auction believe we were a couple?

Jake: I saw him checking you out earlier. I knew he was going to make a move on you. Did you not see how he was dressed? He was wearing chaps trying to impress someone. You don't need to get mixed up with someone like him.

Beth: I neve said anything to him. You got there before I could answer his question.

Jake: I'm sorry. I was trying to protect you. He wanted to do more than just show you around.

Beth: Thanks for looking out for me.

Jake: That's what friends do. Are you coming over tomorrow because if you are there is something I want to talk to you about?

Beth: Yes, I will be over there. We can talk then. I will look for you before I leave if I don't see you before then.

I wonder what he wants to talk to me about. Well, I guess I will find out tomorrow.

CHAPTER 15

Ella took Beth over to Hank's house before she headed to town. She needed to go to the clinic for Doc. He got called away for an emergency. She didn't mind because she needed to go to the grocery store as long as she was in town.

She was on her way back to the ranch when she heard this thump, thump, thump noise. She pulled her car off the side of the road. She opened the car door, got out and walked around the car. She had a flat tire. She didn't have a spare. She got out her cell phone and dialed Hank's phone.

He answered his phone on the third ring, "This is Hank."

"Hank can you come and get me? I have a flat tire. I'm on the main road from town. I am about five minutes from my place."

"Ella, honey, I will be right there. Just give me a couple of minutes."

When he found her, she was standing outside of her car with her arms crossed in front of her. She looked like she was really upset.

He walked toward her with his cowboy hat on and wearing his sunglasses. He stood beside her with his hands on his hips.

Looking all cowboy and sexy.

"Ella, do you have a spare tire?" he asked.

"No, I haven't had the money to get one since I moved here. It is on my list of many things to do." she replied.

"Get your purse and I will get someone to fix your tire for you."

"I have groceries in the car that I need to take home."

He opened up the car door, grabbed the grocery bags then carried them to his truck. "Is there anything else you need?"

Yeah, I could use one of those delicious kisses. Get that thought right out of your head girl.

She got her purse and climbed into his truck. His truck smelled like horse, hay, and Hank. She pulled her sunglasses from the top of her head back to where they covered her eyes. She didn't want him to see the emotions that she was feeling.

They rode in silence to her house. He parked the truck next to the house so that he could unload the groceries. As soon as the door opened, Toby was there to meet them. She let him out in the yard. Hank carried the groceries to the kitchen for her.

When she came back in, she started to put the groceries away. Hank was looking the place over from where he was standing. He could tell that they had been putting in a lot of work into the place." I like what you have done to the place."

"Thanks, it is coming along slowly."

He walked up behind her as she was reaching in the cupboard. Her neck was exposed to him so he placed a feather like kiss on her neck. She leaned back into him. She slowly turned to ace him and his lips brushed hers. She moved her arms around his neck. She pulled him toward her so that she could kiss him. She parted his lips to taste his mouth with her tongue. A deep moan came from him. His hands were on her sides and he was pulling her closer to him. With her arms around his neck she had her fingers in his hair. When they were both having hard time breathing, he finally pulled away from her enough so that he could look in her eyes.

He rested his forehead on hers and asked her in a very sexy deep voice, "Please tell me that you will let me take you over to the house and that you'll stay for supper."

"Yes, I will go over and stay for supper."

"Ella, I'm not the type of person that plays games with people. So please listen to what I have to say. You told me that you don't date. I am very attracted to you, but I don't have time to date because I have a ranch to run. I think you are beautiful, sweet and sexy as hell. Once I get you into my bed, you will be mine. You will be mine, mind, body and soul. Don't encourage me if you don't want this too. You better think about what you want before you kiss me again. I will be honest with you, I don't know how any kisses like that I can handle."

"I will think about what you just said. There is a lot about me that you don't know."

"There is a hell of a lot more that I would like to discover if given the chance. Right now, I need to get back to the ranch. I have Billy coming over today."

"Is it alright if I bring Toby along so that he can play with Wyatt?"

She put Toby's leash on him then grabbed her purse and sunglasses off the counter. They headed out the door to the truck. They were both quiet on the ride to the ranch. He parked the truck by the house since he would be going back out later.

He was talking on his cell phone on his way to the barn. When Ella walked into the house she saw Beth in the kitchen. She told her that they would be staying for supper. She also told her about her flat tire.

Beth told Ella that she was getting ready to go out to the barn to talk to Jake for a few minutes. Ella decided to walk out to the barn with her. When Ella stopped at Baby's stall she noticed that it was empty. Someone must have put her outside in the pasture.

Beth told her she would see her back at the house in a little bit. She walked until she came to the arena. She stood in the doorway so that she could watch Hank. Hank and Billy's dad were getting Billy in the saddle. She watched Hank strap Billy's leg in place.

"Are you ready, cowboy?"

"Yeah."

"Walk Lizzy around the arena two times. She has to get warmed up. Do you understand me Billy?"

"Yeah."

Ella stood there and watched them for about

fifteen minutes. She was amazed at what he was doing and how he made Billy feel. She then walked outside and found Baby in a corral with Star next to the barn. As soon as she walked up to the fence Baby walked toward her. You could see that she was starting to gaining weight. She looked really bad when she first came to the ranch. All of her ribs were showing from not being fed properly.

She put her hand out so that she could touch Baby's forehead then run her hand down the side of her neck. Star saw all the attention that Baby was getting and walked to the fence to get in on the action. Ella rubbed her hand on Star's forehead too.

Hank takes good care of his horses and cattle. I wonder if he would take good care of woman that he loved. He fixes broken animals all the time. I wonder if he would have the patience to fix a broken woman? I have come a long way over the years, but, I don't know if I am ready to take the chance of being rejected once he gets me in his bed. What should I do?

She walked back to the house and let the dogs out. She sat on the step and watched them play in the yard for a while.

He is so damn sexy and such a good kisser. I know he wants me. I can feel his body responding from just kissing me. I can see the desire in his eyes.

Beth walked up to her and asked her what she was

so deep in thought about. She lied to her, by telling her she was thinking about her car. She really needed to get new tires. She was hoping that her car would last one more year before she got another one. She really needed to get something with four- wheel drive.

"I have something that I want to talk to you about. I just talked to Jake, and I think he might be on to something. Jake wants to plant a pumpkin patch in the field behind the house. It won't be a big one. He will have the field plowed so that we can plant the seeds. He will sell the pumpkins this fall when Hank has his fall harvest cookout. We are going to make it more family oriented.

If you say yes, then he will talk to Hank. He has some other things he wants to talk to him about.

Jake likes him a lot. He wants to stay working for him as long has Hank will have him. He has learned a lot from him. Hank is also going to help him raise the cattle that he just bought. He likes that Hank really listens to his ideas, and that they really discuss things together. He doesn't belittle him or make him think that he doesn't know what he is talking about."

"You and Jake are becoming good friends, aren't you?"

"Jake and I have talked a lot in the last couple of weeks. I would like to think that we are becoming good friends. We are both loners. Anything that he tells me, he knows won' get told all over school. I can also trust him with things too. He knows that I want to go away to school after I graduate. "

"You and Jake can plant pumpkins or whatever you want in that field. It would be nice to see something growing in that field besides weeds."

"I'm also going to have him dig me up a garden close to the house for a vegetable garden. I'm going to turn that place into a farm."

"We aren't going to be getting chickens, are we?"

Beth replied "I'm not buying any chickens, are you?"

They both laughed. Beth then told her she needed to get inside to start supper. She asked her if she needed any help and was told no.

Ella sat there for a few minutes thinking about what she should do about Hank. She really liked him a lot.

During supper, Hank talked to Jake about the rodeo. Jake told him he only wanted to do the calf roping and the barrel racing. He had been practicing his roping every chance he got. Ella asked Hank if he was going to enter any of the rodeo events. He told her his rodeo days were over. They all sat there and listened to him talk about his rodeo days. All the events that he was in and how many events he took first place.

After dinner, the girls cleaned up the kitchen then waited for Hank to take them home. He took the girls and Toby home first. On the way to Jake' s house, Jake started talking to him about what he had discussed with Beth. He listened to him talk about his ideas about what he would like to do at the fall harvest cookout.

"Jake, if it's something that you really want to do, then do it. I will help you any way that I can, because I think your ideas are great. All you can do is try it. I think the people will like it."

When Hank returned to the ranch, he went into the den and turned on his computer. He wanted to know if the cameras that he installed on Ella's property earlier this week had picked up anything yet. He didn't notice anything unusual. He decided he would check it again in a couple more days. *Someone is up to something and I will find out who it is.*

He downloaded a couple more pictures of Ella that he took today on his cell phone. He saw her out at the corral where Star and Baby were this afternoon. He also noticed her watching Billy when he was riding in the arena this afternoon. He also saw her deep in thought sitting on the back steps while the dogs played in the yard.

After our talk today, I wonder if she is going to run like a scared rabbit or if she will trust me enough to love her and make her mine. I wonder how long it will take for her to make a decision. I have patience. Good things come to those who wait.

It started raining during the night. It was coming down pretty steady when Hank woke up the next morning. Wyatt didn't want to go outside because it was raining. He was drinking his coffee when Ben arrived. He told Ben that he was waiting on Ella to call so that he could take her to work. He went on to tell him about her flat tire yesterday.

Just then, his cell phone rang. It was Ella calling him telling him she was ready to go to work. He told her he would be right over to pick her up. Ben headed out to the barn and took Wyatt with him who was not happy about getting wet. He put on his cowboy hat then headed out the back door to get into his truck.

He pulled up as close as he could to Ella's back door so she wouldn't have so far to walk in the rain. He reached across the seat and opened the door for her. She climbed into the truck and said, "Good morning, I really appreciate all the help."

"Morning." replied Hank.

He was quiet on the ride into town. He was waiting to see if she was going to mention anything about the conversation that they had yesterday. She just sat there and looked out the window. As he pulled up in front of the clinic he told her that her car should be done sometime this morning. He waited until she unlocked the clinic door before he headed back to the ranch.

I sure would like to know what is going on in that pretty head of hers. She is acting like she is afraid to talk to me. I wonder if she and Beth got into a fight this morning. Maybe she is just not a morning person.

Later that morning, the garage delivered Ella's car. The car had four brand new tires on it and a spare in the trunk. She was busy when they dropped it off, so they left the keys at the front desk. After she got done with work, she walked out to her car to go home. She noticed the new tires on her car.

Holy crap! Four new tires! I only needed one tire. Well, if he thinks these new tires are going to get me into his bed he has another thing coming. It is going to take more than new tires. The man is driving me crazy. I am going to have to say something to him, but, right now I am just too mad to talk him. Maybe by the time I get to his house I'll have calmed down some.

She drove right to his house. Before she got out of her car, she texted him to see where he was because she wanted to talk to him. He told her that he was in the barn in the tack room. Before she walked to the tack room she took a deep breath to calm herself down. When she entered the room, he turned to face her. He leaned back against the small counter. He could tell that she was upset by the expression on her face and he could see it in her beautiful eyes.

She tried to speak in a calm voice, "I want to thank you for buying the tires for my car. I will gladly pay you. I was only expecting one tire, not four."

"You needed the tires for your car. I bought them for you. You don't need to pay me for them. You clean my house and won't let me pay you. It's the least I can do."

She stood there with her hands at her sides knowing that if she moved closer to him or if he touched her, she would turn to putty. He had that effect on her.

"Well, are you sure you didn't buy them for another reason?"

"Ella, what are you talking about?"

"You didn't buy the tires hoping that I would repay you by getting into your bed?"

He replied in a gentle, sexy voice, "I am offended that you would think so little of me, or even of yourself. When you come to my bed, you will come because you want to be there. We talked about this yesterday. When you become mine, you will not go without anything because I will take care of all your needs.

I'm not looking for just sex. I am sure that you will be an excellent lover. I'm looking for a special person who is willing to be my partner, in more ways than one. Someone, who is willing to be part of my soul and let me be part of hers. You would be loved and cherished forever."

Hank walked over to Ella, bent his head and gently kissed her. "You just have to decide if you want to be mine. "

She replied in a voice that was just above a whisper, "What makes you think that I want more than friendship from you?"

"Ella, your body tells me that you do. You are very responsive to me when I touch you or when I kiss you."

"Well, that's only because you are such an excellent kisser. You probably have had lots of experience."

"Ella, what are you afraid of? Are you afraid to

have a relationship with someone?"

"No, I am not afraid of having a relationship with someone."

"Why don't you think about it for a few days? If you have any questions, or want something explained to you, we will sit down and discuss it like two adults. If you decide that you don't want a relationship with me, then just tell me. I will not pursue you or beg you to change your mind. I will not ask you again."

"Hank, you almost make this sound like a business deal."

"I'm sorry if that is what it sounds like. I just think it's better if both of us know what to expect from the other person. You have a very demanding job and I have a ranch to run. You may be seeing someone already. I don't know. I just know how I feel right now. I want you to tell me how you feel and what you want."

"Alright, I will think about it. I will give you an answer this weekend when I come over with Beth."

She walked out of the tack room and stopped at Baby's stall and then Star's stall on her way out.

When she walked in the door at home she found Beth in the kitchen making supper while listening to music on the radio. She told her about the new tires that Hank bought for her car.

Beth turned away from the stove and said, "He really did that for you?"

"Yes, he did, and I stopped over there to thank him and to tell him that I would pay him for the tires. He told me I didn't have to since I was cleaning his house for him."

"That was really nice of him to do that. Before I forget, I need you to take me to meet with Rob Lawson on Saturday. He is giving his sister a graduation party and wants me to cater it. I told him that I would meet him at ten o'clock."

"You know Beth, you really need to think about getting your driver's license, and some transportation of your own. "

"After I get my driver's license I was thinking about getting the truck that is in the barn on the road for me to use. I have already talked to Jake about the truck, and he said that he would come over and take a look at it to see if he can get it started."

"Do you really want to drive Uncle Joe's old truck?"

"If it can get me from point A to point B, I'm all for it. I hate having to ask you to take me places all the time."

"I know and with my crazy work schedule it is hard to plan anything. Now that warmer weather is coming things should quiet down a lot."

"Things maybe quieting down for you, but things are picking up for me. Right now, I have a small wedding and one graduation party in the next six weeks. Plus I have to cook for Hank. I am going to ask him if I can use his kitchen for making food for the events that I have planned since our kitchen is not big enough. Some of the stuff I can make ahead and freeze. The graduation party is having homemade pizza. I can make the sauce ahead and freeze it."

"I am so proud of you Beth. You are really getting into this catering thing."

"The hard part is the planning and making sure that the people get what they really want. I am using the money that I get from working for Hank for the supplies. I am saving most of the money that I get so that I can take a cooking class next summer."

After supper Beth decided it was time to call her friend Libby Adams. She needed to talk to someone about Hank. She met Libby at a group session. Libby knew all of her dark secrets. She was her closest friend. They have been friends for over ten years.

Libby answered on the third ring. "It is about time that you called me. I have not heard from you since you got there."

"What, I don't even get a hello, or hi how are you?" said Ella with a laugh.

"Ok, hi, how are you?"

"That's better. I have so much to tell you. I really, really, need your opinion on something. I have met this guy named Hank. *He is so hot and sexy that you would not believe it.* He has a ranch next to where I live. He raises cattle and works with horses. I told him that I didn't date when I first met him. I told him that because I thought he was going to ask me out."

"Ok, so what is the problem that you have with him if you don't want to date him?"

"He told me that he wants to have a relationship with me. I mean a serious relationship with me."

"How serious is he talking? Are you ready for a serious relationship with him? It has been only about four or five months since you had your last boyfriend."

"You know why I broke it off with Mark, because he cheated on me. You also know why he cheated on me. "

"Tell me about your cowboy Hank. How well do you know him?"

She told her about the fire behind the house and staying at Hank's house. She told her how good he is with horses, how he heals them, trains them and makes them better. She also told her about Beth working for him and that they spend a lot of time on the weekends over at his ranch. She told her about her flat tire and how he took care of it."

After listening to her talk about Hank for ten minutes non-stop, Libby said, "It sounds like you really like this guy. Has he kissed you yet?"

"Yes, he has kissed me a couple of times . He is a very good kisser."

"The kind of kisses that make you melt?"

"Yes. What am I going to do Libby?"

"If you decide that you want to have a serious relationship with him, you are going to have to tell him about your intimacy problems. I think he will care enough about you to be patient and work with you on your issues. If there is chemistry between the two of you he'll be the one to help you, and understand you, because you can't fake chemistry."

"You are right. I will tell him before we start our relationship. I'm good while I have my clothes on, it's when the clothes come off, and they feel and see the scars on my body. I'm still having problems with intimacy. I have come a long way, but, I know it is going to take someone special to help me."

"Ella, I'll make arrangements to visit you in two weeks. I'm working on something right now, and I can't leave because I have a deadline of ten days to get this campaign ad done. As soon as I get it done I will be on a plane. I'll be able to visit you for a week. We will catch up on everything. I want to meet your cowboy Hank. How does that sound to you?"

"I can't wait to see you. Don't pack any fancy clothes because there isn't any place fancy to go out here. I promise I will talk to Hank, there is no sense in putting it off.

"Ok I will let you know of my travel plans when I get them. I'll talk to you later."

I have a few days to figure out a way to tell Hank. I don't want to sound pathetic. Libby is right it is better to tell him now before things get too serious. After I tell him he may not want a serious relationship with me.

Hank did his final rounds in the barn. He was checking on Black Jack when he heard his, great grandfather's voice. "He has recovered very well. The scars will always be visible. He has learned to trust Jake because Jake has treated him well and spends a great deal of time with him. They have bonded quite well. They have been good for each other."

"You're right grandfather, they have been good for each other. I have seen a change in Jake since he has been coming here. "

"I came to tell you that you will be getting more horses within the next couple of weeks."

"Thanks for letting me know."

"Are you still taking a lot of cold showers?"

"Grandfather I told you I was not going to discuss my love life with you. I have everything under control."

"Sure you do, until you get within ten feet of her." His great grandfather had vanished as quickly as he arrived.

Hank said good night to Black Jack and headed to the house. Ella began to creep into his thoughts as he walked. *I just want to run my fingers through her hair and kiss that kissable mouth of hers. I have never wanted a woman so bad in my life as I want her.*

CHAPTER 16

The rest of the week flew by so fast that it was Friday before Hank realized it. He was looking forward to seeing Ella this weekend. He was also afraid of what she might tell him. He would accept whatever choice she made. He was just praying that she would say yes.

Jake helped him finish up the chores. When the chores were done, he had Jake meet him in the arena. He told him to bring his rope with him so that he could see how he was doing with his roping. Hank put a pole in the arena. He then told Jake to pretend it was a calf that he was trying to rope. Every time he got the rope around the pole he had him step back farther from the pole. He worked with him for about an hour before they called it quits so that they could go get some supper.

During supper he asked Jake why he was entering the events at the rodeo.

"I just want to do it one time. I just want to see if I can do it."

"So, you aren't doing this to try and impress someone?"

"No, I am doing this for me. I'm not doing it for the prize or anything like that. I just want to see how good I really am."

"Are you planning on riding Black Jack in these events?"

"If you will let me I would like to."

"You can start training him tomorrow. We will see how he does. He should do ok with the calf roping, but you will have to train him for the barrel racing event. We will time him to see if he is going to be fast enough. If we start working with him now, he should do ok by the time the rodeo gets here."

After supper Jake said that he would do the last check on the horses. Hank knew he wanted to go see Black Jack. Wyatt followed him out the backdoor. The two of them headed for the barn. Hank stood there and chuckled to himself. He really liked Jake. He was more mature than some of the kids his age. He was so smart about some things. He knew that

Jake was going to make something of himself in the ranching business.

Ella and Beth arrived at the ranch after Beth had her meeting with Rob Lawson. Beth called Hank so that he would know that they were there. He told her that they would be in at lunch time.

Ella started cleaning as soon as she got in the door. She was such a nervous wreck. She has had butterflies in her stomach ever since she woke up that morning. She didn't want Beth to notice how nervous she was, so she had been trying not to get too close to her.

When the guys came in for lunch, Hank didn't see Ella. He went looking for her and found her in the formal dining room cleaning the chairs. The sight of her as always, took his breath away. He didn't know what to say to her so he said, "Ella are you ok?"

"Yes, I'm ok."

"Are you going to eat lunch with us, or are you too busy?"

"I'll be right there as soon as I finish cleaning this chair."

During lunch, he noticed that Ella looked tired, like she hadn't been sleeping well. He couldn't wait for them to have their talk his afternoon. She was not going to leave without talking to him. He was just as nervous as she was.

Later that afternoon Ella walked out to the barn to find Hank. It was time for them to have their talk. She found Star and Baby in the corral beside the barn and stopped to see them. She also needed the extra time to gather her inner strength for her talk with Hank.

She found Hank talking to one of the people that boarded their horse there. She was a pretty woman, and she sure was turning on the charm with Hank. He listened to what she had to say. As soon as he could, he walked away from her toward Ella. When he reached her, he bent down and kissed her forehead lightly, "Let's take a walk outside since it is so nice out today."

She walked beside him with his hand at the small of her back. They walked in silence for a while until Hank found a place where they could talk. When he stopped walking, he turned to face her. "So, have you thought about us having a relationship?"

"Yes, I have thought about it. I have thought a great deal about what you said. I think that you are a really nice person. You deserve to have someone that can love you, someone to share your dreams with. I am not sure that I am the right person to do that."

"Can I ask why you don't think you are the right person for me?"

"Hank, something happened to me a long time ago and because of what happened I have intimacy problems."

As soon as she spoke the words, she looked away because she didn't want to see the look in his eyes. She was afraid of what he would see. He took a step closer to her, placed his hands on both sides of her face. He turned her face back to look at him, then he kissed her. Gently at first and then he deepened the kiss.

"I really don't think that we will have a problem with intimacy."

"Hank, you don't have any idea. I am fine as long as I have my clothes on. But, as soon as these clothes are off, it becomes a different story. I don't know if I can put my heart and feelings out there again to be hurt. I know I can't handle one more person cheating on me because I can't satisfy them in bed."

"Ella, I would never cheat on you. I know you have probably heard it before. If we proceed with a relationship, we will be loyal to each other. That is a must on my part, as much as for you. If you have a problem with anything that I say or do, you tell me. You can't fix problems if no one knows there is a problem. Communication is just as important as intimacy is in a relationship.

You will have to have faith in us as a couple, but most importantly, you will have to trust me. Without the trust, there is nothing. If we work at this together, and I mean together, I think we can make it work. I don't want to make any mistakes with you."

"You really mean it, don't you?"

"Yes, I do. I have never wanted to have a serious relationship with anyone in a very long time. You have stirred things in me that I thought were dead. "

She stood there silent for a moment then said, "If you're still willing to try, knowing up front about me. I am going to say yes."

"I am so glad to hear that. I know it was hard for you to make that decision. I will make sure that you won't regret it."

He wrapped his arms around her and kissed her. He kissed her a few more times before they headed for the house. Hank wrapped his arm around her and pulled her close to his side as they walked toward the house.

Beth and Ella stayed for supper. It was now a regular thing that Hank liked very much. He liked spending the time with Ella. He could see that things between Jake and Beth were changing too. They were all becoming comfortable with each other.

Ella was telling them that her friend Libby was coming to visit her next week. She told them that Libby was her oldest friend that she had. She was getting excited about her coming. Libby would only be able to stay for a week before she had to go back to work. She would be there for Memorial Day weekend. Ella asked if the town did anything special for that weekend.

Hank told her that the town put on a barbecue in the town square. There were people that set up booths selling homemade things. They held a dance there at night. "If you are interested in going I would like to take you and Libby. Talk it over with her and let me know."

"It sounds like fun. I will ask her if she would like to go." Ella replied.

After supper Ella and Hank had a few minutes to be alone. They took a walk outside. They walked side by side in silence for a couple of minutes. Hank broke

150

the silence by saying "I would like you to go riding with me tomorrow afternoon?"

"Sure, I would like that."

He stopped walking and turned to face her, "We can go after lunch. We won't be able to be gone for very long because Billy comes tomorrow. That or we can go after Billy's visit, whatever is best for you. I want to spend some time with you."

I will let you know how my day goes tomorrow so you know what will be better. I have to go to the clinic in the morning to check on things there. Then I will call you and let you know."

He leaned down and kissed her. She deepened the kiss and when she did Hank pulled her closer to his body. He wrapped his arms around her and ran his fingers through her hair. After he ended the kiss he stood there and looked into her eyes . He wanted to make sure she felt something too.

They walked back to the house hand in hand. "Do you go to the clinic every weekend?"

"No, Doc and I work it so that we alternate weekends. That way we both get a weekend off or at least try to. Doc usually has some emergency he has to deal with and I am always on call on weekends."

"I hope that things will be peaceful tomorrow

afternoon so that we can go for our ride."

When they reached the house, Beth was ready to go home. He walked them to the car and kissed Ella before she got in. On the way home Beth asked her if something was going on between her and Hank. She told her that they had talked about having a relationship.

"It's about time. I thought he was never going to ask you. I hope that you told him yes."

"How did you know he was going to ask me?"

"Have you seen the way he looks at you? He always wants to know where and what you are doing when he comes into the house if he doesn't see you."

"I wasn't aware of that."

"Well you are aware of it now. They are plowing the field tomorrow and digging my garden so I can plant some vegetables. Jake and I are going to plant the pumpkin seeds tomorrow after they plow. He's already bought the seeds. He is also going to help me plant my garden. I think it is going to be fun."

"Hank and I are going to go for a ride tomorrow afternoon. We won't be gone long because he has so much to do. I also have to go to the clinic in the morning. At least you won't be here alone if they are coming over to plow the field."

"Well I am going to my room I have some things to plan out for the graduation party and then I am going to go to bed. I will see you in the morning."

As soon as Beth got in her room and closed her door she texted Jake to let him know about Ella and Hank.

The next morning Ella left early for the clinic. She wanted to get done early if she could. She couldn't wait to get back to the house because she knew that Jake and Hank were going to be there. She was excited about spending some time with him.

She was at the clinic for a couple of hours before she got a chance to leave. As she was driving home her thoughts had drifted to Hank. All of a sudden a black SUV came up beside her car. The SUV started coming over into her lane. She thought the SUV was going to hit her. She took her foot off the accelerator to slow down the car, hoping that the SUV would pass her. The SUV also slowed down next to her car. She pushed on the accelerator to speed up and the SUV sped up. She was trying not to panic. Her knuckles had turned white where she had her hands on the steering wheel. She saw a car coming in the opposite direction headed right for the SUV. The SUV hit the front of her car causing her car to spin off the road. *Please don't let me die! Please don't let me die!* She tried to press on the breaks but was so afraid that she might roll her car down the embankment. The

SUV sped up and kept on going. As soon as the car slid to a stop she let out her breath that she did not realize that she was holding. With shaking hands, she got out her cell phone. She called Hank.

The car that was going in the opposite direction stopped and the man ran to Ella's car. He knocked on the driver's side window. When Hank answered his phone, he heard Ella screaming. He started running toward his truck.

"Ella, Honey are you all right? Where are you?"

"I'm just down the road. Someone ran me off the road and there is a man pounding on my window."

"Tell him that you are ok, and that you have someone coming to help you. Do not get out of the car and do not unlock your door. I will be there is just a couple of minutes."

He called the County Sheriff's office to report the incident. The sheriff's office told Hank that they would send someone right out.

He found Ella sitting in her car crying. She kept wiping her tears away with the palm of her hands. As soon as she saw Hank she opened the car door and ran to meet him. He opened up his arms to hold her. He stood there holding her until she stopped crying. His voice was soft as he was talking to her.

"Ella, are you all right? If you are all right that's all that matters." He kissed the top of her head. He continued to rub his hand up and down her back trying to calm her.

"The SUV came out of nowhere. I saw the car behind me a few miles back, but I didn't think too much of it. The next thing I knew it was trying to hit my car." She started crying again.

The man who was in the car that saw everything and stopped walked over to Hank.

"Is she ok?"

"She is just shaken up some. Thanks for stopping Kyle. Did you happen to see a license plate or see who was driving the SUV?"

"The windows were all tinted dark so that you couldn't see in. The plates on it were from out of state. I think it had Nevada plates. It was a black Cadillac Escalade. I'm not sure what year but it didn't look to be that old."

A County Sheriff's car pulled up behind Hank's truck. The sheriff got out of his car and walked to where the three of them were standing. The sheriff asked what happened and who was involved. Ella told the sheriff the same thing that she told Hank. Kyle also told the sheriff what he saw. The sheriff then walked over to Ella's car and looked at the damage that was done to her car. He asked her if she was hurt and needed to be seen by a doctor. She told the sheriff that she was fine.

The sheriff went to his patrol car to get the papers to fill out for the accident report. He asked her a couple more questions before he finished filling out the paperwork. He handed Ella a business card with his name on it. He told her that if he had any questions that he would contact her.

Hank asked her "Are you all right to drive the rest of the way home? If not, I will drive you home and we will come back and get your car later."

"I can drive my car home. Please follow me."

"I will be right behind you."

Hank gave her a hug and kissed her forehead. He watched her get into her car before he turned to get into his truck. While he followed her home, he was thinking. *Why would someone run her off the road? First the fire and now this. Someone is really out to scare her and is doing a good job.*

When they got to Ella's house the field in back had been plowed. Jake had also plowed a small area near the house for Beth's garden. Jake and Beth were planting pumpkin seeds. Jake was telling Beth that they were going to have more pumpkins than they figured. He hoped that they could figure out what to do with all of them.

Hank parked his truck next to her car. He got out and walked up to her. He asked her "Are you sure you're ok?" He wrapped his arms around her. He just wanted to hold her and comfort her.

She looked up at him "Yes, I will be ok. It just scared me a little. I'm just glad that my car wasn't damaged more than what is was. At least I can still drive it."

"When is your friend Libby coming to visit you? You will need something better to drive, why don't you use one of my trucks."

"She will be here toward the end of next week. She hasn't called me yet with her final travel plans . I think she is going to rent a car to drive while she is here."

"Ella, if you and Beth feel at any time that you are not comfortable about staying here. You know that you can come and stay at my house. There is plenty of room for you girls to stay there. I will admit that I would enjoy seeing you more. I will give you all the space that you need for you and your friend."

"Thanks, that means a lot to me." replied Ella.

"I need to get back over to the ranch. There is a lot going on today. I want to be able to spend some

time this afternoon with you. I hope that you still feel
like going riding with me today."

"Ok, I will see you later." She kissed him before
he got into his truck. After he left she walked out to
where Beth and Jake were planting the pumpkins. She
decided to help them so that they could get over to
the ranch sooner.

After Billy's visit Hank saddled two horses. He
called Ella and told her that the horses were ready and
to come to the barn. After they mounted the horses
they headed toward the stream. As soon as they were
alone he asked her if she was doing ok.

"I am doing fine."

"What made you decide to move here Ella?"

"My Uncle Joe's attorney contacted me. He told
me about the property. He told me I could sell it or
do what I wanted with it as it was left to me. I was
his only living relative. He suggested to me that I
should come and look at the property before I
made a decision. I was not in a position to do that
right away.

I had just ended a relationship with someone a
few months before that. I was ready to make a change
in my life. I also thought that it would be good for
Beth. She hated the school that she attended. She was
withdrawing more and more from me.

I talked it over with Beth. We decided to give it a try. We sold and gave everything away that didn't fit in my car. I quit my job and we moved here to get a new start. I had talked to Doc before we moved here. He told me that he could use an assistant. I had a job if I wanted it.

I have never been to the property that I can remember. My parents might have brought me here when I was little but, I don't remember. I had no idea what the place looked like. I just figured it couldn't be any worse than where we were living. Things just had to get better and so far, they have.

Beth has changed so much in the last month I can't believe it. She is talking to me again. She doesn't stay in her bedroom all the time. I think her friendship with Jake has helped her a lot. That and the way you treat her. Thank you for having faith in her and giving her a chance."

"I am glad that you decided to move here. Things will get better for both of you. You just have to have a little faith in yourself and in her."

"I just hope that you will have a lot of patience with me. I like you a lot. You are so different from all the guys that I have dated. You haven't pushed me into having sex with you the first time that you were alone with me. You have been honest and upfront with me. I like that."

"I 'm not like other guys, I know what I want and will not settle for anything less. I want you very much, but I also want you to want me.

Since I have asked you a question it is only fair that I answer any question that you might have about me."

They had arrived at the stream. They both dismounted and stood next to each other as the horses drank from the stream. He put his arm around her and drew her closer to his side. He couldn't wait to touch her hair. He started running his fingers through her hair as he said,

"What no questions?"

"I have several questions, I just don't know which one to ask. You told me that it has been a long time since you have had a serious relationship with someone. What happened to that relationship?"

"Yes, it has been a very long time. I dated and fell in love with my high school sweetheart. We had talked about getting married and having a future together. Right after graduation she got ill. The doctors told her she had cancer. The cancer was so advanced that she was told she only had six months to live. After she died it took me a long time to get over her death. I loved her very much.

When I went to college, I had dated a few women

but they didn't stir anything in me. After I returned home I decided to build up my ranch instead of chasing women."

They mounted the horses again and rode back to the barn. They rode side by side. He noticed how the sun shined behind Ella and it made her look like an angel. *His angel. He was already falling in love with her. She just didn't know it yet.*

When they reached the barn, they dismounted. He led the horses into the breezeway by their stalls. While he took care of the horses, Ella stopped at Baby's stall and then Star's stall. He walked up beside her, "I think you have made some friends here. Star is now saddle broke and I think she will let you ride her. The next time we go riding I will let you ride her."

"Do you really think she will let me ride her after what I did. I didn't know what happened to her, or I wouldn't have let the dogs come into the barn."

"She has become really good friends with Wyatt. He comes and visits her all the time now. She looks for him when I put her out in the corral. Now that Wyatt is getting bigger he is starting to be playful with Star. You should watch them sometime.

You visit her whenever you come over. She likes you, so I am sure that she trusts you. I don't think you will have any problems riding her."

"I would like to try to ride her the next time we go. I enjoyed our ride today. I have forgotten how nice it is."

"I would like it if you would find the time to go riding with me every Sunday afternoon. It will be a good way for us to get to know each other."

"That is something for me to think about."

CHAPTER 17

On Wednesday night Ella's phone rang. Libby called with her travel plans. She was going to be flying in on Friday afternoon. She would rent a car to drive to Ella's house. She would be there by supper time. Ella decided that she would stop by Hank's after work tomorrow, to tell him about Libby's plans. Also to tell him that she wouldn't need to borrow one of his trucks. She was also anxious to see him since she had not seen him since Sunday.

After she pulled into Hank's driveway she parked near the house. She took out her phone and texted him.

Ella: Where are you?

Hank: I'm in the arena working with Moondance. Where are you?

Ella: Heading your way. I just got here.

A few minutes later he saw her. *He saw his beautiful angel. As always, she took his breath away when he saw her.* He stopped working with Moondance when he saw her stepping into the arena to stand by his side. "What is going on?"

"I came to tell you that my friend Libby is arriving tomorrow."

"Will you still be coming over here on Saturday and staying for supper?" He moved closer so that he could touch her. He placed his free hand on her arm and moved it up and down.

"I won't be doing any cleaning while she is here. I want her to meet you. I think you will like her. I will talk to her about coming over for supper."

"Does she like horses? If she does you two can go riding."

"I know that she knows how to ride, but, I think it has been a long time since she has. Are we still going to the celebration in town this weekend?"

"The cookout and dance is on Sunday. I will be happy to take you girls. Jake and Beth can use one trucks and meet us there. If that is ok with you. "

They walked holding hands back to Moondance's stall. He let Moondance into the stall and turned so that he could kiss Ella. What a sweet kiss it was. When he moved his mouth to the side of her neck and began kissing her she let out a soft moan. He returned to her mouth and kissed her one more time before he drew her into his arms. He waited until their breathing returned to normal before he spoke to her.

"I am so glad that you came over. I missed you. If I didn't see you today, I was planning on going over to your house to see you. It is getting hard for me to go a week without seeing you. We need to do something about that. I think we need to see each other at least once or twice during the week so that I can make it till the weekend." *She has no idea what she really does to me. I have to do this right or she is going to run like hell.*

"After Libby goes home we will talk about it. I would like to see you more too." *He has no idea how he makes me feel. I want to be able to trust him.*

Friday afternoon Hank got a call from Doc. He told him that he would be right there. He hitched up the horse trailer to his pickup truck. He headed toward the interstate. He didn't have to drive far before he found the overturned truck and horse trailer. After he pulled his truck off the side of the road, he climbed out of his truck to go looking for Doc.

He saw Ella first, *his beautiful angel*, he walked toward her. She explained to him what happened and that there were three horses in the trailer. They walked down the embankment together to help Doc. The driver of the truck was taken to the hospital.

Doc was trying to figure out the best way to get the horses out of the trailer. The trailer was on its side and Doc had crawled on the top to look into the window. He needed to see how bad the horses were. Doc crawled down and told Hank to take a look to see what he thought. He climbed up and took a look in the window. "Let's see if we can get the back door open."

They both walked to the back of the trailer and tried to open up the back door, but it was jammed shut. Hank went to his truck to get a crowbar to pry the backdoor open. They worked on getting the back door loose so that it would open.

"Ella go to my truck and get some lead ropes. As soon as this back door opens they are going to want to run. We can't have them running along this highway. Doc you might want to get down here and help me with the horses as soon as this door opens up."

Doc got up on the trailer to check on the horses one more time. Doc got down from the top of the trailer. He stood by the back doors next to Hank. Ella had returned from getting the lead ropes and was standing next to the side of the trailer.

He looked at Doc, "Are you ready?"

Doc nodded his head yes. He gave the door one good pull. The door came open. One of the horses started backing out toward the door. He stood there talking in a soothing voice to the horses. The first horse made it to the door. Hank quickly attached a lead rope around the horse's neck. Doc was given the lead rope so that he could move the horse out of the way so he could check out the horse more thoroughly.

The second horse had a harder time trying to get out. Hank could hear the horse trying to stand up but was having a hard time getting his footing. He went into the trailer to see why it was having such a hard time.

The horse was trying to move backwards to get off the horse it was on top of. He could hear the horse underneath moving his head from side to side trying to see what was going on. He continued talking to the horses trying to calm them down. He needed to get them to calm down so that he could get them out of there without getting hurt.

He needed to get the horse on top to move back a couple of feet to get it out of there. Once he got it moved back it could swing around to get out of the trailer. Hank told Doc that he had a plan that might work to get the horse out.

Hank crawled over the side of the horse so that he could get in front of it. He attached a lead rope around his neck. He was trying to get a place where he could put his feet in a position so that he could use his strength to help push the horse backwards. He threw the lead rope to Doc. Doc moved to the back of the horse trying not to get too close, he would pull if he had too.

"Ready Doc?" asked Hank

"Ready" replied Doc.

He got in front of the horse and put his hands on the horse's front shoulders. He spoke to the horse telling it to move back. When the horse started to move he pushed on his shoulders to help it move back. The horse started moving backwards, it was back far enough so that it could better footing to get up without hurting the other horse.

He immediately went to the horse that was left in the trailer. He could tell the horse was in a lot of pain.

"Let's try and get you out of here girl so that we can see how bad you are hurt. Ready girl, let's go. "He gave her enough room so that she could get up and turned around to get out of the trailer.

He told Doc that she had some broken ribs and that she was in a lot of pain. I don't know what else is wrong with her, so look her over pretty good.

Now that the horses were out of the trailer, and out of the way. The people that were standing around watching were ready to go to work on getting the truck and trailer out of there. Hank noticed one of the men had stopped to talk to Ella. He immediately walked over to her and put his arm around her. He kissed her forehead and told her that Doc was going to sedate the horses so that the ride to the ranch would be more comfortable for them.

"Do you want to ride back to the ranch with me or are you going with Doc?"

"Libby is due to arrive around seven o'clock. I think I will ride to the ranch with you. I will help you with the horses and then you can take me home. I will pick up my car later. It will also give me a chance to spend some time with you. Let me go tell Doc."

They got the horses loaded into the trailer. Doc told him that the horses were going to be sore for a few weeks while their bruises healed from the accident. One horse does have several broken ribs and they will take a few months to heal. You will have to keep a close eye on them to make sure that there is no internal damage. If you see something unusual, call me, and I will come right out.

Ella climbed into the cab of Hank's truck. *I love the smell of his truck. Does he know how good looking he is? That sexy voice of his makes me melt inside.*

As soon as he had the truck on the main road heading back to the ranch he reached over and grabbed Ella's hand and held it in his. "What are you thinking right now? You have been quiet since you got into the truck."

"Not much. I'm just anxious to see Libby. I have not seen her for a while and she is my best friend."

"Tell me a little bit about her."

"I met her when I was going to college. She is now working for an advertising company. She has been working there for a couple of years."

"Does she have someone special in her life?"

"Not that I am aware of. She would tell me if she was seeing someone. She hasn't had anyone special in about a year."

"How long is she going to visit?"

"I not sure of her schedule, but I know she will be here all weekend. I think she plans on leaving Wednesday or Thursday."

When they arrived at the ranch he drove up to the birthing barn. They put the horses in the corral next to the barn until he could get the stalls prepared for them. He wanted to keep them separate from the other horses until he got to know more about them. He would keep a close watch on them for the next twenty -four hours to make sure they were going to be alright.

Doc would be by in the morning to check on them, and hopefully would be able to tell him more about the horses. Tonight, he would make special rubs to help them with the pain. Tomorrow he will soak them in warm water to help with the bruises and the stiffness of the muscles.

When they were done he told Ella that he would take her home when she was ready. They stood next to each other at the corral fence looking at the horses. "Thank you for your help with the horses."

"I am glad I could help."

"I need to walk up to the barn to grab them some feed do you want to walk up there with me?"

"Sure, I will walk up there and help you."

He walked to where the feed was stored. He got three feed buckets and filled them. He also grabbed three buckets for water. Ella carried the empty water buckets and he carried the feed buckets. They walked back down to the birthing barn . He would get Jake to put down some straw in the stalls for them.

When they were done he pulled Ella into his arms and kissed her. He had one hand behind her head holding her in place and his other hand rested around her waist. She could feel him getting aroused. She was also getting aroused. Her breasts were starting to ache. He moved away from her as he did, she let out a soft moan. In a husky, sexy voice he said, "I better take you home now."

Hand and hand they walked out of the birthing barn to the truck. Ella was quiet all the way home. *You have no idea how you make me feel. The smell of him in this truck is doing strange things to me.* He finally asked her if something was wrong. She told him that nothing was wrong. He leaned toward her to gave her a soft kiss on her lips before she climbed out. "I will see you tomorrow." As he turned his truck around he was thinking *tomorrow can't come fast enough.*

When Ella walked into to the house she found Beth in the kitchen cooking. Toby was glad to see her so she took him outside for a few minutes. *I don't want to blow this relationship with Hank. He makes me feel safe when I am in his arms. I have never felt that before with anyone.*

She walked back into the house and headed straight to the shower. *I wonder what his hands will feel like when he touches me. When there is nothing between us and it is skin touching skin. I hope that I don't freeze up on him. He is such a good kisser. He has been patient with me so far. He is so sexy and he smells so good. I think about him all the time. I just don't want to get my heart broken again.*

After Ella got dressed she walked back to the kitchen to talk to Beth. She was cooking supper when she looked at her. She told her that she was fixing chicken alfredo for supper. "What time will Libby be here?"

"She told me she would be here around seven o'clock. I hope she won't mind staying here. I will have her take me into town tomorrow morning to get my car. I left it at the clinic. We had an emergency out on the interstate. A truck with three horses in a trailer went off the road. I rode with Doc to the scene. I went to Hank's with him to unload the horses and then he brought me home. I didn't want to be late since Libby's coming."

"I'll sleep on the couch tonight and Libby can sleep in my room. I have to go over to Hank's in the morning anyway. You know I could stay over there this weekend so that you and Libby can have all the girl time you need."

"That is not fair for you to have to give up your bedroom for Libby. I guess she could sleep in mine and I could sleep on the couch."

"I don't mind staying over at Hank's house. I've already talked it over with Hank and he said it was not a problem. After we eat I will pack a small bag and call him. I'm sure that him or Jake can come and get me."

"Alright, if you really don't mind, I guess you can stay at Hank's house."

A car horn was beeping outside. Beth and Ella both went to the door to see who was there. They saw Libby closing the car door. Ella ran off the porch to give Libby a hug. "I have missed you so much. How was your trip?"

Libby hauled a large suitcase out of the trunk of the car. She sat it down on the ground as she closed the trunk. Ella picked up the suitcase and carried it into the house. She sat it down inside the door. Toby went to greet them at the door. Ella reached down to pet him.

"We were just about to eat supper, have you had anything to eat yet?" asked Beth.

"No, I haven't had anything to eat. What is your dog's name?"

Ella told her the story about Toby and Wyatt. She can't believe how much the dogs have grown since she brought them home.

After supper Beth went to her room and packed a small bag to take to Hank's. She called him and he said that he would send Jake over to pick her up. Jake was there in ten minutes. Beth told the girls to have fun and she went out the door.

Libby asked where Beth was going. She explained to her that Beth was going to spend the weekend over at Hank's house. Libby said to her "You better start spilling your guts girl because I am totally confused. Is it safe for her to stay there?"

"Yes, it is safe for her. She cooks for Hank on the weekends. Maria, Hank's housekeeper and cook got called away for a family emergency. Since she has been gone Beth has been filling in for her. We have been eating supper there on Saturday night for over a month. He wants us to come over for supper tomorrow night so that he can meet you."

"I was wondering when I was going to meet him. Have you told him yet?"

"Not really. I wanted to know what you thought about him first. Right now, we only see each other on weekends. We did go for a ride last Sunday. It gave us some time alone and we talked a little. We are taking this real slow. I mean real slow. He has only kissed me. *What a good kisser he is!* I am beginning to wonder what he is doing. He hasn't tried to touch me in any way."

"What did you tell him about your problem? "

"I told him that I had intimacy problems. I told him that I was fine with my clothes on, it was when they were off that the problem occurred."

"So, he doesn't know that you were raped?"

"No, I haven't told him. I don't want him to look at me any different than he does now."

"What makes you think he would look at you any different?"

"Wait until you meet him tomorrow, and then tell me what you think about him. We will eat supper at his house. Tomorrow you will have to take me into town so that I can get my car. I left it at the clinic. On Sunday, there is barbeque and dance held in the town square. Hank said he would be glad to take us."

"Ella, are you already falling for him, and I mean really falling for him?"

"I really do like him. I am scared that I will get hurt again. I have these mixed feeling because he makes me feel safe when I am with him. He has already told me what kind of a relationship that he wants to have with me. He is so different from any man that I have ever had a relationship with. He wants the whole package deal. He doesn't want a fling with someone. He wants a partnership with someone, mind, body and soul. He wants someone to share his life with, stand by his side and someone that he can love and make love to."

"I get it the making love part scares you because you turn to ice between the sheets. Maybe he is the one that can help you. Have you ever thought of that? Think about it, and we will talk some more tomorrow, right now I need some sleep."

Hank was in the kitchen getting a cup of coffee when Jake entered. He had been lost in thought about the new horses. He received a phone call from Doc last night. He learned more about the horses and their owner. Their owner had a broken arm and a concussion. He would be released from the hospital today or tomorrow.

He was telling Jake about the new horses. He was expecting a phone call from the owner to arrange transportation for them. He told Jake that he was sorry to see the one with the broken ribs leave because the horse needed so much care. He wondered what kind of care the horse would get once it left there.

Beth had wandered into the kitchen wearing her pajamas. She had her hair pulled back into a pony tail. She told the guys that she would have some breakfast ready in about fifteen minutes. She went to work getting some pans out and pulling things out of the refrigerator.

Jake took a quick glance at her over his coffee cup as Hank was talking to him. *I wonder if she knows how beautiful she really is. I know it is okay to look but don't touch. She will be gone before you know it. We can only be friends.*

She served them breakfast and only heard half of what they were saying as her mind started wandering. *I wonder if Jake is a good kisser. I wonder what kind of a boyfriend he would be. He is so good looking and his body is getting really nice to look at. I love to hear him talk. I don't know why I am thinking about all this, we are just friends.*

Hank asked Beth if he knew what Ella's plans were for today. She said that they were going to go into town to get Ella's car and probably do some shopping. She said that they would be here for supper tonight. "Is there something special that you want me to make?"

"No, anything you want to make will be just fine." replied Hank. *I can't wait to see my Angel.*

Hank and Jake left to start their day out in the barn. He wanted to do a treatment on the horse with the broken ribs before the owner arrived to take her home. When he went to the birthing barn he found the mare laying down in her stall. She sounded like she was in a lot of pain. Hank called Doc and told him what was going on. The mare was pregnant and was having a miscarriage.

Doc told him to call Ella because she was closer than he was as he just arrived at the clinic. He then called Ella and told her what was going on. She told him that she would be right over. He gave her something to help with the pain. He was in the stall talking to her when Ella arrived.

After Ella examined her she told Hank that it wouldn't be much longer. We just ave to make sure she aborts everything. I don't think that she is that far along in the pregnancy, so hopefully everything will go smoothly. The accident yesterday caused her to miscarry.

He told her that Doc would be out as soon as he could. He just arrived at the clinic when he called him. Ella told him that she didn't have any supplies with her. She asked him if he had any rubber gloves that she could use. He told her that he did have some and left to go get them. He returned a few minutes later with the gloves.

Doc arrived about an hour later and talked with Ella about the horse. The horse will be ok and I will give her some medicine to help her. This poor horse has been through a lot in the last couple of days. Doc asked Hank if he had heard from the owner of the horses yet. He told him that he had not heard from him yet. This horse shouldn't go anywhere for a couple more days. Doc told him that he would contact the owner to let him know what was going on.

When it was time for them to leave Hank walked out of the barn with them. He asked Ella if she was still working today and she told him no. Good because I want to kiss you so bad. He covered her mouth with his. "You taste so good Ella." He kissed her again before he let go of her.

Just then Libby walked out of the back door of the house. Hank still had his arm wrapped around Ella when she approached them. Ella said to Libby "I want you to meet Hank and Doc."

Doc said to Libby "Nice to meet you. I hope that you enjoy your visit. Well I have to be on my way I have another call to make before I can take this afternoon off. I will see you in town later." He walked over to his truck and got in.

Ella noticed that Libby was watching Doc with a strange look on her face. *I wonder what is wrong with her?*

Hank asked Libby if she was enjoying her visit so far. She told him that she was having a good time and that she was just talking with Beth. "I didn't know that Beth was such a good cook."

"You won't hear any complaints come out of my mouth. I like everything that she cooks." said Hank. "I need to get back to work, so I will see you two later." He bent and kissed Ella on the side of her forehead before he walked away.

Ella wanted to go home and take a shower before they went into town to get her car. Ella walked into the house and asked Beth if she needed anything in town.

The town was all decorated with red, white and blue banners. The town square had vendors set up selling their wares. The girls walked to the park to look around going from table to table. Libby found a nice leather purse that she bought. Ella found a straw hat that she liked.

As they walked around the park Libby asked questions about Doc. Ella told her that he was a wonderful boss. She had learned a lot from him about the larger animals that they serviced. She told her about the fawns that were born along the highway after their mom was hit. She told her that they had to nurse the fawns until they could find a place for them. She also told her that he serviced a lot of people outside of the county because he was so good at what he does.

When they arrived at the clinic Doc's car was parked beside Ella's. They walked into the clinic so that Ella could show Libby around. They found him in the back of the clinic cleaning out one of the pens that had a sick dog in it. The dog was a mess and needed a bath. He was picking up the dog and carrying it to a large tub filled with warm water. He was talking to the dog as he was placing the dog in the tub and did not hear them come into the room.

He looked up and smiled at them. He asked what they were doing here. Ella explained that they came to get her car. Since they were there she decided to show Libby around the clinic. She asked a couple questions about the dog that he was bathing.

"I can't tell if this little guy is going to make it or not. The medicine that I have given him doesn't seem to be helping him. I'm going to have to try something else. I will take him home with me so that I can watch him more closely."

They talked for a few more minutes before they left Doc. They walked around town then went into a restaurant called "Stella's Place". As soon as they walked in a waitress named Donna told them to find a place to sit, and that she would be right with them. They found a booth to sit in and when Donna came to the table they placed their order.

Donna was in her late thirties with brown hair pulled back into a ponytail. She knows everyone in the county. She returned shortly with their drinks and said to Libby, "You are new in town. I haven't seen you before."

Libby explained to her that she was here visiting Ella for a few days. Donna went on to tell them about the events that were going on in town for the weekend. She hoped that the women would have a nice time.

As they ate their lunch Libby asked Ella how she liked living in a small town like this. Ella told her that she liked it. "You have to do some adjusting to things and get use to how they do things here. The pace is a lot slower. Everyone knows everyone which is actually kind of nice. The people here care about everyone and their town. You might have to go thirty miles to a mall but the stores in town try to carry everything that you might need. This is a farm town not a city, and the life style is a lot different.

When we first moved here I thought that Beth was going to fight with me because we moved to the middle of nowhere. As soon as she started working for Hank and realized that it doesn't matter where you live that your dreams still can come true. I had no idea that she wanted to go to cooking school. She is already saving money to go to a school next summer for a cooking class. She is establishing herself as a caterer already. If we didn't move here who knows what would have happened to her."

Libby then asked her " What are you going to do when Beth gets out of school and moves on with her life. Are you going to stay single forever or are you going to make things work with Hunky Hank?"

"I haven't really thought about it. I have been so focused on just getting her through school and keeping a roof over our heads to think about things like that."

"Here is something else that you might want to think about Ella, what kind of a future do you want with Hunky Hank?"

"There might not be a future with Hunky Hank once he gets me between the sheets."

"I think that you are wrong with this one. I think that he is the one that is going to help you, not hurt you. He already cares about you."

CHAPTER 18

When Ella and Libby arrived back at the Rocking R Ranch Beth already had supper cooking. The house smelled amazing. The table was set, there was a fire going in the fireplace in the living room. The girls made themselves comfortable in the living room while waiting for Hank and Jake to join them.

They were talking about Libby's job when Hank walked into the living room. He asked Beth if he had time to take a shower before supper. She told him that he did. They heard him walk down the hall to his bedroom as they resumed their conversation. A few minutes later they heard Jake come in the back door. Jake went right to his room to take a shower.

Fifteen minutes later they all sat down to eat supper. Jake was asking Hank about the new horses that were there. He wanted to know how the one with the broken ribs was doing. Hank had given her a mud bath and put another rub on her to help her with the pain. He also gave her the antibiotic that Doc left for her. I think we will see a change in her in a couple of days. She has been through a lot in short period of time. I still haven't heard from her owner yet. So hopefully she will be here a few more days to get her strength up.

After supper Jake and Beth cleared away the dishes and cleaned up the kitchen. They were talking about some of the ideas that Jake had for the fall cookout. He had a lot of ideas. He wanted this to be something everyone would remember.

They all returned to the living room to enjoy the fire that was still burning in the fireplace. Hank and Jake got their guitars and started playing music. The girls began to sing along with the music.

Sunday afternoon Hank arrived to take them to the BBQ and dance. Ella had on a dress and wore her hair down. Hank could not take his eyes off of her. She just keeps taking his breath away with her beauty every time he sees her. *She is so beautiful and I can wait to touch her hair. Her beautiful blonde hair that feels*

like silk and smells like flowers.

Hank opened up the truck door for them. Ella got in front and Libby got in the back. They talked about the town and some of the people that lived there. Everyone knows everyone because it is a small town. The town was growing smaller slowly all the time. Hank was telling the girls the town needed to do something to bring in the tourist back into town during the summer months and keep them there until winter.

When they arrived in town he found a place to park the truck. They had to walk a couple of blocks to the town square to the park. They found tables were already set up. The band was setting up in the town gazebo. The Fire Department had the BBQ cooking. After they found an empty table to sit at, Hank went to get them something to drink.

When he brought the drinks back to the table Ella and Libby were talking to a couple of guys. One of the guys was Kyle. He was asking Ella if she ever found out anything about who had run her off the road. She told him that she had not heard anything and he doubted that she ever would. After a few more minutes of talking with the girls and Hank they left.

Ben and his wife Sara joined them. Sara is pregnant with their first child. She was introduced to

187

everyone. It was clear to everyone why Ben was smiling every day. You could see the love that they both had for each other. Ella and Libby asked her all the normal questions about her pregnancy, when are you due, do you know the sex of the baby? She laughed at them and answered all their questions.

Beth and Jake joined them just as the BBQ was starting to serve the food. The band was getting ready to play and a wooden floor had been made so that people could dance. People were coming from all over to hear the band and to dance.

Hank was thinking that he had to keep a close eye on Ella because she was so beautiful. The dress that she wore showed off her beautiful long legs. With her hair down, she looks like an angel. She was his angel. He couldn't wait to get her on the dance floor just so he could hold her.

The first slow dance that the band played he asked her to dance with him. He led her to the dance floor where he put his arm around her and touched her beautiful hair. When the dance ended, he whispered in her ear "You really look beautiful tonight."

He lowered his mouth to kiss her as they stood on the dance floor. It was just a quick kiss that left her wanting more. He put her hand in his as they walked off the dance floor. By the time they reached the table where the others were sitting he noticed that

Doc had joined them and was talking to Libby.

Doc had asked Libby if she would like to dance. When the next song started he grabbed her hand and lead her to the dance floor. Hank and Ella followed them to the dance floor.

Beth and Jake decided to walk around for a while. Jake put his hand that was closest to Beth in his pants pocket. He was thinking about how nice it would be to hold her hand. *I will ask her to dance with me later. I am so asking for trouble with her. I just have to keep telling myself that we are just friends.* Beth interrupted his thoughts when she asked him if they would be able to go riding tomorrow. She enjoyed the riding lessons.

The first chance Jake got he had Beth on the dance floor for a slow dance. She wrapped her arms around his neck. He grabbed her one hand and placed it in his as they danced. He didn't speak to her as he was enjoying the sweet smell of her. Their bodies moved together as if they had danced together before. She was light on her feet.

"I didn't realize that you were such a good dancer Jake."

"You are a good partner and you just make me look good." He said teasingly.

"There are so many things about you that I don't know. You keep surprising me all the time."

"I just hope that you don't judge me from what people say about me. I' m not really a bad person. "

Beth stood in front of him and looked him in the eyes and said "I don't care what other people think about you. I know for myself what kind of a person that you are. I have seen a side of you that not too many people have seen. I like what I see and that is all that matters to me."

"We better get back to the others. I'll need to get back to the ranch soon."

They returned back to the table where everyone was still sitting. He told Hank that he was going to go back to the ranch soon. Hank looked at him and asked him if everything was alright. He nodded his head yes. "There are some things that I want to get done at the ranch."

Jake turned to Beth and said "You can ride back to the ranch with them or you can go with me."

"I'll ride back with you if that's ok."

Jake got up from the table and started to walk toward the truck. He took few steps and waited for Beth to catch up with him. They walked together to the truck. When they arrived at the truck he opened up the door for her and waited for her to get in. He then walked around the truck to the driver's side and slid behind the wheel.

Beth looked out the window at the passing landscape. They rode back to the ranch in silence. The only sound that could be heard was the radio playing some country music. They were both deep in their own thoughts.

As soon as Jake parked the truck Beth jumped out and headed for the house. She went upstairs to changed her clothes. She put her hair in a ponytail. He followed her upstairs to change his clothes. When she got to the kitchen she noticed that Jake was already heading toward the barn. She watched him walk across the yard. *I hope that I haven't said anything to upset him. I have replayed everything that I have said to him today and I can't think of anything that would upset him. But, something is bothering him I just wish I knew what.*

June was going to be a busy month for Beth and she needed to get started on making things for the wedding that she had in two weeks. She had final exams and then a graduation party to cater.

Jake went into the tack room to get a blanket and saddle. He then headed to find Black Jack. He found him in his small corral. Black Jack was glad to see him. As soon as Jake saw him and touched his friend his mood changed. He put the saddle on Black Jack and led him to the arena. He only had five weeks left before the rodeo, they needed to practice.

After their practice he headed Black Jack toward

the stream. When they got to the stream he dismounted and let Black Jack get his drink of the cold water. *I really need to keep my distance from Beth. I knew I shouldn't have danced with her. She smelled so good. I just wanted to touch her.*

Just thinking about her had caused changes to his body. "Damn it! I have to think about her in a different way. Ok, let me think here for a minute. I know I'll think of her as a sister. That's it, as a sister. Black Jack I can't let her know how I really feel about her. She doesn't feel the same way. Next summer she will be out of here and who knows where she will be. Our goals in life are so different. I don't want to get hurt, and I don't want to hurt her. I have to keep my distance from her. Thanks for listening Black Jack."

Black Jack responded by moving his head up and down. He mounted Black Jack and they headed back to the barn. When he rode up to the barn he noticed that Hank's truck was there. He tied Black Jack up in the breezeway and took the saddle and blanket off. He put them in the tack room. As he was brushing down Black Jack he heard Hank come up behind him.

"If you don't mind me asking, what was the reason you left town to return to the ranch?"

Without turning around to face Hank, he continued brushing Black Jack "I wanted to get some more practice with Black Jack."

Hank stood there watching him a few moments before he spoke again. "The way you acted you couldn't get out of there fast enough. Did something happen between you and Beth?"

"No Sir, nothing happened between Beth and I, we're just friends."

"So, you say. I see the way you keep looking at her. Does she know how you feel about her?"

"No and I don't want her to know because we can't be anything more than friends."

"Alright your secret is safe with me. If you ever need someone to talk to you know you can talk to me."

"Thanks, that is nice to know."

Hank walked over to the birthing barn to check on the horses. He wanted to check on them before he made another rub mixture for the one horse.

CHAPTER 19

Ella was saying good bye to Libby. She couldn't believe how fast the days went by. Libby told Ella that she would try to come back before the end of summer.

Saturday morning Ella went into town to the clinic. There wasn't a lot to do since they didn't have any animals staying there. After she got her work done, she drove to the Rocking R Ranch. Beth was there working in the kitchen when she arrived.

"You are here earlier than I thought you would be. I haven't made lunch yet so you can join us. Before you even ask, he is out in the barn. Text him so that he knows that you are here."

She looked at Beth and said "Why do I need to text him? He knows about what time I get here? Is something going on that I need to know about?"

She took out her phone and texted Hank to let him know that she was there. He was in the birthing barn attending to one of the horses. He told her where he was and asked her to come out there.

She walked to the stall that Hank was in with one of the horses. He had just let the others out into the pasture. He was examining the horse with the broken ribs.

"Ella, what do you think, I want you to come and look at this one spot on her."

She opened the stall door and walked over to where he had his hand to get a better look. She put her hand next to his on the horse.

"I think that she is going to heal just fine. She has only been here for a week. Her breathing is better."

Before Ella could say another word, he pulled her into his arms, and kissed her. His lips touched hers gently at first. After he tasted her lips he deepened the kiss. When he ended the kiss, he looked into her eyes and saw the glazed look in her eyes. She responded to his kiss like no other woman had. *I'm falling more in love with her every time I see her.*

He rested his head against her forehead. "I have missed you this past week. I couldn't wait for you to get here today."

195

"Hank, we need to talk."

"We can talk now or we can talk later." replied Hank. He still had her in his arms.

She moved her head so that she could look up at him. She started placing kisses along his jaw line until she heard a groan come from him. She could feel his arousal against her body.

"Sweet Ella, you are playing with fire. When we make love, I don't want it to be in one of my barns. I want you in my bed where I don't have to be worried about being interrupted by an animal or someone."

"Alright, I didn't realize that just a few kisses would get you so aroused." She said in a sexier voice that she didn't know that she had.

"I don't think that I'm the only one here that is aroused. It is a good thing that I'm a patient man."

Ella's phone rang. It was Beth telling her that lunch was ready whenever they were ready to eat. He told her to go ahead and go back to the house he would be there in a few minutes. He wanted to finish up there before lunch. He also needed a minute to calm his body down.

She has no idea what she is doing to me. Boy, do I need to slow things down a bit, because I don't want to screw this up. I wonder what she wants to talk about.

As Ella was walking back to the house, her mind was on what she wanted to say to Hank. They really needed to talk before either one of them got hurt from this relationship. She really did like him a lot, but if they couldn't make a go of it between the sheets, they needed to end this relationship before they got too emotionally involved.

Later that night after supper Hank asked Ella to take a walk with him. The night air was warm as they walked toward the barn so that he could check on the horses one last time. As they entered the barn he said to her "What did you want to talk to me about?"

She explained to him what she had been thinking about. "Please hear what I have to say before you say anything. Sex is a very intimate thing between two people. I have an issue with intimacy because I was raped when I was attending college. I tried to explain it to you when you first asked me to have a relationship with you. You told me not to worry about it that you didn't think it would be a problem. But I do worry about it because if I don't satisfy you in bed then you won't want to have a relationship with me. I think we should find out soon before we get too emotionally involved with each other."

He turned so that he was facing her. Their hands

were joined together. Slowly he said "Ella, I'm not like other guys. I'm not going to pay the price for something that someone else did. I'm glad that you told me so that I will know how to proceed with our relationship. I don't do sex. We and I mean WE will make love to each other when you are ready and not until then. It will be because you want it and need it. When you are truly ready to take our relationship to the next level let me know. I will wait for you to be ready."

"You understand that we should do this before we are emotionally involved, because the longer we're together the more the rejection is going to hurt."

He moved his hands to place them on each side of her face. He looked her into her eyes and said "I'm sorry Ella, but I want you to be emotionally involved with me or this is not going to work. I need you to want me more than just physically. I want to be in your mind and in your heart. "

"I'm just afraid that you are going to hurt me just like the others have."

"I'm not going to hurt you. You have to be able to trust me because, if you can't trust me then we might as well end this now. Do you trust me Ella?"

She stood there looking at his face trying to see if he was being honest with her. After a few seconds she replied "Yes, I trust you."

He pulled her closer to him so that he could kiss her. He kissed her in a way that left her no doubt about the way he felt about her. A soft moan escaped her lips as he kissed her. He shifted his stand so that she wouldn't notice his arousal. He could feel her body starting to surrender to his touch.

He took in the scent of her hair and left a trail of kisses down the side of her neck. He flicked his tongue against her ear lobe to feel her response. She pressed her body closer against him as she wrapped her arms around his neck. He found her lips one more time before he put some distance between them. *I want her so much it hurts.*

As he walked down the breezeway he looked into each one of the stalls to make sure that the horses had enough water. Ella made her way to Baby's stall. Baby was there waiting for her with her head over the door looking for some attention. "Baby is looking better. She hasn't been here that long and you can already notice a difference in her."

He walked up beside her to stand next to her. "Yes, she is doing really well. She is getting so that she rust us with her care. She still needs to gain some more weight before we can ride her."

He ran his hand down the side of Baby's neck and

then back up to rub her by her ear. Baby looked at them both with her soft brown eyes that said more please.

"Are you ready to go back to the house?" Hank asked.

"Whenever you are, what about the other horses?"

"Jake will look after Blackjack and I will take a look at the horses in the other barn after you leave."

Later that night he walked her to her car when it was time for them to leave. He gave Ella a quick kiss and told her he would see her tomorrow. He stood there and watched *his angel* leave and fade into the night.

The more he was around her the more he wanted to get to know her. He wanted to know everything about her. He asked her questions about her childhood. In exchange he told her about himself. He looked forward to their Sunday afternoon rides together.

The month of June was a busy time around the ranch. The planting was done. The people that had their horses boarded there were coming out to the ranch more since the days were longer and the weather was nicer.

The second weekend in June, Hank had a group of

father and sons coming for an overnight trail ride. They were to arrive at one o'clock. Ella and Beth arrived on Friday night to start putting things together for a wedding the next day that Beth had to cater.

Saturday morning Hank went to get things together for the trail ride. Beth made some food and got it together for the trail ride. She didn't want the group to go hungry. She made a pile of plastic containers for him to pack. She told Hank to make room them.

Ella stood in the yard as the group left for the trail. Jake and Beth were on the other side of town setting up for the wedding reception. She took her phone out and sent a text to Beth to see if she needed any help. Beth texted her back saying that they were just about done setting up.

She walked back into the house to do some more cleaning. An hour later Beth and Jake arrived.

"How did things go at the reception?" she asked Beth when she saw her.

"Things went pretty good. I'm pleased with the way things went."

"Where did Jake go?"

"As soon as we got out of the truck he headed for the barn. It was like he couldn't get away fast enough.

He has been acting kind of strange lately. He has been on the quiet side for the last couple of weeks."

"Have you tried to talk to him to find out what is bothering him?"

"No, I haven't had a chance to talk to him and when I text him messages he has been giving me short answers. He isn't telling me anything."

"Maybe it is time to have a talk with him. If it is really bothering you then go and talk to him. There is a reason he is acting the way he is. You just have to find out why."

She took Ella's advice and headed out to the barn in search of Jake. She found him out in Black Jack's corral. He was standing there talking to Black Jack while running his hands over Black Jack's neck and side. She walked up to the corral fence and asked him if he had a couple of minutes because she wanted to talk to him.

"What do you want to talk about?" asked Jake.

"I want to know what is going on with you Jake. Have I done something wrong or said something that has hurt you. If I have I'm sorry because you are the last person on this earth that I would want to hurt."

"I don't know what you are talking about? I'm not mad at you."

"Jake please turn around so that I can talk to you. I hate talking to your back. Something is going on and I want to know what it is. You have always been able to talk to me and lately it is like you are trying to avoid me. Why?"

"I'm not trying to avoid you."

"Then what would you call it? You don't speak to me at school anymore other than saying Hi. Do you have a girlfriend and didn't tell me? Are you sweet on someone?" Beth held her breath until he answered her question.

"No, I'm not sweet on anyone *just you*. I have just had some stuff that I have been dealing with. I'm fine and I will let you know if I need to talk to someone. You will be the first person that I will call."

"What kind of stuff are you dealing with? You can talk to me about it you know I'm here for you."

"It's stuff about school and my family. I will be ok." *I can't let her know what is really going on. If you knew how much I really like her, I will just be asking for trouble. She's not going to stay here, she will be going off to cooking school before we both know it.*

"Well, I'm going to go and start supper. I will call you when it is ready."

He watched her walk away and head toward the

house. *I think this is going to be harder than I thought. I need to keep things friendly between us so that she won't ask me any more questions. Think of her as a sister. Think of her as a sister.*

As soon as supper was over Jake went back out to the barn to practice on Black Jack. He never saw Beth standing in the breezeway watching him. She stood there watching him for a little while before she headed back to the house. *I would really like to know what is really going on with him.*

Hank rode up to the barn and tied his horse on the corral fence. He watched the others dismount and tie their horses to the fence by his. Ella walked out on the back porch to watched them. His eyes made contact with hers. *There is my Angel. I have missed her more than she will ever know.*

She walked toward the group. She wanted to get closer to Hank. He was talking to the group giving them instructions and thanking them all for coming. The leader of the group stood there talking to him for a few minutes. He just wanted to put his arms around Ella and kiss her. As soon as she reached his side he breathed in the scent of her hair and her special smell.

Oh, how I have missed this smell. He placed a quick kiss on the side of her forehead.

Later after the group had left. He had a few minutes so he went to find Ella to talk to her. He found her at the corral fence petting Star. He walked up next to her and slid his arms around her. "You know that you can ride her anytime you want."

"I know that you will let me ride her. I think the next time we go riding I will ride her. She is getting so that she really likes me."

"The leader of the father and son group has asked me to take them out again. They are going to get back with me with a date. Things went really well."

She turned so that she could look at him. "I'm glad things went so well. How many of these overnight events do you do?"

"Right now, I have one booked in June, July and August. When Mr. Scott calls back with a date that will make four. I'm thinking about asking one of the older guys that helps me out from time to time if he would be interested in doing it. I don't like spending so much time away from the horses and the ranch. But, the money is good that I get from the group rides."

"There are so many things that you could do if you wanted to expand your business here."

"I like keeping things the way they are. I don't need more responsibility for things like that. I just want to focus on the horses and my cattle."

"If you ever change your mind let me know. With a little bit of advertising you could do really well. I would have my friend Libby help you. I'm sure I could talk her into working for real cheap if money is a problem."

"I'm doing just fine, but thanks for letting me know" replied Hank.

They walked toward the barn so that he could check on a couple of the horses. He also wanted to find Jake and see how things were while he was gone. He didn't get any phone calls so hopefully everything went well.

Ella returned to the house and found Beth in the kitchen as usual cooking up a storm. Beth found a cooking class that she wanted to take that was a couple of hours away. She was trying to figure out a way to take the class. It was for three weeks just after the fourth of July. It would be to her advantage to take it because it would help her catering business so much. She just needed to figure out a way to do it and have Ella approve of it.

Beth had several pans on top of the stove cooking. She was stirring something in one of the pans. Ella knew that something was bothering her just by seeing the expression on her face. She asked her if things were getting any better between her and Jake?

She told her that things haven't changed that much. That he still only talks to her when he needs to ask her something. He has been so busy with things here at the ranch that she hardly saw him.

"What do you want to do about the fourth of July? Do you want to go to the rodeo and watch Jake in the events or do you want to do something else?"

"Yes, I want to go to the rodeo and watch him ride. I care for him as a friend. I think it will be fun. It is something that I haven't done before."

"When the time gets closer I will ask you again just to make sure you still want to go." She then left the room to get some more cleaning done.

As she was cleaning Hank's bedroom she was thinking about how she could get him between the sheets. *There has to be a way that I can seduce him. I want more than just him kissing me! I have to figure something out before this house starts filling up with more people. We will never get any time alone.*

Hank walked into his bedroom to take a quick shower when he found her standing in the middle of his bedroom deep in thought. He knew she did not hear him come into the room. As he walked up to her he spoke in a softer voice than normal. "What a pleasant surprise to find you here. I have always wondered how I was going to get you into my bedroom. I hope that one day it will have nothing to do with you cleaning it."

She turned toward him and replied "I'm looking forward to the time that we share your bed together." She placed her hands on hips and grabbed his tee-shirt. She started pulling the shirt up toward his chest. Her warm hand were sliding up his sides until she couldn't move the shirt anymore. She admired the skin that she had revealed.

Hank moved his hands to her waist and puller her closer to him. "So, you want to undress me, do you? You can only take my shirt off. If you like what you see I will allow you to touch me."

She slid the shirt above his broad shoulders and let it hit the floor. She then placed her hands on his chest. He had a small patch of dark hair in the middle of his chest that narrowed as it proceeded down his body to the top of his jeans. His arms were developed well from all of the work that he did. The tight muscles of his stomach tightened even more from her touch.

She heard his breathing change as she moved her hand across his chest. She could feel his heartbeat pounding in his chest. She put featherlike kisses across his chest where her hands had been. She raised her head so that she could kiss him on the lips. She deepened the kiss until a moan sounded in his throat.

"Sweet Ella you know that you are playing with fire. Come closer and let me feel you against me. I want to feel your skin against mine." He raised her tee-shirt up so that her breasts were exposed to his eyes. He reached around and unhooked her bra then pushed it out of his way so that he could see her breasts.

"I'm going to touch your breast Ella. Don't be afraid of my touch. I will not hurt you. If you want me to stop just say so and I will stop. I want to love on you a little bit. You are so beautiful that I just want to taste your skin."

Her body stiffened when he first touched her skin. He placed his hand on her breast and his lips were putting light kisses just above his hand. She liked what he was doing to her. Her body started to relax against him. She had put her fingers in his hair to pull his head closer to her. As her body began to melt against him her breathing had changed. She wondered how far he would go.

After he teased her breast with his touch and his mouth. He raised his head to seek her mouth for another kiss. He moved his head back far enough so that he could look into her eyes. He saw her eyes filled with lust. "Are you okay honey?"

She couldn't speak so she just nodded her head up and down. He hooked her bra up for her and pulled her tee-shirt back into place. "I'm going to go take my shower now. You can finish cleaning while I'm in there."

She couldn't believe her ears. He was just going to walk away from her after he kissed her senseless. She watched him walk into the bathroom. He left the door partly open while he stripped off his jeans. She couldn't resist a quick peek. *Oh my! Oh my! Such a sexy man and he is so nice to look at. She touched her mouth to make sure she wasn't drooling.*

Hank knew that she was watching him. He purposely didn't let her see the front of his body. He turned on the shower and stood there with the cold water flowing over his body. He was going to have to endure the cold water for a few minutes until his body started to cool down.

After his shower, he walked into his bedroom to put his clean clothes on. He was surprised to see her still there. He walked over to his dresser and pulled out a pair of underwear. He slipped them on under the towel he had wrapped round his waist. He grabbed a pair of jeans and put them on. He threw the towel at her and said "Next time I will put on a better show for you, but right now I have to get back out to the barn and get some work done. I would love to stay here and kiss you all day and night but I have work to do."

She didn't say a word she just looked at him. After he walked out he door she went to the bed and sat down because her legs would no longer hold her up.

CHAPTER 20

When school let out for the summer Beth was glad, but she was also sad because she would no longer have the chance to catch a glance of Jake at school. She now had to wait until the weekend to see him. Beth realized how much she would miss him. She hoped that he missed her too.

The rodeo was getting closer and Jake was spending more time with Black Jack since he was now staying at the ranch most of the time. He wanted to stay at the ranch so the he could work with Black Jack as much as possible. A couple more guys were coming to the ranch to stay for the summer right after the Fourth of July.

The owner of the horses that were in the accident came to take them home. He was very surprised by the way the horse with the broken ribs had healed. He was told not to ride her for at least another month. He was impressed with the care of the horses. He told Hank that he would tell his friends about him. He traveled the rodeo circuit most of the summer.

The day of the rodeo Hank and Jake drove over to the rodeo grounds with the Black Jack. They were going to meet up with Ella and Beth at eleven o'clock. Jake got registered for the two events that he was going to be in. Black Jack was unloaded and tied to the side of the trailer.

Jake was excited and nervous at the same time. He was just hoping to be able to complete the events without making a fool of himself. He knew that these guys have been doing these events for years. This was going to be his one and only chance to do this. Hank kept talking to him reminding him of what to do.

"Don't worry about the score, just worry about doing it right. You aren't doing this for points like most of the guys here. They have been doing this for a long time and this is your first time. Always think about Black Jack's and your safety first." Hank patted him on the back.

Beth and Ella found them standing by the horse trailer when they arrived. Hank smiled at them when he saw *his Angel* walking toward them. Ella walked up to Hank so that he could place a kiss at her temple and stood there with his arm around her waist. Hank saw someone he wanted to talk to, he grabbed Ella's hand so that she would go with him.

Beth helped Jake pin the numbers on his shirt. As soon as she touched him she felt the butterflies in her stomach. He tried very hard not to look at her face. He kept looking around to see who was arriving and registering for the events. She also was looking around and noticed a couple of guys from school that she didn't like. They were always saying rude remarks to her. She took a step closer to Jake and slid her arm around him so that her back was toward the guys. Jake whispered in her ear "What are you doing Beth?"

"Just play along with me for a couple of minutes. I will explain later."

He placed his arm around her and kept whispering in her ear which sent more butterflies to her stomach. *Why is he causing my stomach to act up like this?*

When he was whispering in her ear he got a good smell of her hair. He was losing *control* fast where she was concerned. *I've missed the smell of her. As much as I would like to bury my face in her hair I know this doesn't mean anything.*

She placed a light kiss on his cheek. *Oh, what sweet torture this is. Jake smells of horse and some manly smell. Whatever it is he smells so good.*

They stood there until it was time for them to get some seats to watch the events. Hank agreed to get them something to drink while the girls found them a good seat in the stands. The first event was the barrel racing event. Jake was the seventh one to ride.

Jake and Black Jack did well. They ended in the top three. Jake had walked Black Jack back to the trailer to get him some water. It was getting hot and he wanted to get them both out of the sun. He tied Black Jack to the trailer then he went inside to get him some water. When he came out of the trailer Tommy Stewart and Ty Wilson came up behind him. Tommy was the one who spoke. "I don't know what you think you are doing but you better stay out of my way."

"What are you talking about?"

"You know what I'm talking about. Are you doing this impress Beth? She sure is a pretty little thing. You better watch it or I will steal her away from you."

Before he could reply, Tommy and Ty walked away. The more he thought about it the funnier it got. Tommy has his eye on Beth. If they knew the truth they wouldn't have wasted their time. But, it also bothered him to know that someone else had their eye on her. *Beth is my girl for right now. Now where did that come from.*

After the calf roping event which Jake placed sixth, Hank, Ella and Beth met him back at the horse trailer. They were all so happy that he did so well. "Do you want to hang around here for a while or do you want to go back to the ranch?" asked Hank.

"I'm ready to go back to the ranch. I'll take Black Jack back and cool him off and take care of him." replied Jake.

"I'll ride with Jake so that you two can come back whenever you want." said Beth.

"Okay we will see you in a little while. I want to talk to someone before we leave." said Hank.

On the way back to the ranch Jake asked Beth why she acted like they were a couple today at the rodeo. She explained to him that she saw Ty and Tommy and that Tommy was always saying crude remarks to her every time he would walk past her.

"What kind of remarks did he say?"

"He would say stuff like, I bet you are an easy lay, or did you ride someone last night. Those kind of remarks, just turn me right off because he doesn't even know me."

Anger was building inside of Jake as he spoke "No, Beth he doesn't know you and no decent guy would ever say those things to a girl. I'm glad you turned to me for some protection against him."

"Well maybe he will get all the girls he wants this summer doing the rodeo thing that guys do. They always get girl followers that are happy to share their bed with them."

He smiled a little and said "They are called buckle bunnies. Now that he has graduated from school you won't have to worry about running into him that much."

When they got to the ranch, he pulled the truck up next to the barn. He got out and walked to the back of the trailer. He unlatched the back door and let it fall to the ground so that he could walk into the trailer to get Black Jack out. He took Black Jack to the back of the barn to where there was a water hose. He ran the water over Black Jack's back to cool him off.

Beth came around the corner of the barn to see what he was doing. When he was spraying the water on Black Jack he didn't see her until it was too late. He soaked the front of her tank top. The top clung to her body and her breast showed very nicely to Jake. The sight of her breast made him go hard in an instant.

He turned to Beth and said "I'm so sorry Beth I didn't see you until it was too late. Honestly, I didn't do that on purpose."

"Jake can I see the hose for just a minute?" Before he could answer her, she took the hose and sprayed the front of his shirt. She laughed and said "Now we are even."

He laughed and said "I deserved that."

Black Jack turned his head and pushed her right into Jake. He caught her with both his hands on her waist. When she looked up at him, he bent his head and kissed her on the mouth. Her lips were soft against his and he wanted more. He took his tongue and traced the line between her lips until she parted them. He then put his tongue inside her mouth and tasted her. A soft groan came from her mouth. He ended the kiss, as he pulled away from her he looked into her eyes to see if she was upset with him. Her eyes were a shade darker. He didn't know if she was upset or not.

She had never felt anything like that before in her life. She had been kissed by a few guys but none of them made her feel that way. She felt that all the way to her toes.

"I'm sorry Beth I guess I shouldn't have done that. It won't happen again."

"It's okay. I know it was one of those, spur of the moment things. It didn't really mean anything right?"

Before he could answer her, she started walking

toward the house. As she was walking she was thinking *I guess you can't say it any plainer than that. We can only be friends. All I need to do now is to convince myself of that. That kiss we just shared was something else. I hope he didn't see the hurt in my eyes before I left.*

He returned his attention back to Black Jack. He took Black Jack back to his corral as he put him in the corral he was thinking out loud *she can't find out how I really feel about her. She is beautiful is so many ways. She has plans for the future that don't include me. She's not going to be happy staying around here. She will want to move to a city.*

CHAPTER 21

The next morning Jake was surprised to find Beth in the kitchen fixing breakfast. She was humming some song as she was cooking up some eggs and bacon. She had already poured him a glass of milk. She handed it to him on his way to the coffee pot.

"What are you doing here this morning?"

"As you can see I'm making breakfast. Hank asked me last night if I would be interested in cooking for the group of guys that are going to be staying here. He realized that he didn't have someone to cook for them this summer. I told him I would if he would let me use his computer to take a cooking class that I wanted to take this summer. So, it looks like we will be seeing each other more than what we thought."

"What kind of a course is it?"

"It is about decorating cakes, cupcakes and cookies. I think it will be something I will be able to use in the future. You know for birthdays and special holiday parties. Speaking of birthday's, when is your birthday?"

"It's in a couple of months. I'll be seventeen."

"Good it will give me some practice to make you a birthday cake. "

Just as he sat down at the table to eat his breakfast Hank walked into the kitchen and then the back door opened and Ben walked in. They discussed what they were going to do today. "When the boys get here we will start repairing the fencing in the north pasture."

Hank looked over his shoulder and told Beth that he was expecting three guys. Two of them would be staying and one would be going home every night. So, we will be having two more for supper. As soon as they get here let me know. I'll go into town to get the rest of the posts for the fence. While I'm gone you two can get started on the barns. Let the horse s out into the pasture for the day. Beth is there anything that you need at the store?"

"No, I think I have everything that I need." She

returned to cleaning up the kitchen. The guys all left the house leaving her alone in the kitchen. *I'm so glad that I will be seeing Jake every day.*

Brett and Seth arrived mid- morning and went to the barn to see who was around. They found Ben first. Ben talked to them a few minutes. He told them to unload their horses and where to put them.

Garrett arrived at lunch time. Hank walked out on the back porch when he heard a truck door shut. He told him where to put his horse and to come into the house when he was done. He offered Garrett some lunch. Beth quickly made him a sandwich and set it on the table in front of him. Garrett looked at her and thanked her with one of his award-winning smiles.

Jake noticed the look that Garrett gave Beth. *He better not make a move on her. I know his reputation with girls. Beth is not like that. If she kisses anyone, it's going to be me. I hope that Hank keeps him as far away from her as possible.*

After lunch Jake walked up behind her and put his arms around her waist and drew her closer to his body. He was just going to hug her then she turned her face to say something to him but before she could, he quickly kissed her pretty little mouth. He made sure that Garrett was watching him. "Lunch was good, but dessert was better." Jake left to join the others. *Beth was off limits to all of them. The smell of her just drives me crazy. She is my girl. What have I gotten myself into now.*

Beth watched him walk away from her. I wonder what that was all about. Just yesterday he had made it quite clear that they couldn't be anything more than friends. But, I will take those amazing kisses any time he wants to give them to me.

After work Ella stopped at the Rocking R Ranch to pick up Beth. She went searching for Hank just so that she could see him. She stopped at the corral beside the barn to see Baby and Star. They came to the fence to see her. She stood there petting them and talking to them when she heard Hank's voice behind her. "What a beautiful sight."

"How did you know where to find me?"

She stepped closer to him so that she could wrap her arms around his waist. She looked up at him and smiled. Before he bent his head to kiss her he said, "You are so beautiful. I can't wait to make you mine."

"I am yours more than you know." replied Ella as she deepened the next kiss that they shared.

They walked to the house together. She was telling him about her day. Then he told her about the work that they got done today.

"You know, I'm going to like seeing you every day. It just makes my day a little bit better." He told her.

"Only a little bit better?"

Just then Hank's cell phone rang. It was it was a woman that had an injured horse. She wanted him to take a look at it. He told her to bring the horse over. When he finished the call, he looked at Ella and said "I'm glad that you are here. I have an injured horse coming here. We will both get a look at it. I hope you and Beth aren't in a hurry to go home tonight."

"I don't have any plans for tonight so I guess we could stay. I don't believe Beth has any plans either."

"I'm going to go take a quick shower before dinner. You can join me if you like."

"You know I won't join you with Beth being in the kitchen."

He walked to his bedroom to take his shower. Ella stayed in the kitchen to talk with Beth. Beth told her that she has been doing some light housekeeping during the day since she is there all day. She informed Beth that someone was bringing an injured horse and told her that Hank wanted her to stay until they looked it over.

A truck hauling a horse trailer stopped in the yard out back. A tall woman with long black flowing hair got out of the cab of the truck. She was very pretty. She wore a pair of jeans as if they were her second skin. Hank walked out the back **door** to meet her. He wrapped the woman in a hug. Ella came out and stood behind him.

Jasmine told them that she was riding him on a trail that she normally rode on when King stumbled and started limping. She explained that she almost fell off the horse. I walked him back to the barn and then called you. I know how good you are with horses. I hope that he will be ok and that I will still be able ride him."

"I'll put him in the barn so that I can watch him for a couple of days to see what is going on. I will wrap his foreleg with some medicine. We will see how he does. Hopefully there won't be any permanent damage."

Jasmine walked closer to Hank and put her hand on his arm and said, "We can work this out can't we."

"We always work things out Jasmine." Hank told her that he would find out what was wrong with King's leg and would let her know as soon as possible. He grabbed King's halter and led him toward the barn.

Jasmine looked at Ella and said, "I'm not blind and I'm guessing by the way that you are looking at him that you have some kind of feelings for him."

"Yes, I do have feelings for him. We have been seeing each other for a couple of months."

"Don't get your hopes up too high because he hasn't gotten serious with anyone in a very long time. Good luck to the woman that can capture his heart."

Jasmine turned climbed into her truck and drove back down the driveway. Ella watched her leave. *I think I should call Libby and see what she thinks. It's not like my heart hasn't been broken before.*

Hank had put King in a stall and was looking at his leg when Ella found him. "Ella come and take a look to you see if anything is on his leg."

She walked into the stall and crouched down beside him. She touched the horse's leg with her finger tips. She lifted the horse's foot up so that she could look to see if the horse had a stone stuck in or under his shoe. She turned to Hank and said "He feels warm to the touch which means that there is an infection going on, but I don't see where the skin is broken anywhere."

She stood back up and looked at Hank "You want

me to go and get my bag out of my car?"

"No, that won't be necessary. I will make up a paste to draw out the poison and then wrap his leg for tonight. We will see how he does in the morning."

She followed him out of the stall and down the breezeway to the tact room. He entered the tact room and went to a door that was at the back of the room. Ella never noticed it before. He walked into a long narrow room that had shelves with jars on it. The jars had dried herbs, berries, and roots in them. There were also medicine bottles that had horse's names on it that were in a cabinet that was locked.

She watched him pull several jars from the shelf and watched as he mixed them until the mixture consistency was like a paste. He then took out a large gauze pad and placed the paste on it, then he grabbed some medical tape. Ella never said a word to him while he was doing this, she just watched in amazement.

He walked back to the stall and applied the paste with his fingers, then wrapped the horse's leg. "We will see how this works. I think he stepped on a snake and the snake bit him. The fang marks are so small that we can't see them. I will check on him in the morning to see how it looks then. The paste should draw out a lot of the poison. I will reapply some more paste to get the rest of it out. This paste will work faster than anything that you have in your medical bag."

After they were finished in the barn they went to the house so that Ella could tell Beth that it was time for them to go home.

As soon as she arrived at home she called her friend Libby.

"Libby, how are you? I need your opinion on something and I know you will tell me the right thing."

"Does this have something to do with your Hunky Hank?"

"Yes, it has to do with him."

"Have you gotten between the sheets with him yet?"

"No, I haven't."

"Okay tell me what your problem is. I will see if we can't figure this out. But, first of all tell me if you really have fallen in love with Hank?"

"I will admit that I am falling in love with him. I'm just afraid to fall too deeply in love with him for fear of getting hurt when things don't work out when we do get between the sheets."

"As long as you have that invisible wall up around your heart you will never fall that deeply in love with him. Let the wall down and have more faith in the relationship that the two of you are building. He will know when the wall comes down because he will feel it when you respond to him. It is something that you can't fake. He will know the difference if you are just going to sleep with him out of lust or if you really love him. Your body will give you a way."

"Do you think this is what he is waiting for? I mean he only kisses me he doesn't even touch me intimately. Most guys by now have run all the bases and the relationship is over."

"Ella, he's not like other guys I think he is really into you. He is just waiting for you to give him the signal that you are ready to deepen your relationship with him."

"I'll think about what you said. Have you gotten yourself a new man yet?"

"No, I haven't gotten a new man yet but, I'm thinking about it. I'm not going to say anything more until I decide on what kind of a relationship I want. I'm really getting tired of all the losers that I've been dating lately. I really miss you."

"You know that you can come and stay with me anytime that you want to get away. How are things going at work?"

"Let me just say that I'm ready for another vacation. I'm thinking about making a change in the work area too. I'm starting to get a plan together. I will tell you more after I have made a final decision. I'm still in the thought process. I may just come for another visit in September over Labor Day weekend. I will see how things go here before I can make any commitment."

Hank had just walked out of his bathroom when he heard "You made the right call on King. He should be okay in a couple of days."

"Thank you, Great Grandfather for letting me know."

"I also wanted to warn you about that Garrett fellow. You better keep a close eye on him because I think he is going to start a little trouble. Jake likes Beth and he is letting it be known with the other guys. I don't think Garrett really cares. He is going to try and get her alone."

"Thanks for letting me know I will keep him away from the house as much as possible. I will let Garrett go as soon as the fencing is done. I don't want Jake to get into a fight with him. He has changed so much since he has been here I don't want him to turn back into what he was before."

Great Grandfather replied, "He has changed a lot since he has been here. He is falling in love with Beth and he has been fighting it all the way because he knows she plans on leaving when she gets out of school. As you know, your first love changes you as a person, even when you know that you have to let them go in the end."

"I know how he feels about Beth. She has no clue how he really feels about her. I hope she finds out soon."

"How are things going with you and Ella? Are you still taking a lot of cold showers?"

"Great Grandfather I have told you I'm not going to discuss my love life with you."

"She is going to make you a good wife and mother for your sons."

Hank was standing alone again in his room. *Man, I wish that he could let me know when he is going to make a visit. At least this time I had some clothes on.*

I know he is right about Ella. I'm trying to be patient with her and take things as slow as possible with her. I just need her to realize how much I love her and that she loves me.

CHAPTER 22

Hank was looking at his computer at the pictures that the cameras had taken of the person that had planted the cannabis plants on Ella's property. He took out his cell phone and called the Sheriff's office. He finally got a good picture of him.

The next call he made was to Ella. He needed to talk to her about what he found. He wanted the Sheriff there when he told her what was going on. They needed to know about the information that he had.

Ella left the clinic and drove straight to the ranch. She just got out of the car when Hank was walking out the back door to meet her. She took his breath away as he looked at her. He noticed that she had her beautiful hair pinned up on her head. She had blue jeans on that fit her just right with a tee-shirt. He walked up to her and kissed her on the forehead.

"What is going on Hank?"

Sheriff Gomez was just driving up to the house. "Just a minute I will let you know."

They watched as Sheriff Gomez got out of his patrol car and walked toward them. Hank and Al Gomez exchanged greetings. Hank explained to the Sheriff and to Ella that after the fire he went over to her property to have a look around to see if he could find any clues about the fire.

He explained that there were several paths where someone was taking a different path every time that he visited the property. He also found another set of footprints down at the other end of the property where the fire started. The footprints were two different sizes. I made a cast just to make sure.

I couldn't understand why things were happening to Ella. I knew the Fire Chief would only investigate the cause of the fire. The Sheriff that investigated the incident where she was run off the road wouldn't be able to find anything out.

I went over to Ella's property take a closer look. That is when I found that someone had planted cannabis plants on her property. I set up a few hunting cameras on her property so that I could find out who it was. I finally got a good enough picture of the person on my computer. I also wanted to know how often he was going to her property.

Ella listened to all of this and said "Someone is using my property for growing illegal drugs? Why would someone do that?"

Hank said "Think about it. No one had been using that property for a few years. You moved in and they thought if they scared you enough that you wouldn't stay. If you did stay then you would have to prove that you didn't plant it."

Al Gomez spoke up and said, "Let's take a look at what you have on your computer. "

They all went into the house to the den. Hank turned on his computer. The first thing that they saw on the screen were pictures of Ella that he had taken with his phone. She was so surprised to see all the pictures of her. "When did you take all of these pictures?"

"They are pictures that I have taken of you over the last few months."

"I had no idea that you took pictures of me."

He typed something into his computer. The program started that had the pictures on that he was looking for. Hank explained to Al that he had been keeping track of how often that person was coming out to the property. The person was coming out every three to four weeks to check on the plants. The person would not come at the same time every time. Sometimes he would come here during the week and sometimes it would be on the weekend. The time was always just before dark.

Al asked Hank to print him out a picture of the person. He also wanted to know if he could download everything so that he could use it in court. Hank printed out the picture and downloaded everything off his computer for the Sheriff.

Al turned to Ella and said, "Now that we know who we are looking for I want to watch him for a few weeks. I want to find out who he is selling this to. Don't say anything to anyone. Ella, don't change anything that you are doing. I don't want him to know that we are on to him. Have Beth stay over here if you have to go out without her for any reason. "

Do you think that he would hurt either one of us? He hasn't made any attempt to so far."

"I don't really know if he would or not. I just think it would be better if neither one of you were left there alone."

"Ok, I will make sure that we aren't alone at any time."

Al turned to Hank and said "He is going to start harvesting it pretty soon. If you see him over there cutting it down call me and I will get here as soon as I can. I'm hoping we have enough time to figure out his whole operation and see who he is dealing with. I will contact the DEA with this information."

After the Sheriff left, Hank pulled Ella into his arms and held her. "I hope you understand that I put the cameras over there so that I could help keep you safe. I don't want anything to happen to you because I love you very much." He bent his head so that his lips met hers and kissed her to prove to her that he really did love her. He kissed her until she was breathless. He held her for several minutes until his emotions were under control.

"I need to sit down for a minute. This is all too much for me to take in at one time. I need to process all of this."

"Baby, I'm right here and I'm not going anywhere. Please look at me and tell me what you are feeling right now."

She sat down in the nearest chair that she could find. Hank kneeled down in front of her. He took her hands in his and held them. Her eyes slowly met his eyes when she said "I don't know what to think about all of this. I have so many emotions going on right now that it is hard to explain it all."

"Just sit here for a few minutes."

He left the room and returned with something for her to drink. He pulled a chair up in front of her to sit in. He handed her the drink and held her other hand in his. He waited for her to talk to him. Several more minutes had passed before she spoke.

"I'm mad and hurt to think that someone would plant pot on my property. I'm so against drugs because I have lost friends due to drug use. The man that raped me was on drugs at the time and he thought it was okay because he wasn't in his right mind. The more I screamed the more he hit me. He told me that I was nothing but a whore and no one would ever want me.

I have gone through years of counseling and had to learn to trust men again. I changed schools. I've moved. I even changed my career because of it. I tried to have a relationship a couple of times only to be hurt in the end because I could not please them in bed. I get frigid, I have been called the "Ice Queen", just to find out that they have found someone else. I caught my last boyfriend in bed with one of my so-called friends.

A little over two years ago a drunk driver hit my brother's car. Mike and his wife Pam were killed on impact. That is why I have Beth living with me. She is just starting to be herself again.

I hope to hell that the police catch this person and

put them behind bars for a long time. I don't want drugs to ruin my life any more than it already has. I have fought long and hard to become the person that I have become today.

I moved Beth and I here so that we could start over again. To put all the bad stuff behind us. It seems like it has followed me here."

Hank pulled her onto his lap and wrapped her in his arms. "Baby, none of this is your fault. There are bad people all over this world. I love you and I 'm going to protect you the best that I can. That is why I called the Sheriff. I wanted him to know that you didn't know anything about what was going on at your place. Who knows how long it has been going on over there since the place has been empty for a few years.

I want you to trust me. I will never hurt you physically in any way. When the time comes for us to become sexually intimate together I will only do what you are comfortable with. I want to know your body very much and I'm looking forward to it. If you scream my name it will be from the pleasure that you receive and not from pain. I could never hurt you because I love you."

"I'm falling in love with you too and I'm so scared of being hurt again."

"Please don't be afraid because I want us to be able to plan a future together. I'm so in love with you already that I'm afraid that if I do the wrong thing that I will lose you. I don't want to live without you. I love seeing you here every day and I hate it when we are apart. "

"How can you say all of this? We haven't even been sexually intimate with each other yet."

"I will try to explain this to you the best that I can. Love is a word until someone gives it a meaning. You have opened my heart up again and given it meaning. You have a big heart and are a very caring person. I know this because you have your niece living with you. You could have let her go into the foster care system but you chose to give her a home.

I have seen how you are with the horses that are here. You seek out Star and Baby every time you are here. It's like you know how they feel and they need the extra attention. You are bonding with them. I have seen the longing in your eyes that you want someone to love you.

You clean my home and won't let me pay you for doing it. You are a strong woman because of the things that have happened to you. I have fallen in love with you because of the person that you are.

The best of our relationship is yet to come. When

you are ready and want to be sexually intimate with me then it will happen, not until then. Your heart has to be in it or it will not happen. I will know the difference. As much as I want you and love you I'm willing to wait until you are ready.

I'm going to be here for you, and beside you, because I love you. I hope that you will someday love me as much as I love you. Please open you heart and let me in. I want to feel the love in your heart."

She looked into his eyes and felt his arms encircle her. She could feel his heart beating in his chest. She closed her eyes before the silent tears fell down the side of her face. He moved her away from his body so that he could wipe the tear s from her face with his fingers. His kissed her tenderly so she would know how he felt. "Are you ok honey?' he asked in a low caressing voice.

She nodded her head up and down because she couldn't speak. When she found her voice again she said "I think I will see if Beth is ready to leave."

Ella and Beth left to go home for the night. She had a lot to think about. She had to tell Beth about what was going on and that she didn't want either one of them on the property alone.

She also had some serious thinking to do about what Hank had told her. He was very much in love with her. *Can I le t down the wall so that I can return his love?*

Later that night Hank thought about the conversation that he had with Ella. *I love her so much. I've probably scared her. I hope that she isn't going to run like a rabbit and hide in the brush. Maybe it is a good thing that she knows how I feel. I'm not going anywhere and I'm going to continue to show her how much I love and respect her.*

CHAPTER 23

The next morning when he got a chance to speak to Ben alone he told Ben to keep an eye out for any movement on Ella's property. If you see anything unusual call my cell phone. Ben told him that they were almost done with replacing the fence line that needed to be replaced.

Mid- morning Beth wandered out to the barn looking for Jake. She was walking down the breezeway in the barn when Garrett stepped out of the tack room. When Garrett saw her, he stopped outside of the door way "Hello there beautiful did you come to see me?"

She stopped walking as soon as he spoke to her. He stepped closer to her and said, "Don't be afraid I won't hurt you. I know you want me and it was just a matter time."

Beth stepped back from him to put more distance between them. With a brave voice as she could speak she asked him, "Where is Jake?"

Garrett gave her one for his famous smiles and said, "I'm not sure where he is right now but I'm sure I can make you forget about him for a few minutes."

Hank had come from the arena and saw Garrett talking to Beth. As he walked down the breezeway toward them he said, "What are you doing in here Garrett? The guys are waiting for you outside. I think you better not keep them waiting any longer."

He watched Garrett leave the barn before he spoke to Beth. "What are you doing in the barn Beth you normally don't come out here, is everything okay?"

" Just came out to speak with Jake for a minute . I didn't mean to cause any trouble. If I had known that Garrett was in the barn I wouldn't have come in here. I don't like him. I thought that they had left already."

"Beth, I don't care that you come out here I just want you to be careful. If any of the guys give you any trouble please let me know. I will handle it. That includes Jake too."

"I will try to be more careful. Where is Jake?"

"Jake is in the other barn cleaning out stalls the

last time I saw him."

She told Hank thanks and went on her way to find him. She found him a few minutes later right where Hank said he was. As soon as he saw her he stopped what he was doing and walked to her. "Beth is something wrong?"

"No, nothing is wrong, I just wanted to get out of the house for a few minutes so I thought I would come out and ask you what kind of cake do you like?"

He wrapped his arms around her, pulling her close as he hugged her. He rested his chin on the top of her head before he spoke. "I would like any kind of cake that you make for me." He stood there holding her for a few seconds enjoying the smell of her hair. He kissed her on the forehead before he moved away from her.

"I miss our rides that we take. Will you be able to take me riding again soon?"

"I will see what I can do maybe later we will be able to go for a short ride how will that be. I will let you know okay."

Later that afternoon Jake sent Beth a text.

Jake: I have the horses saddled come out as soon as you can.

Beth: I will be right out.

She found him by the barn. They saddled up and headed toward the stream. She liked being alone with Jake, he was the only friend that she really had. The more they were together the more she liked him, and she liked him a lot. They talked about the fall event and about the pumpkin patch.

When Hank came into the house for supper that night he told Beth that he wanted to talk to her. He wanted to take his shower first. Beth was busy cooking when he left the kitchen and walked down the hall to his bedroom. When he returned to the kitchen Ella was there. He walked over to her and placed a kiss on the side of her forehead as he slid his arm around her. He talked to Ella for a few minutes before he returned his attention to Beth.

"I have another group coming this weekend. Do you think that you could pack up some food for this group to take on their weekend ride?"

"Sure, is there anything special you want me to pack for them?

"No, I will leave it all up to you as to what to send with them. I'm sure that they will appreciate anything that you send. What you sent with the last group was really good. I got a letter saying that it was the best food that they ever had on a trail ride.

This group is willing to pay extra for the food. So, I will let them know that we will provide the food for them. You will get paid extra for this. This group is going to be ten people. They will be gone for two nights. They will be leaving on Friday afternoon and returning on Sunday."

"Are you going to be going with group?"

"No, I hired a guy to do this group and if it works out, he will do the rest of the groups that are booked. I have too much going on right now to leave the ranch for that length of time. They will be taking a wagon with them that will have tents and the food. I will get out the coolers for you so that you can pack then with the things that need to be cold. We should also put a couple cases of water on the wagon."

Beth asked "Who is doing the cooking?"

"His name is Sam Walker. I will give you his phone number so you can call him. Between the two of you, I'm sure you can figure out what to make and pack. If ou need to go into town for anything let me know. I will take you or have Jake take you to get what you need."

"I will call Sam right after supper."

"I'm going to email the group leader and tell him that we will provide the food."

Beth and Ella were just putting supper on the table when the rest of the guys entered the kitchen. Beth sat down by Jake and Ella sat down beside Hank. Ella was thinking about how nice it was. They were all like a happy family. She hoped that someday she would be having a family like this of her own.

They had just finished eating when Hank's cell phone rang. "This is Hank. She is here with me. Yes, I know the place. We can meet you there in about twenty minutes."

Hank turned to Ella and said "That was Doc. We have to go and meet him. I have to hook up the horse trailer. Beth you stay here until we get back. Jake, don't leave her alone, you stay by her side until we get back."

As Hank and Ella were walking to his truck he started to tell her what was going on. He told her to grab her medical bag. There was a barn fire at the Lawson place. I'm not sure what we are going to see when we get there. Doc asked me to bring a horse trailer with me. I know that we will be bringing a couple horses back with us.

When they arrived at the Lawson place the barn still had smoke coming out of the back of the barn.

The firemen were still trying to put the fire out. They were still hosing down the barn with water. After several minutes what was left of the barn was smoldering from the fire.

They found Doc talking to Rob Lawson. Rob was telling Doc that they got out as many of the horses that they could get to. He knew that a couple horses didn't make it out of the barn. We put them in the corral over there. The fire spread so fast and it was filled with smoke we just opened up the stall doors and let them run out the door that we had opened. The heat was so intense that we had to get out.

Doc, Hank, and Ella walked to the corral where the horses were. Doc and Ella looked over the horses together while Hank looked over a horse that had burn marks on his back and hind quarter. They found another horse that was badly burned with burns on her legs.

They told Rob about the two horses that were burned so bad that they would need care. Rob agreed to let Hank take the horses to his place. Doc gave the horses a sedative to help with the pain. They loaded them into the horse trailer that Hank brought. Doc told Hank the names of the horses and a little bit about what he knew about them.

Hank and Ella got into the truck and headed home. They were both quiet on the way back to the ranch. They were almost back to the ranch when she asked Hank "What do you know about Rob Lawson and his family?"

"The Lawson family has been in this area for a long time. The ranch was first started by his father who is now in a nursing home. He had a heart attack out in the barn a few years ago. He can no longer use his right hand and he drags his right foot when he walks.

Their mother died from cancer some years back. Rob went to law school and became a lawyer. After his dad went into the nursing home Rob took it upon himself to take care of his brother and sister."

"I know that his sister just graduated from high school. She will be leaving soon to go to college. I didn't know that he had a brother."

"The brother, Dan, is a couple of years older than his sister. He is the one that has been taking care of running the ranch."

Hank turned the truck onto the gravel driveway on his property. He parked the truck close to the barn. Ella climbed out of her side of the truck and walked around the front of the truck. He told her to text Beth to let her know that they were back. He walked to the back of the trailer to get the horses out. He tied them to the fence post while he closed up the trailer.

He led the horses to the side of the barn where the water hose was. He turned on the water and started cleaning the horse named Rocket. He let the water run down the length of Rocket's back to get the soot and smoke smell off of him. He cleaned around the burns on his back and on his legs the best that he could.

Ella was holding on to Rockets halter and talking softly to him while Hank was taking care of him. Hank moved to his head to wash his mane when he noticed what Ella was doing. *My Angel was being an Angel to Rocket. I keep falling more in love with her every time that she takes my breath away like she is now and she doesn't even know it.*

She worked side by side with him until both of the horses were cleaned and inspected to see how bad they were really burned. He put the horses in a small corral by Black Jack. When he got them settled in the corral he walked to the main barn to the tack room.

He opened the door to the medicine room. He started pulling jar after jar from the shelves. He placed the herbs into a mortar bowl using a pestle to turn the herbs into a paste. She watched him as he was mixing them. "What are you making?"

"If I tell you my secrets I will have to marry you. They are family secrets and have to stay in the family. What I'm making is something to put on the burns to make them heal faster." He handed her a key out of his pocket "Find an antibiotic in there to give the horses to fight off any infection."

She took the key from him and opened up the cabinet. She noticed the bottles on the right had the horse's names on them and the ones on the left didn't. She found what she was looking for and took it out of the cabinet. "I found something."

They walked to the small corral where the horses were. He told her to give the horses the antibiotic. She held onto the halter as he put the paste on the burns. He explained to her "The paste will help soothe the pain so that tomorrow we can see how badly that they are really burned. I will be able to scrape some of the dead skin off and cut some of the hair around the burns to prevent any infection."

She looked at him with soulful eyes before their eyes met when she said "Does this mean that you have to marry me because of what you just told me?"

"Ella, my Love I will ask you to marry me when the time is right. You are not ready to hear those words yet. I'm still working on earning your trust." He moved closer to her so that he could wrap his arms around her. His lips met hers in way that she knew how much he cared for her. *He is such a good kisser. My lips just seem to melt against his.*

He stepped away from her to look at her. He was looking at her as if he could see all the way to her soul. Without thinking she grabbed the front of his shirt to draw him closer to her so that she could return the kiss that he gave her. She tried to show him how she felt about him with her mouth. "Ella my Love you better stop before we get into trouble. This is not the place for you to be kissing me that way. I have more respect for our love than to throw you down to the ground where you stand. I think it is time to go to the house."

When they walked into the kitchen Hank noticed the house was all dark. He turned the light on so that they wouldn't trip over the dogs. Toby and Wyatt were laying on their rugs. They wagged their tails at them when they saw them. Hank noticed a note on the counter. He picked up the note and told Ella that everyone had gone to bed. He looked at the clock and noticed that it was almost midnight.

"I don't want you going home tonight. There is an empty bedroom upstairs for you to sleep in. I will go get you one of my tee-shirts for you to sleep in. You can go get some clean clothes to wear in the morning." He walked down the hallway to his bedroom to get her the shirt. When he returned with the shirt in his hand. As he handed it to her he said, "You know that you can take a shower with me and sleep in my bed tonight if you want."

"It is late and I don't think that we would get much sleep if I did that. Not only that the house is of full of people and what would they think?

"I thought I would give you the option, and to answer your question they probably would think that I got really lucky. But, you are right I would not sleep too much because of the sexual tension and frustration that I would create in my mind about you as you lay next to me. I'm going to go take my shower now. I will see you in the morning. "

Cold shower here I come. I need to get that image right out of my head and fast.

She climbed the stairs and entered the empty bedroom. She took a quick shower and washed her hair. She was glad that she didn't smell like smoke anymore. As she slid Hank's tee-shirt over her naked body she was thinking what kind of a lover he would be.

She grabbed her dirty clothes and towels. She went down stairs as quiet as possible to put them into the washing machine. As she turned to go back upstairs she saw him leaning against the wall in the hallway looking at her. The lights were all off but, she felt his presence. In a soft voice he asked her, "Everything ok Baby?"

"Yes, I hope I didn't disturb you?"

"No, I was just getting into bed when I heard you. Please go upstairs and get into bed. Try to get some sleep." *Damn, she looks so sexy wearing my shirt. How am I ever going to get some sleep now? I just want to strip the shirt off her and run my fingers thru her beautiful long hair. Kiss her senseless and carry her off to my bed. She has no idea how much she is tormenting me.*

She went upstairs and crawled into bed. She had visions of Hank kissing her going through her mind as she fell asleep.

As the new day was beginning, Hank got out of bed. He headed to the bathroom to turn on the shower. When he made his appearance in the kitchen everyone had been seated and had started to eat breakfast. The girls had just put the food on the table and were getting ready to sit down. He walked up to Ella and kissed the side of her forehead. "Good morning."

She looked at him and nodded. "Can I go with you after breakfast to look at Rocket and Patches? I want to see how they are doing this morning. I already called Doc and told him I would meet up with him later this morning."

Hank told Jake where he put the horses. He told him what had happened to them. "We will have to keep a close eye on them for the next couple of days. If you see them acting strange let me know."

After breakfast they walked to the corral where the two horses were. He opened up the gate for them to go in. He walked up to Rocket and was looking at the burns on his back while Ella held on to his halter. He noticed that some of the burns were not as bad as others. The heat from where the skin was burned had subsided so the burns were easier to see how bad they were. He held on the halter so that she could take a look. She looked at Hank and said, "How did you do that? I know that I was with you when you treated them last night. What was in that mixture that you made?"

He looked at her and replied with a slight chuckle in his voice "It's a family secret and I would have to marry you. I told you that last night."

"I have never seen anything work so fast on a burn before. You are amazing at what you do with the horses. I'm not talking just about these two horses but I have seen what you have done with many of the horses that have been here."

"I'm glad that you approve of what I do here. I have worked hard to make this ranch what it is and

I'm still not done. There are still more things that I want to do to this place."

"What more do you want to do here?"

"I want to install solar panels on the barn roofs to help produce electricity to the barns. I want to put in heated flooring for the horses when it gets cold and a heating system to keep the barns from getting so cold in the winters. All of it is going to take a lot of money. I'm hoping that the solar panels will pay for themselves in a short period of time."

"Are you turning this place into a resort for horses?"

"That is not a bad idea. We could give them massages , mud baths and braid their hair. We could also fit them with new shoes. I'm sure they will tell their owners take me to *"Hank's Place"* I need a day of pampering." he laughed.

"I'm serious, people would pay for that for their horses. We could put in a spa for the owners so that the owners could get pampered too."

"That is not quite what I pictured for this place."

"Well, it was just a thought. If you change your mind we could get Libby to do the marketing on it for you." She was trying very hard not to laugh.

"I like things the way they are around here. I will keep the suggestion in the back of my mind. I have a lot to do today. Are you going to meet Doc?"

"Yes, he is checking on a horse that has colic, so I'll see him at the clinic later." She walked up to Hank and gave him a kiss and told him that she would see him later.

He watched his Angel walk away from him. *She is one hell of a woman. She takes my breath away every time I see her. I can't wait to be with her again tonight.*

As Ella walked away from him she could feel his eyes on her back. She knew he was watching her leave. *I hope he likes what he sees, because he is one sexy cowboy. He really knows how to kiss a woman. I really have to figure out a way to get him between the sheets.*

CHAPTER 24

Sam Walker arrived at the Rocking R Ranch mid-morning on Friday. He pulled up close to the house. Beth came out of the house to take a look at the covered wagon that had stopped with two horses pulling it. On the wagon seat sat a man in his twenties wearing a dark brown Stetson, blue jeans with a work shirt. She watched Sam climb down from the wagon. She was expecting someone older than the man who stood in front of her. He extended his hand and said in a deep voice, "I'm Sam Walker you must be Beth?"

"Yes, I am. You are not at all what I expected after I talked to you on the phone."

"I'm sorry. Did I disappoint you?"

"No, I just thought that you were much older than what you are. I pictured in my mind a man that was in his late thirties to early forties. What is a nice way to say a little out of shape?"

Sam stood in front of her and lifted his arms out from his sides. He looked down his body and said "When I checked in the mirror this morning I wasn't that old and out of shape."

"No, you are not." She said with a little chuckle.

"Well if it helps you aren't anything what I expected either."

Beth remembered her manners and said, "It's nice to meet you. I have all the supplies in the kitchen that you will need. I got everything on your list." She turned around to go into the house. Sam walked beside her to the porch steps. He stopped walking when he heard Hank calling his name.

Hank told him that he had some tents stored in the barn. He thought that it would be a good idea to take them since it might rain. Sam told him they could put them in the back of his wagon so that they wouldn't have to take another wagon on the trip. They walked to the barn to where the tent s were stored.

"Hank, you didn't warn me that you had such a beautiful cook working for you."

"You better keep those eyes, and hands to yourself because she is too young for you. Besides Jake is awful sweet on her. I think he is fighting falling in love with her. By the looks of things I don't think either one of them has ever had a serious relationship before. He is very protective of her."

He told Sam about Ella and Beth moving into the Smith property. He explained that Ella inherited the property from her Uncle Joe. Beth was working for him since Maria left to take care of her father. You won't be disappointed in anything that Beth makes she is a good cook and wants to go to a cooking school when she gets out of school.

They walked back to the wagons to load the tents when Beth came out of the back door. She stood on the porch and watched them. "Can I get you guys anything to drink?"

"You got any coffee?" asked Hank.

"No, but I can make a pot really quick for you."

"Thanks, that would be nice."

Hank and Sam stood outside and talked about the group that was coming. Just as they were getting ready to go into the house Ella pulled up in her car. As soon as she got out of her car she walked up to Hank. As she reached him he pulled her into his arms for a quick hug and kissed her.

"Hi Sam, how are you?"

"I'm good."

They all walked into the house. Beth had made a pot of coffee for them. When Sam entered into the kitchen he saw all the supplies in crates. There was also a big ice chest ready to be filled with food.

Beth was so organized that Sam couldn't believe it. She had all can goods in one crate. She had paper plates, napkins, plastic cups and plastic silverware in another crate. She made biscuits that morning and put them in a plastic bag and then in a plastic air tight container. She also packed brownies, and cookies that she made.

Sam finished his coffee and asked Beth if she would like to see his wagon. She told him yes. They walked out to the back of his wagon. Sam reached up to unlatch the cupboard door that folded down to a table. The back of the wagon was now a big open cupboard with a place for his cast iron pots and lids. There were smaller shelves at the top that held can goods there was also a spot for tin plates and a drawer that held cooking utensils and silverware.

On one side of the wagon was a big wooden box which held fire wood. On the other side she noticed there was a wooden barrel. She climbed upon on the seat to look inside the wagon. She found a bed on one side. He had a small dresser that was built- in with two drawers. She noticed a couple of folding chairs, and the tents that they put in earlier. He had plenty for room for the plastic crates.

As Sam and Beth were loading the wagon people were arriving that were going on the trail ride. Hank, Jake and Ben were there to help the group. They unloaded their horses and were told where to park the trucks and horse trailers for the weekend.

Dave Brown was their guide for the weekend. When the group was ready to go, Dave mounted his horse. The group of rider formed behind him with the chuck wagon driven by Sam, following behind them. They headed northeast toward the state land.

Beth was standing next to Jake with his arm around her waist pulling her to his side so that he could kiss her forehead. "Jake what do you think about us asking Sam to join us for the fall event? He could put on a demonstration or something. I think he would be a good addition to the event?"

"We can ask him when he gets back. He makes a good pot of chili served with some corn bread that makes my mouth water."

"I'm getting so excited about this fall event. I just hope it will go as well as we have planned it."

"I have talked to my brother, Josh, plus Brett and Seth. They have all agreed to help us with the event. It is going to take a lot of work, but I'm sure we can make it all happen."

She looked up to look into Jake's eyes at the same time he looked down at her. Their lips were just inches from each other when he moved his arm away from her waist and said "I better get back to work. We will talk about it some more later."

As she watched Jake walk to the barn she was thinking *I wish he would have kissed me. His lips were so close to mine before he pulled away. I would like just one really good kiss to see if he is a good kisser.*

After supper that night Beth asked Jake to talk to her while she cleaned up the kitchen. She had some things to discuss with him. He told her he would help her. They decided that they would have a small meeting with Brett and Seth to get their ideas on the fall event.

They all sat at the kitchen table. Beth got out her notebook that she started with her and Jakes' ideas written down. Their ideas were becoming a reality with their help. They had eight weeks to put this all together. They even came up with ideas for posters for the event. The posters would go up in four weeks to announce the event. The event is now being called the "The Fall Festival."

It had started to rain early on Sunday morning. The trail group returned to the ranch that afternoon. The riders were wet and couldn't wait to get dried off. The leader of the group found Hank in the barn. He told him how well the trip went and how good the food was. They would definitely be back next year.

Sam had pulled his wagon close to the house so that he could unload the plastic crates. He told Beth that everyone enjoyed the food. He told her if she ever got tired of working for Hank that she could work with him anytime. She told him that she would keep that in mind.

She decided to talk to him about the fall festival. With a smile on her face, she asked "Would you be interested in doing a little demonstration of your chuck wagon cooking? It will be a good way to promote what you do. If you say yes, we have one small request on what you cook. Someone already requested that you make chili and cornbread. I have heard it is very good."

She held her breath while she waited for him to answer her. He looked away from her for a couple of minutes before he answered her. "When did you say this event was?"

"It's on Saturday, October tenth. From ten o'clock a.m. until four o'clock p.m."

"For you, young lady I will do it. You have my phone number. Just text me the date and time so that I can put in on my calendar." He tipped the corner of his cowboy hat to her and walked back to his wagon.

Beth was so excited that she sent a text to Jake telling him that Sam said yes. While doing a happy dance in the kitchen this is going to be the best event ever.

CHAPTER 25

As soon as Libby made her plane reservations she called Ella to let her know when she would be arriving. She would be arriving on September first. Libby also told her that she would rent a car to drive to her house. Ella told her to call her so she would know where to go when she got here because she might have to go to Hank's house to wait for her.

Summer was coming to an end. The nights were getting cooler and the days were getting shorter. Everyone had so much to do. Ella was cleaning the living room in her home when she realized, that her and Beth seemed to be just sleeping there.

Beth would be returning to school soon.   She

still needed to take her shopping for school supplies and buy her some clothes for school. Maybe while Libby was here they could go to a mall and do some shopping. She needed some girl time very much with her BFF and Beth.

When Beth found out that Ella had planned a shopping day she started making out a list of things that she wanted to pick up. She had also started ordering a few things on the computer with Hank's permission for the fall event that was now turning into a fall festival. Things were starting to come together with the extra help they had.

Beth had been emailing Libby and asking her questions about making small cards that they could put out in the stores in town to advertise the event. Libby suggested that they also put them in the hotel and the B&B in town. She told Beth that she would bring them with her when she came to visit.

The last week of August the men were working out in one of the fields when Ben got the call from Sarah to come and get her. He left the group and headed home. Sarah was in labor. She was trying to wait until he got home, but the pains started coming quicker and quicker. He was nervous because the closest hospital was thirty minutes away. When he arrived home, he found Sarah pacing the floor in the kitchen. She stopped walking when one of the pains would hit her. He asked her how ar apart her pains were. She told him when she called him that they were about five minutes apart. The pains were now about three minutes apart. With the pains being so close he called the clinic in town and talked to Dr. Jones. The doctor told him to bring her to the clinic. She would not make it to the hospital. He carried Sarah in his arms to his truck and away they went.

As soon as they arrived at the clinic they took her to a room in the back where they prepared everything for her and the new baby. Dr. Jones asked Ben if he wanted to stay or wait in the waiting room. He told Dr. Jones he was not leaving her.

Jason Baker was born twenty minutes later. Dr. Jones told Sarah and Ben that it would be best if they stayed at the clinic tonight. If Sarah and the baby were doing well in the morning, they would be able to go home.

Later that afternoon Ben called Hank and told him about Sarah and the baby. Hank told him to take a couple of days off so that he could spend some time with Sarah and the baby. He told him that he would drop by after they got home to see the baby and check on them.

When Ella arrived at the ranch they told her the news about the baby being born. "I want to go see the baby. When are they going to be home?"

Hank informed her that the four of them could go over this weekend to see the baby if they wanted. They made plans go after lunch on Saturday?

Early Saturday afternoon the four of them went to visit Ben, Sarah and baby Jason. Sarah was glad to have female visitors. Ella and Beth spent time talking to Sarah and taking turns holding the baby.

Hank and Jake got Ben caught up on everything that was happening at the ranch. The guys were cutting, bailing and putting up the hay in the barn. The Lawson barn was just about done being built. The horses that belonged to them would be going home soon. Dan had been over to check on his horses. He couldn't believe how much they had healed from the burns.

On the way back to the ranch Ella reminded Hank that her friend Libby was coming or another visit. Libby would be there for a week. She would be arriving on Thursday. Ella asked him if they could think of anything the girls could do while she was here. One day the girls were going to go shopping at a mall in a nearby city. Beth was so excited. She hadn't been to a mall since they moved here.

When Hank laid in bed that night he thought about seeing Ella holding Jason in her arms. *She was going to be a good mother. He couldn't wait till the time came when Ella wanted to carry their child. He realized he had never thought about that with no else but her. I love her so much and I can't believe that every time I see her she still takes my breath away.*

Libby arrived at the Rocking R Ranch on Thursday night just as planned. Ella came out the back door as soon as she saw the car pull up next to the house. She waited until Libby reached the steps before she gave her a hug. "I have missed you so much."

"I feel the same way as you do. But why oh, why did you have to move so far away? I must admit it feels good to get out of the city for a few days."

When they entered he kitchen, Beth asked Libby if she wanted anything to eat or drink. She settled on a bottle of water. She told them about her flight out there. There was a guy on her flight that was on the loud side. He tried to pick up some woman on the flight. He was so rude and obnoxious that the woman asked if she could change her seat. With a chuckle Libby said, "He wasn't even that good looking." The girls all burst out laughing.

Hank and Jake walked in the back door as the girls were talking at the kitchen table. Hank walked over to them. He greeted Libby as he bent over to kiss the side of Ella's forehead. Jake had disappeared down the hallway to the back stairs without saying a word.

Friday morning after breakfast the girls got ready to go shopping. They got into Libby's rented car and headed to the nearest mall. When Beth told Ella that she wanted to shop for a pair of boots Ella couldn't believe what she heard. She explained to Ella that Jake had been taking her riding when he had the time and she wanted some boots to wear instead of her sneakers.

The girls enjoyed their day shopping. They arrived back at the ranch in the late afternoon. Beth took her stuff up to the room that she used at Hank's since she would be staying there until Libby went back home.

As soon as Hank finished his chores he walked to the house to see his Angel. He missed seeing her all day. He found the girls in the living room talking. He went over to Ella to kiss her on the side of the forehead and give her a little hug. "Did you girls have a good day shopping?"

"Yes, we did and we bought so much stuff we didn't think it was all going to fit in the car."

"I think you girls should go shopping more often."

"Hank, what are you trying to say?" asked Ella.

"I think by the looks on all your faces that you

enjoyed your day being with each other and doing something that you all enjoyed. You should do things that you enjoy more often. I hope the next time Libby comes to visit that you will be shopping for something special."

"I would make a special trip for that any time if the occasion is presented." replied Libby. She looked at Ella with a questioning look.

Hank left the room so the girls could talk. He went into the den and turned on the computer. He turned the cameras on that watched over Ella's property. There was movement going on. Someone was there harvesting the plants that they planted. He got on his phone to call Jake to the house to stay with the girls.

The next phone call was to Sheriff Gomez. He walked out of the den and told the girls not to leave the house until he got back. Sheriff Gomez told him he was on his way with backup.

Hank took off toward the wooded area along the back part of Ella's property. He slowly approached the area where the men were. He had walked up behind a tree to get a better look at who was on the property. There was a total of three men that he could see. They were all busy cutting the plants and trying to get out of there as fast as they could. Hank was trying to figure out a way to stall them until the

Sheriff Gomez got there. They were putting the cut plants into big black plastic bags. He heard one of the guys say "You just about done over there so we can get the hell out of here?"

One of the men caught a glance of Hank moving behind the tree. As he walked closer toward the tree he motioned to one of the other guys to hurry up and pack the bags so that they could get out of there. The other guy he wanted to circle around to the back of the tree to come up behind him.

Hank knew what they were doing. As quietly as possible he moved to a different spot. He heard a gun go off. Hank felt the pain as the bullet grazed his arm. He wasn't counting on them having a gun with them. If they caught him he knew that they would not hesitate to kill him. He just had to keep them there long enough for the Sheriff to arrive. He pulled his knife from his belt and threw it at the man that was headed toward him. The knife landed in the man's shoulder. The man yelled to someone that he had been hit before he fell to the ground. He told someone, "Get me the hell out of here. I'm bleeding pretty bad. He got me with a knife."

One of the men had taken some of the bags to the van that was parked at the other end of the field. When Sheriff Gomez and a couple of deputies arrived upon the scene. They found the man that was loading the bags into the van. He had his back toward them putting the bags inside of the van when they came up behind him. Trying not to make a lot of noise to alert the other two men they got him down on the ground to search him and to put the handcuffs on.

Sheriff Gomez and one of the deputies went to go look for the other men. When they found them, the two men were together. The man with the knife wound was sitting on the ground leaning against a tree. The other man was looking at the man's shoulder. As soon as the man that was still standing saw the Sheriff he left the man sitting on the ground. He took off running in the opposite direction.

He ran in Hank's direction. Hank ran after him and tackled him. He drew his gun and was going to shoot Hank when Sheriff Gomez shouted, "Put the gun down, you are under arrest." Sheriff Gomez had his gun pointed at the man on the ground. Hank disarmed him as the deputy took the gun. Hank got up and the Sheriff put handcuffs on the guy. They all left the wooded area and walked to where all the cars were parked.

All three men were arrested on multiple charges. The man with the knife wound was taken to the clinic to be seen by Dr. Jones. The other two were taken to the jail. Sheriff Gomez asked Hank to stop by his office in the morning to give him a statement for the record. He also thanked Hank for all his help with this case.

Sheriff Gomez said to Hank, "Let me give you a ride home."

"Sure."

When Hank got into the patrol car Sheriff Gomez realized that Hank had been shot. "You need to go see Dr. Jones about your arm?"

"Nope, I just want to go home."

CHAPTER 26

When the Sheriff's car came to a stop behind the house the back door opened. Ella walked out on the back porch. Right behind her stood Libby and Beth with Jake standing as close to Beth as he could get without touching her. As soon as Ella saw Hank get out of the patrol car she stepped off the porch and went down to the steps. She walked right into Hank's arms.

He put his arms around her pulling her close to his body so that he could kiss her forehead. *He loved seeing her. She took his breath away just looking at her. I love her very much.*

"Hank, you're bleeding!"

"Just a little, it is just a flesh wound. I will be alright."

"When we get into the house I want to see how bad you are hurt."

Hank turned to Sheriff Gomez nd thanked him for the ride home. He told him that he would be in town first thing in the morning to give him his statement. Sheriff Gomez said good night and drove away.

They all walked into the kitchen. Hank sat down at the kitchen table. While Ella looked at his arm he told them what had happened. He only gave them a brief description. Ella was busy cleaning his wound and putting a bandage over it. He told the girls that he wanted them all to spend the night just to be on the safe side. He had a feeling that this wasn't over yet. He would feel better if they stayed. They all agreed that it would be best.

As he laid in bed he was thinking about how things would be changing again around the house. School would be starting up which means he needed to talk with Jake and his mother about Jake continuing to work at the ranch. Jake had changed so much in the months that he has been there. He has turned into a good worker. He was also really good with the horses. He listened to everything that he told him about the horses.

If Jake stayed around for the next year working at the ranch he was going to talk to him about going to college. He wanted him to learn about animal husbandry. He could go for two years and get his Associates Degree. He could use his knowledge here at the ranch or make more money at another ranch if he chose to.

It also meant that Ella and Beth wouldn't be spending as much time at the ranch. He needed to figure out a way to keep them at the ranch. He wanted to see his Angel every day. Ella hasn't revealed her true feeling to him as to how she really feels about him. She hasn't told him that she was in love with him. He knew that she was scared to put her heart out there one more time, but, I think if she looked really close she would see that her heart is already attached to me. I just need to figure how to get that last wall around her heart to go down so that she can love me freely.

I know that the sexual intimacy is a big thing with her because she was raped. I have gone slowly with her because I want her to fall in love with me first before I take her to my bed and make her mine.

I can vision her laying in my bed with her beautiful silky hair covering my pillows. I love touching her silky hair. Her blue eyes will turn darker in color as her passion grows. Her pretty lips will part as her breathing changes and I take advantage to run my tongue across her lips until she opens her mouth more to allow my tongue to enter and deepen the kiss that we share.

I will continue to kiss her mouth, neck and a start to leave a trail of kisses as I move down her body to kiss and suckle her breast with my mouth. I will pay equal attention to her other breast as they are a part of her beautiful body. I will continue to work my way down her body kissing her and telling her how beautiful she is. I will work my way to her navel still kissing her and licking her with my tongue. I can't wait to taste her sweetness that has been building between her legs.

With a groan, Hank rolled out of bed and headed to the shower again. As he stood in the cold shower he realized that it was not helping him much. He didn't know how much more a normal man can take before he had to do something to relieve his sexual tension.

When he walked into the kitchen for his morning coffee, he noticed an empty cup in the sink next to the coffee pot. Must be Ella was up already or maybe Libby was. Ella walked into the kitchen as Hank was so deep in thought he didn't realize that Ella was that close to him. She walked over to him a gave him a

Good Morning kiss. "Good morning Beautiful." he said.

"Good morning yourself cowboy."

"I was just wondering who made the coffee this morning. When I saw the empty cup in the sink. I wondered if you got called out on a call first thing this morning."

"Libby went out about thirty minutes ago. She was telling us last night that she brought her camera with her so that she could get some photos of the horses and the cowboys. The everyday things that go on at a ranch. She also wanted to take picture of some things around town and the area around here."

"What does she want the pictures for?"

"I not sure. She didn't really say."

Beth walked into the kitchen and asked if they would like some breakfast before they started their day. She could make a quick breakfast. She opened up the refrigerator pulling the items out that she would need.

Jake entered the kitchen and walked over to the coffee pot to pour himself a cup. Beth had already poured him a glass of milk and placed it in front of him at the table when he sat down. She also placed a plate of food in front of him.

Hank told Jake that he would help out with some of the chores this morning then he had go into town to talk to Sheriff Gomez. He asked him to stay close to the house while he was gone since it was Ben's day off. Ella told him that she would like to go into town with him.

After their visit to the sheriff 's office, Hank ask Ella if she would like to get a cup of coffee and something to eat at Stella's Place? They walked into the restaurant and found a place to sit. Donna waited on them and asked Hank a couple of questions before she left to place their order.

Ella was telling him how relieved she was that the worst part of the ordeal with the growing of illegal drugs on her property were coming to a close. She couldn't wait to be able to go back to her own home. He told her he enjoyed seeing her every day even if it was for a short period of time every day this summer. He wished he could have spent more time with her.

He also told Ella that he wanted Beth to continue to cook for him until he could find someone else. He didn't want Beth to spend all her time working at his ranch. This was her last year of school and he wanted her to be able to enjoy it. She told him he would have to ask Beth what she wanted to do. She didn't have any problems leaving things the way they were. She liked seeing him every day too.

She has no idea how much I need to see her every day. I don't think I can go back to seeing her only a few times a week. I'm so in love with her and I know that I have to wait for her to come to me. She needs to want me in her life as much as I want her in mine.

When they returned to the ranch they noticed that Libby had returned. He gave Ella a swift kiss and told her that he was going to the barn. She walked into the kitchen and found Libby at the table eating some lunch. She was talking to Beth. Beth noticed that Ella wanted to talk to Libby so she left the kitchen so that they could talk.

"How did things go for Hunky Hank at the Sheriff office?" asked Libby

"They have got the FBI Drug Enforcement Unit involved. Hank gave them a copy of the pictures from the cameras that are on my property. It looks like there is more going on with this operation than we realized. A lot more people than the three men that they arrested. The police asked if we could stay here at Hank's for a while until they arrested more people. They said it was a precaution because of the people that are involved in this. I'm not to make any house calls without Doc being with me."

"I'm sure that Hunky Hank won't let anything happen to you or Beth. He's already proved that he would protect you with his life. He is so in love with you Ella, I hope that you are going to be happy with him. You need to give him a real chance and let down the wall around your heart."

"The walls are slowly coming down. I'm falling in love with him too. The more I'm around him the more I'm falling for him."

"Have you let him know how you feel?"

"I'm trying to let him know how I feel. I think it is time I really told him. I already know that he loves me. I also know that he would ask me to marry him but he knows I'm not ready yet for that commitment. I have to get him to make love to me first and that is what scares me."

"Ella, Hank is different from any man that you have ever dated. What I see is a man that is very much in love with you. He's not some guy that wants to take you to dinner or a movie just so that he can get you into a bed. If that were the case, he would have already tried to get you there."

"I know that you are right. I will tell him how I feel after your visit the first chance that I get."

"No, you don't have to wait to tell him after I'm gone. Why not do it now, you know he is out in the barn so find him and tell him."

"Boy, you are getting bossy my friend." Ella got

up from the table and walked to the back door.

She walked toward the barn and stopped at the corral to say hello to Baby and Star. When they saw her approach the fence they both walked over to her to get some attention and maybe a carrot. "Sorry I don't have any treats on me right now but, I will get you some I promise. I'm on my way to talk to Hank. Wish me luck."

Star moved her head up and down like she was answering her. She stood there for a few minutes to get the nerve to go talk to Hank. When she entered the barn, she could smell the hay and the horses. The barn looked pretty clean for the stalls were all cleaned out and had new straw.

She didn't see him anywhere so she got out her cell phone and sent him a text message asking where he was. He told her to go beyond the second barn and she would find him at the mud pit.

He had just put Rocket into the mud pit to soak for a few minutes. He would then clean him off before he treated him again. Ella couldn't believe what she was seeing. Rocket was standing in a hole up to his chest, that was filled with muddy water.

She stood beside Hank looking at Rocket and asked him if he had a couple of minutes to talk to her. He pulled her closer to him so that he could place a kiss on the side of her forehead. "I will always make time to talk to you. What is on your mind?"

"You know, I was just kidding about the spa thing with the horses, but it looks like you already have it going on."

"It is part of Rocket's treatment. I know you didn't come looking for me just to tell me that."

"Hank, I want our relationship to go to the next level."

"Ella, what are you trying to tell me?"

"I'm trying to tell you that I have fallen in love with you. I want you to make love to me soon."

He turned so that he could look into her eyes. He placed his hands on each side of her face as he looked into her eyes. "Are you sure that you are ready for this? Once I get you into my bed I won't be able to let you go. You will become mine."

" Yes, this is what I want."

"I love you and this means so much to me that you are really going to give us a chance. You will not regret it my love." He bent his head so that he could give her a kiss. It was a kiss to remind her how much he loved her and it took her breath away.

She stayed there watching him take care of Rocket.

She followed him as he took Rocket to clean him off. She realized how careful he was with touching and caring for Rocket.

I hope that he is that kind and patient with me. The thought of his hands working their magic on me gives me goosebumps and makes my skin tingle.

A soft moan escaped through her lips. He looked at her and knew where her thoughts had been. Her eyes had a faraway look and her body was giving her away. He could see that her body was getting aroused just by watching him.

He moved closer to her so that he could whisper in her ear, "I will make it so good for both us, that you will want more."

Her face had turned a pretty shade of pink. "I hope so." She turned and walked to the house before she embarrassed herself anymore.

Hank watched his Angel walk away with a smile on his face. He finished taking care of Rocket before he did the same treatment on Patches. The horses would be going home soon.

CHAPTER 27

When she returned to the house she found Libby at the kitchen table with her lap top computer. She was looking at the pictures that she had taken that morning. Ella walked up behind her. She was looking over her shoulder when she said "I didn't know that you were so good with a camera. These pictures are fantastic. What are the pictures for?"

"I haven't decided what I'm going to do with them yet. The first time I came to visit, this place just called to me in a way that I can't explain. The small town's atmosphere and the beauty of the area. Seeing the cowboys working with the cattle and the horses."

"How much do you know about this town Ella?"

"I don't know a lot yet since we've only been here for about six months. I'm just getting to know the people here. I guess I should say the ranchers in the area. I haven't met too many of the women yet. I'm too busy working to socialize with the women. I know some of them from coming into the clinic. That is just about it. I don't get into the town gossip if that is what you want to know."

"I stopped in town to get lunch at Stella's Place. Two women approached me and asked me to join them at their table. They introduced themselves as Eva Baker and Sadie Ballinger. I was wondering if you knew anything about them?"

"I think that Eva Baker is Ben's mother. I don't know anything about Sadie Ballinger."

"They wanted to know if I would be interested in doing some work for their group. I asked how I could help them since I wasn't from the area. They heard thru the gossip grapevine that I worked in the marketing industry. I told them that yes, I did work for a marketing company. They asked me to meet with their group on Tuesday morning at ten. Sadie said to Eva that the women in their group would be pleased. They never did tell me about their group and I was wondering if you knew anything."

"No, I'm sorry that I don't know anything about a group of women. I wonder if Hank would know anything. We can ask him when he comes in for supper. They also mention a place called Cupid's Falls that is not far from here. That I should make a point to go there and take some pictures. Do you know where this place is? "

"I have never heard of Cupid Falls before. There is probably some story behind it if they call it that. Another question that we can ask Hank."

"I'm anxious to hear how these ladies think that I can help them."

Ella left Libby at the kitchen table while she went to go clean Hank's bedroom and bathroom. They have become her favorite rooms to clean. As she opened up the bedroom door her lungs filled with his scent as she knew they would. She loved the smell of him.

She put his dirty clothes in the basket that she brought with her so that she could do his laundry. While she was cleaning the bathroom, her mind started wondering and thinking of Hank. *I want this relationship to work out so much. I don't think that I could handle another relationship that didn't. He has no idea how I felt when I saw that he was hurt yesterday. I was glad that it was nothing serious. I don't know what I would have done if I had lost him. I don't know when I fell so much in love with him. I guess it is time that I let him know how much I love him. I just hope that we can get the intimacy part of our relationship to work for us.*

She had just finished cleaning his rooms when he

came into the house. She heard him speaking to Libby in the kitchen. She walked down the hallway to the kitchen. She noticed the look on his face as the tightening in his face muscles relaxed as soon as he saw her. The look in his eyes softened as he looked at her.

He walked up to her and placed a light kiss on her lips that left her wanting more. He told her that he had to go the Wheeler ranch to pick up a foal that had just been born. Doc had called him to ask him if he could take the foal. He wanted to know if she wanted to go with him. He already had the horse trailer hooked up to his truck. She decided to go with him. They told Libby where they were going and would be back shortly.

Hank pulled into the driveway of the Wheeler ranch about ten minutes later. The property was pretty much like the other small ranches in the area. He parked his truck close to the barn. They got out of the truck and walked into the barn hand in hand looking for Doc.

They found him in a stall in the back part of the barn. He looked up at them when they stopped outside of the stall door. Doc told them that the mare had been in a long and difficult labor. She was an older horse and her heart gave out after she gave birth. Mrs. Wheeler was concerned and knew something wasn't right so she called me. I thought that she was going to lose both of them. I managed to save the foal but not the mare.

"What did Mrs. Wheeler say about the foal? What kind of plans does she have for the foal?"

A woman of slender build with brown hair pulled back into a neat bun at the back of her head appeared at the stall door. Tears were silently falling down her cheeks. " Please call me Melissa. Please excuse my behavior as I just lost my horse. I rode her every day when the weather allowed. I got her when she was just a foal and was able to leave her mother. She was such a mild natured horse. I loved riding her. To answer your question Hank, I had no real plans for the foal. I didn't want her to get pregnant at her age.

I had gone on a trip with some of my friends for a couple of weeks, so I took her over to the Double T ranch to board her for a month while I was gone. Shortly after she came back I found out that she was pregnant by one of Trevor's horses. I was not happy."

"Does Trevor know about the foal?"

"Don't take me for a fool. If he knew he would charge me a stud fee plus more. He thinks he only raises the best horses in the area."

"I'm willing to take the foal to my place. I have a

horse that gave birth a few months ago. We can see if shea will foster the foal. If not, then we will feed her and raise her. I have some mares that will adopt her and take care of her."

"Hank I think that would be best, that way Trevor will never know about the foal."

Hank walked over to Mrs. Wheeler and said "You can come to my ranch to visit her any time you want. I will let you ride one of my horses any time you want. If you decide to get another horse I will be happy to help you find the right one. You can keep your horse at my ranch if you go out of town again."

"Thank you, that means so much to me. Since my Josh passed away it is nice to know that there are still some nice men out there that really do care about a woman's feelings and needs."

While Hank was talking to Mrs. Wheeler, Ella was helping Doc get the milk from the mom's milk sack before her body temperature dropped too much and the milk wouldn't be any good. They needed to feed it to the foal as soon as they could. Hank walked back out to his truck to get a nursing bottle so that they could feed the foal.

After the foal was fed they put her in the horse trailer and headed home. Hank brought Sandy in from the corral and put her into her stall. He brought the new born foal into the stall to see what Sandy would do. The foal laid in the straw in the corner of the stall. She watched every move he made.

He approached Sandy and told her that the foal needed a mom. He knew she would be a good mom because she was a good mom to her own colt. He was running his hand down the side of her neck as he was talking to her.

He heard the voice of his great grandfather. "You need to put Sandy's scent on the new foal. Sandy needs to smell the scent on it so that she knows it is hers. She knows she didn't give birth to it but she will take care of it because it has her scent on it. Make sure after you touch Sandy that you touch the foal. Then move out o the stall and see what Sandy does. She will either accept it or refuse it."

Ella watched him in the stall with the Sandy and the foal. Then he opened the stall door to stand on the other side of the door to see what Sandy was going to do. After a few minutes Sandy moved over to the foal. She bent her head and started nudging the foal to stand. After a few attempts, the foal stood up on wobbly legs.

He heard great grandfather say "Let them bond for a couple of hours before you return her colt to her. She will worry about her colt until she is reunited with it."

"Ok, I think this is going to work. We just have to wait and see if Sandy will encourage the foal to let her nurse her."

"I have an idea that she will." replied great grandfather. "Oh, by the way you know that Ella is going to be a great mom too.!"

Ella heard a small chuckle come from Hank's mouth. She asked him "What is so amusing to you?"

"I was just thinking of something. I will bring in her colt in a couple of hours so that Sandy will be with it. I will keep both of them with her tonight. We will see how she does with both of them tomorrow."

Hank's cell phone received a text message stating that supper would be ready in fifteen minutes. He told her that it was time to go the house. He wanted to get cleaned up for supper. He knew that Jake also got the text message.

After everyone was seated at the kitchen table Hank started telling Jake about the new foal. We will have to think of a name for her. Jake told him that he would go out to the barn and look at her. Maybe a name would come to him.

Libby asked Hank about Eva Baker and Sadie Ballinger. She wanted to know if he knew anything about their group. "Eva is Ben's mother. I don't know too much about them. Ben was telling me that these women, and I think that there are about five of them get together about once a month. They are all widows. Ben has named them "The Widows Club of Cedar Creek."

Melissa Wheeler, the lady that gave us the foal is part of that group. I think that Mrs. Parker and Mrs. Graves also are in it. Last year they all went on a trip together for two weeks. I don't know anything more than that.

"What can you tell me about Cupid Falls?" asked Libby.

"Well there is a story that goes with the falls. I will give you directions to the falls but you can't take Ella with you."

With a confused look on her face she asked "Why?"

"I want her to go with me. The story of the falls is that when a single woman goes to the falls if she tosses a silver coin into the pool of water she will see an image of the man that she is going to marry. If they haven't met, they will meet before one year goes by. If a couple go to the falls and they enter into the pool of water together they will have eternal love for each other."

"What a cute romantic story. Does it really work?"

"They say it does. I'm hoping that Ella will go into the pool with me. After chores in the morning I will take you ladies to Cupid Falls".

After they finished eating, Hank and Ella went for a walk to the corral that had Sandy's colt out by the barn. They got the colt back into the stall with Sandy. They made sure that there was enough water and hay in the stall for her. Ella made her visit with Baby and Star. Baby was starting to look better. When she arrived at the ranch she was so thin from being abandoned by her caretaker. She was starting to gain weight. In a couple more months you would never know how neglected she was.

Before they left the barn he pulled her into his arms and kissed her. "I have been waiting all night to kiss you." He kissed her again until he heard a soft moan a come from her mouth. He ran his fingers through her hair. "I love the smell of your hair. The feel of your body when it is close to mine."

She pulled his mouth to hers for one more kiss. "I love the way you kiss me. The way you make me feel safe in your arms."

"Honey I'm so glad that you have decided that you're ready to take our relationship to the next level."

CHAPTER 28

Sunday morning came with the sun shining with a warm breeze in the air. Hank was already doing the morning chores when he spotted Libby and Ella down by Sandy's stall. Libby had her camera with her taking pictures of the new foal.

Ella asked him if he wanted Baby and Star to be let out to the side corral. He told her it was okay to let them out. She grabbed a lead rope to put around Star's neck. She opened up the stall door. Then led her to the side door to let her out. She repeated the same process with Baby.

She spotted a truck with a horse trailer behind it coming toward the barn. Hank also heard the truck coming. After the truck came to a stop, Jasmine got out of the truck. Jasmine had her hair loose under a cowboy hat. She looked as beautiful as ever. Hank went to meet her. Ella watched as he embraced her in a hug. Libby stood behind her and asked, "Doesn't that bother you the way he hugs her?"

"Nope, not after I found out that Jasmine was his cousin. The first time I met her she pretty much told me that no one was going to capture Hank's heart. Let just say that she put on a good performance. No one told me that they were related. I found out from Doc when he mentioned it one day."

They watched as Jasmine got King out of the horse trailer. She led him around the back of the barn to one of the smaller buildings out back. King had lost a shoe and she wanted Hank to put a new shoe on him.

She changed the subject of their conversation back to what pictures did Libby want to take of the ranch and of the surrounding area that she had not already taken. Since she had driven around the area on just about every back road in the county, she was trying to think of some good places for her to take pictures. "Do you want pictures of the rustic homesteads of the past, or more of the up to date life on a ranch?"

"I've taken a few pictures of old barns and some of the newer ones. I have taken pictures of the cowboys working the cattle out in the pasture. I have pictures of the hills in the area. Pretty soon they will be full of color when the leaves change. It is really a beautiful place here. I can understand why you moved here."

"As you know I didn't know what I was getting myself into when I moved here. I just knew that Beth and I needed a change. It has been good for both of us. She has changed so much from the person she was. She was headed for the darker side of life and I didn't want that for her. She has grown in so many ways. I think that she is falling in love too with a special guy who is fighting falling in love with her. It has been interesting to watch."

"If that is all it takes to fall in love I would move here in a heartbeat. I'm just so happy for you and Beth."

They left the barn and walked to the house. "Who knows maybe you will find out who you are going to marry today when we go to Cupid Falls."

"The way my love life has been there probably won't even be an image for me. I think I'm doomed to be single. I'm so tired of the dating scene. With men just taking you out on a date hoping that they can get you into bed. As you know that is not our style to fall into bed with a strange man. I refuse to go to a bar anymore because of the date rape drugs that are out there that men can get their hands on. I have already been raped once and I will not let it happen again."

"Maybe you just need to find yourself a good ole country man."

"Well that is going to be hard to do since I live in a big city."

"I know that there is someone out there for you. When you least expect it, the right man will find you."

"Yeah, and I will be old and gray when that happens."

When Hank finished putting a new shoe on King, Jasmine walked him back to the horse trailer. He walked back with them and gave her another hug before he went into the house. He told Ella that he would take them to Cupid Falls after he took a quick shower. He told Ella to grab her bathing suit and he would get the towels.

They me in the kitchen a few minutes later. They walked out the back door to Hank's truck. Ella sat up front next to him and Libby sat behind them. After he got on the road he put his hand on Ella's thigh. She covered his hand with her own. Letting him know that it was okay.

He explained that Cupid Falls is hidden from the public. Not a lot of people know about the falls because of the legend. A lot of people don't believe in it and others think that a mysterious spell is put on the falls. They say that if you go out there in the spring the smell from the flowers and the greenery is very intoxicating.

The pool of water that is at the base of the falls is kept warm all year round from the hot spring that feeds into it. The water is never hot, but it isn't ever cold either. It is really hard to explain why the water is always pleasant.

He drove for a while before he turned his truck down a dirt road. He followed the dirt road for a couple of miles before he parked the truck. When they got out of the truck, he took hold of Ella's hand. He told her to follow him because the path wasn't very wide. They walked until they reached a clearing.

Ella couldn't believe her eyes. There was a waterfall that had to be the most beautiful thing that she ever saw. All of the greenery around to falls was still so bright with color. The flowers were still in bloom in many different colors. The smell was intoxicating. There were some wild flowers scattered around the clearing.

The color of the water that cascaded into the pool of water was so white. The pool of water at the base of the falls was a pretty shade of blue. Someone had made paths thru the greenery to some of the large boulders.

Hank tuned to Ella before he spoke to her,

"Please go into the pool with me."

She told him that she would. As soon as they had their clothes off he asked her if she was ready. He took her hand and led her into the pool of water. She was surprised at the temperature of the water, it was warm. He took her to the base of the falls before he took her into his arms. He lifted her out of the water as he turned her toward him. She slowly slid down the front of his body until they were face to face.

He looked into her eyes and said, "Ella I love you very much, more than you will ever know. From this day forward I will love you until I take my dying breath."

She moved her hand from his chest and cupped his face. She looked into his eyes "I love you too. I will love you until the day that I die."

He kissed her with such care and love that she knew without a doubt how he felt about her. "I can't wait for you to become my wife and life partner. All you have to do is say the word because I'm already yours. I can't wait for you to become mine."

"I know and we just have one more thing to do before you put that ring on my finger. I want you to be able to make love to me. I also want to be able to have babies with you. I know that is something that we haven't discussed yet. I want to have children at least two and I hope that you will agree to it."

"You can have as many babies as you want. I will be more than happy to do my part." He kissed her again before they got out of the water. When they reached the shore line he took her hand as they walked out of the water together. He walked to where the towels lay. He picked one up so he could wrap it around her shoulders. Then he placed a gentle kiss on her lips. He stepped away from her so that he could put some space between them. They needed to get out of their wet clothes.

Libby stood on the shoreline taking pictures of Hank and Ella in the water. It looked so romantic that she couldn't help herself. She was hoping that someday she would fall in love. Maybe today she would see an image of the man she would marry.

Hank decided that after they changed their clothes that they would leave Libby there for a few minutes that she could throw her coin into the pool. We will just be down the path a little way just enough so that you can have some privacy.

Libby stood there for a minute and was hoping that it would be so exciting if she saw an image. She turned her back to the falls and threw the coin over her head into the pool of water. She closed her eyes and slowly turned around. She opened her eyes and saw an image of a man. She could not believe her eyes. She blinked her eyes to make sure that her mind was not playing games with her. The image disappeared as soon as she blinked.

Libby walked down the path where Ella and Hank were waiting for her. As soon as they got into the truck Ella looked over her shoulder and asked Libby "Did you see an image?"

"Yes, I did see something, but I really don't think it is the person that I'm going to fall in love with. Let me rephrase that I could probably fall in love with this person but I really don't think that we would get married.

"So, you are saying that it is someone you already know.?"

"Yes, I know who the person is and that is all I'm going to say."

Later that night Hank was looking at the pictures that Libby took at Cupid Falls. "These pictures are really good. I'm going to pick out some and have you send them to my computer. This one I'm going to have enlarged so that I can hang it on the wall in my den. I'm so glad that you got some good pictures."

Ella walked into the kitchen and heard the end of the conversation. "What picture are you going to put on your wall?"

Hank pointed to the picture of him and Ella in the pool of the water with the waterfalls in the background. He had lifted Ella into the air by her waist. She was looking down at him. The next picture was of them looking into each other's eyes. When he had declared his love for her. "That is the picture." The next picture was when Ella had her hands on both sides of his face before she moved them down to wrap them around his neck as he kissed her. " I want her to send me all of the pictures that were taken I like them all. But, I really like that one."

Ella looked at the pictures that he was looking at. She couldn't believe what she was seeing. They looked like a couple having a romantic moment. The picture that he chose took her breath away.

CHAPTER 29

On Monday morning Ella, Libby and Beth decided to take a short ride on horseback. Ella had Jake saddle them some horses. He had them all ready by the time they got to the barn. He helped Beth get up into the saddle. When she looked down at him he smiled at her and patted her leg in a friendly gesture.

The three women rode side by side until they reached the far end of the pasture where Ella got down to open the gate for them to go through. They went as far as the stream. They all dismounted as the horses got a drink.

Libby was looking at the scenery when she spoke to Ella "When are you going to marry Hunky Hank and put that poor man out of his misery?"

"Is it that obvious?"

"I have been here less than a week and I can you tell that man is having to deal with some sexual tension between the two of you. The air just about crackles. "

Beth added "You should see how he looks at her when he thinks no one is looking."

"You have that man's heart and soul." Libby said.

"But."

Before she could say another word Libby said, "I don't want to hear that word come out of your mouth unless you are talking about the man's fine backside which mean his nice butt. There should be no more doubt in your mind whatsoever."

"I know that he loves me and he has been so patient with me."

Libby turned to her and said "Then start loving him back. Your heart is already there. It is your mind that is causing the trouble and needs to catch up with your heart. You need to start thinking about the positive things and let go of the negative things that are holding you back. I want you to find true happiness."

"Please tell me you will marry him before I leave for school next summer. I don't want you to have to live alone. I don't want to worry about you while I'm gone. I don't know how long I will be gone or where my schooling is going to take me." Beth said.

The three of them moved together for a group hug. Libby was the first one to speak "It is really a beautiful place here. You are right Ella, the life style out here is so different from city life. You and Beth have adjusted so well. The more I come here the more I hate going back to the city."

"You know you could always move here and stay with us."

"I could and what would I do for a job? Cedar Creek is a small country town that doesn't have any marketing jobs and I know nothing about ranching."

"You could always freelance. You could live here and travel when necessary for a job."

"Actually, I have been thinking about something similar to that. I need to do some more research when I get back to the city."

"So, when were you going to tell me about this. Does this have anything to do with all the pictures that you have been taking?"

"I not going to say any more until I get a better plan put together. Right now it is just an idea that is going thru my head right now."

The girls mounted the horses and rode back to the

ranch, talking and laughing. When they rode through the last pasture to the barn they were riding side by side. Jake saw them first, and he hollered to Hank that the girls were back. Hank saw them and said, "Have you ever seen anything more beautiful than that?" As he took another picture for his collection. He then patted Jake on the back and said, "Let's go meet them."

When the girls came to a stop and dismounted Jake and Hank were standing just beside their girls and taking the reins. Hank kissed the side of Ella's forehead and asked, "Did you have a nice ride?"

"Yes, we did."

The girls walked together toward the house. Ella looked over her shoulder and saw the two men looking that their backsides. Jake made some comment to Hank that she couldn't hear, but she heard him laugh. She hoped that he was enjoying the view.

Later that night Hank cooked their dinner outside on the grill. Just before they sat down to dine on the side patio Doc arrived. They all talked about how their day went. After dinner, the guitars came out and the music started flowing through the night air. Someone had turned on the small patio lights and started a fire in the fire pit. The night air was starting to get cooler since the sun had set. The day was coming to an end.

The next morning when Libby entered the kitchen the house was empty. Beth had gone upstairs to take a shower. The men were already out in the barn. She received a text on her phone for the address as to where she would be meeting the women of "The Widows Club." She was deep in thought about what they would want to talk to her about when Beth returned to the kitchen.

She finished her cup of coffee. She was dressed in a pair of dress slacks and a blouse. She even took the time to curl her long dark hair. She didn't know what kind of meeting this was or the place where she was meeting these women. She asked Beth if she thought she looked alright or did she think she over dressed for the meeting?

Beth told her she looked fine. She let out a loud breath of air from her lungs before she headed to the back door. She got in her rental car and headed toward town.

She arrived at the address that she was given. The house was at the end of one of the side streets off Main Street. There were a couple of cars already parked in the driveway. She parked behind the last car. She walked up the steps to the front porch. She took one more deep breath before she rang the doorbell.

Sadie Ballinger opened the door with a smile on her face. "I'm so glad you agreed to meet with us today. Please come in and I will introduce you to everyone."

She entered the house and followed Sadie to the kitchen. There were four women sitting around the table drinking coffee and eating sweet rolls. Sadie motioned for Libby to sit in a chair that was empty at the table while she took the other empty chair.

Sadie introduced Eva Baker who is Ben's mother who sat to her right. Next was Zara Graves, who owns a B&B in town. On Sadie's left sat Lilly Parker who owns The Formal Affair. Melissa Wheeler was next to Lilly. Ladies, this is Libby Adams. I think she will be able to help us out.

"We want you to help us bring our small town back to life." replied Sadie.

All the women had turned to look at Libby to see what her response would be. This is not what she had expected. With a questioning look on her face she said, "You want me to give you some ideas on how you can get more tourists to the area?"

Sadie explained to her that Cedar Creek was just a

small farm town, but it also has so much more to offer. We want you to help us be more than a small farm town that is dying. We are open to any suggestions that you might have. We are willing to pay you for your work, but we would also like it if you moved here for one year. We want you to get to know the people in this town. You will get free housing as you can stay in my guest house as you work on the projects. You work in marketing and we thought you would be able to help us.

The five of us will help you out as much as we can. We will all agree on the things that we think will work. Our identity must be kept secret as long as possible. We will refer you to the right people when the time comes to make things happen.

"Doesn't this town have a Mayor or someone in charge of what goes on in the town? We might not be able to do the things that you want to do. It might have to go in front of a town council or something."

Sadie explained that they would handle the Mayor if she agreed to help them. They sat around the table discussing some ideas. She left telling them that she wanted to think about what they were offering her. She would let Sadie know her answer in the next couple of weeks.

When Libby returned to the Rocking R Ranch everyone was in the kitchen eating lunch. She was surprised to see Ella there. "What are you doing here this time of the day?"

She explained that she went on a couple of calls with Doc this morning. He told me to go home and spend some time with you before you have to leave. She asked her how her meeting went as she was very curious as to what the meeting was about. She briefly told her what "The Widows Club" meeting was about.

Ella was so surprised and excited at the same time. "Are you going to do it? If you do we could see each again like we used to. It would be so nice to have you here. I know that you have got a lot to think about."

"Yes, I have a lot to think about. I already had a plan that I was working on before I came here to visit. I have been thinking about working for myself, starting my own company. I have a couple of loyal customers who don't want anyone else to work on their accounts. If I keep them and work for "The Widows Club" I could make a decent living."

There were so many things to think about, like what to do with her apartment in the city. She really had to think about how much her life would change if she chose to quit her job. Her mind was just overwhelmed with everything.

CHAPTER 30

Libby left to return to the city. Jake moved back to his mom's house because of school. Ella had returned to work. Beth had gone to school. The Rocking R Ranch was quiet. Ben and Hank were out cleaning the stalls in the barn. He knew that the time was coming when Ella and Beth would be moving back to her house.

He was trying to think of a way to keep them in his home. He was running out of ideas. Now that Ella was wanting to take their relationship to the next level, he knew it would be harder to not see her every day once he got her into his bed. He wanted their first time to be special. He also knew that she was going to need special care.

After school Beth got a ride with Jake to the Rocking R Ranch. He bought a used truck to drive to school. He wanted to be able to go to Hank's after school so that he could see Black Jack and take care of him. He also did some chores around the ranch.

Beth was telling him that she wanted to get her driver's license before she graduated from school. He told her that he would take a look at the old truck in the barn to see if he could get it running for her. He told her that he would let her drive his truck around the ranch so that she could practice her driving.

He dropped her off at the back door to the house. He parked his truck near the barn. He walked into the barn texting Hank to let him know that he was there. He found him in the second barn tending to one of the horses. He asked him what chores that still needed to be done. He was hoping that he would have time to take Black Jack for a short ride.

The first chance Jake got he went to see Black Jack in his corral. Black Jack walked over to the corral fence to see his friend. He talked as he petted Black Jack telling him that he would be back to take him for a ride. He fed him a treat before he left to finish his chores.

Hank told Ben to go home early that he and Jake would finish up the chores that needed to be done. Ben enjoyed spending as much time as he could with his new son. He told Hank something about Jason every day.

After supper Jake helped Beth clean up the kitchen. He talked to her about the fall festival that they were planning. It was hard to believe that the festival was only a month away. He told her that he found a band that would play for them at no charge. He also told her that he was given a name to contact to see about a square dance caller. He told her he knew who the man was and would contact him this week. They decided that they should have a meeting with Brett and Seth to see how they were coming along with their ideas.

Beth reminded Jake that this weekend they had another group coming for a trail ride. She had extra cooking to do. Sam Walker was going on the trail ride to do the cooking. She had already called Sam to see what she had to prepare for the weekend.

She knew that Jake's birthday was this weekend. She was planning on making his birthday cake on Saturday. She bought him a leather bracelet that she thought he would like. She thought about how much he had changed just since she had met him. He was still a loner at school. At the ranch, however, he was a different person. He was turning into a cowboy, a very sexy cowboy.

The long hours of working in the sun had turned his skin to a golden tan. His dark hair had natural highlights from being exposed to the sun. His chest and abs had grown in size from all the ranch work.

He even walked with more confidence.

On the ride home from school she noticed how handsome he was when he put on his sunglasses. She hated it when she couldn't see his beautiful blue eyes. She didn't know for sure, but she was pretty sure that she had fallen in love with him. As hard as she tried not to because she had plans after she graduated from school. Having a relationship was not in her future. The most that she could hope for is that they would remain friends.

She wouldn't let him know how much she cared about him. He was still keeping her at a distance which was a good thing for both of them. She still would like it if he kissed her. But, knew it would be harder for her to leave at the end of the school year.

Ella walked out to the barn with Hank. He wanted to take another look at the horse he was treating earlier. She loved the smell of the barn, horses and hay. He walked into the stall to look at the horse's front leg where he bandaged the cut. As he unwrapped the bandage he asked Ella what she was so deep in thought about as she was being quiet tonight. She told him that she was getting anxious about them making love.

He walked out of the stall. He placed his finger under her chin so that he could look straight into her eyes. He then placed his hands on her shoulders as he spoke. "You will always be in charge of us making love. I will never force myself on you. I will never touch you without your consent. I respect you and more importantly is that I love you. You will come to my bed because you want to be there."

"When do you think, we should do this?" she asked.

"When you feel the time is right Ella, not until then." He moved his hands to cup her face. He lowered his lips to meet hers to kiss her. He kissed her until a soft moan escaped her mouth. With his forehead resting against hers he looked into her eyes. He then released her so that he could finish his work.

After he finished his work in the barn. He asked her if she was ready to go back to the house. As they were walking back she said, "Pretty soon Beth and I will be moving back in my house. I feel that I have spent more time at your house than I have mine since Beth and I have arrived. I'm wondering what the people in town think of our living arrangements. "

"You know you could move in permanently if you like. We can even make it legal. Whenever you are ready."

"Hank, is that a marriage proposal?"

He stopped walking and faced her with his heart in his eyes and said "I know what you are going to say

S.L.McPherson

and you are right. You are not ready yet. But I'm hoping that after you come to my bed that I will be able to ask you properly. I won't be able to give you up after you become mine. Not for any length of time."

"We still ave many things to discuss before we even think about marriage. Planning the wedding alone will be a chore. It has to be something that we both want. But, first we have to get one of the most important part of the marriage to be good for both of us."

"I'm not worried about that. I'm sure that I can pleasure you in that area. We will let it happen naturally. I don't want us to plan it because you will only stress about it. But I will make it very special for you. I love you and I want you to want me as much as I want you."

"You know how much I want this to work . I have never felt safe with anyone before. I know that you won't let anything happen to me. I also know how much you love me. I'm hoping that we find a way to make things work."

"We will my love, we will. I have faith in us." He brushed his lips against hers in a kiss to reassure her.

They continued walking to the house holding hands.

When they entered the kitchen, it was empty. Jake had gone home. Beth had gone upstairs to her room. He asked her if she would like something to drink before she headed upstairs. Actually, I was going to ask you if you wanted to watch some tv before we went to bed tonight. He followed her into the game room. He turned on the tv. A special weather alert came across the screen stating a severe thunderstorm with damaging winds were headed their way. It was showing pictures of fields and roads being flooded where the rain had already destroyed things on the path though the previous states.

"This doesn't sound good. We might get a couple of calls tonight. If you have to go out Ella, let me know and I will take you. I don't want you trying to drive your car into water covered roads. You don't know the area like I do."

She told him that she would let him know if she got called to go out. She knew that Doc would handle all the emergencies that he could before he called her. She told him good night and headed upstairs to get some sleep just in case she got a call.

The rain started and was coming down quite hard. Ella could hear it hitting the window in her room as the wind picked up. She had been tossing and turning since she laid down. She was trying to figure out a way to get comfortable with being in the same bed as Hank without having a panic attack or just freezing up on him.

She decided she would sneak down to his room and get in his bed while he was sleeping. She would see if she could lay there without acting like a fool. He would never know that she went into his room. If she did this a few times than she knew she could do it when the time was right and he was awake.

She went downstairs and stood outside of Hank's bedroom door. *I can do this, I can do this. Please don't wake up Hank. This is stupid, no I can do this.*

Hank heard his bedroom door open. He didn't open his eyes or move. He knew it was Ella. He wanted to see what she was going to do. He was wondering if the storm had awakened her, scared her, or if she had gotten a call to go out. After she closed his door she didn't move contemplating on what she should do now that she was there in his bedroom.

She moved to the opposite side of the bed where he was lying and pulled back the covers ever so slowly as to not to wake him. She laid down on the bed as close to him as she could without out waking him. *I love the smell of this man. I hope this plan of mine works.*

She stayed in his bed about ten minutes before she got up and quietly left the room. She returned to her own bed and slept until morning. It was a start and no panic attack.

When she came downstairs for breakfast she sat next to Hank at the table. He was the first one to speak "Good morning my Love. How did you sleep last night? Did the storm wake you?"

"I slept pretty good last night and how did you sleep?"

"I slept good. Did you get any calls last night?"

"No, I did not get any calls. I did get a text from Doc asking me to open up the Clinic today. After I'm done with breakfast I will be headed to town. Does anyone need me to pick up anything?

"No, I can't think of anything."

Ben came in the back door. After he got a cup of coffee he turned to them and told them that the storm that came thru last night had done some damage to some of the businesses and homes on the south end of town. He told them that his mother had called him this morning to let him know the town was without electricity. They cancelled school today because some of the kids couldn't make because of the flooded roads and no electricity.

Ella rose from the chair next to Hank and told them that she would go tell Beth about school. Hank kissed the side of her forehead and told her he would talk to her later. As the guys walked out to the barn they decided to let the horses out into the side corral. Then they went into town to see how bad things really were. The first place they stopped was at Ben's mother house so that he could check on her.

Hank told Eva Baker that she could come and stay at the Rocking R Ranch if she wanted to. He explained that there was plenty of room and she didn't even have to lift a finger to do anything. She didn't think that would be necessary as the electric would be turned back on sometime today. She had a backup system for heat if it turns cold.

After they left Eva's house they stopped at the Animal Clinic to see Ella. The clinic didn't get much damage. The animals were all safe. There was some structural damage outside the clinic that wouldn't take much to fix.

After they left the clinic they drove around to see how much more damage had been done to Cedar Creek. They had learned that the elementary school lost part of it's roof. A couple of empty shops had broken windows on Main Street. The Dusty Spurs Saloon got quite a bit of damage. It had several windows broken out and the roof had a lot of damage. When they looked down the side street they could see where tree branches had landed across the street and knock down the electric lines. It looked like there were people working everywhere.

Hank parked his truck at the curb. They walked to the first crew that they saw working and asked where they could help. They worked several hours trying to clean up the fallen trees so that they could open up the street again. They want to be able to get the electric turned back on.

When they returned to the Rocking R Ranch they walked into the barn. They found the stalls all cleaned out. They walked down the main breezeway until they got to the tack room where Jake had walked out of the room and was headed out the side door. "Jake what are you doing here today? I didn't expect you here until later."

"Since there wasn't any school I decided to come out here and work. When I got here Beth told me that you two went to town to have a look around. She told me she would help me with the chores. We got to work and cleaned the stalls. She went back into the house to take a shower and do some cooking for the fall festival. Tomorrow I'm going to take her to Shiloh Bend to an orchard so that we can pick up some apples.

By the looks of the town I don't think we will be having school the rest of this week. So, I'll do some chores around here if you and Ben want to go into town and help out. We can work out a time when I can take Beth to Shiloh Bend."

Hank told him that would be fine if he wanted to work. Ben had gone to the other barn to check on one of the horses. Hank then went to check on one of the horses that he had been treating.

Jake grabbed Black Jack's brush on his way out the door. He was brushing down Black Jack as he talked to him. Beth had walked to Black Jacks corral. He heard her say "Did you get a chance to talk to Hank about us going to Shiloh Bend tomorrow?"

When he looked over his shoulder he saw Beth standing there looking beautiful as ever. His heart started beating faster in his chest. In a calm voice as he could he replied "Yes I talked to him about it. We will talk tomorrow morning and I will let you know when we can go."

"I'm also going to have you stop so that I can get some more baking supplies. I need more flour, butter, sugar and eggs. I'm going to need more baking pans also. If I can sell even half of the things that I will be making, it will be worth all the effort that I have put into all of this.

Since the storm has done some damage to the town, I think this festival just might be the thing that this town needs to bring everyone together. It will be a good way for families to take a break and have some fun for a few hours. Seth and Garrett are creating things for the kids to do. Seth said that he was even painting some cutouts to put up so that they could take pictures of the kids."

Jake walked to the fence and placed his hand over hers on the fence. "Of course, we will stop and get you the supplies that you need. Just tell me where you want me to take you."

"I've been talking to a bakery in Shiloh Bend. They are going to sell me the sugar and the bags of flour. There is a farm where I get my butter and eggs."

"It sounds like we are going to be busy all afternoon. I just hope that I get to sample all of this food that you are going to be making. Next weekend we will get you some pumpkins from our pumpkin patch."

CHAPTER 31

Jake decided to spend the rest of the week at the Rocking R Ranch. It has become his second home. He enjoys being there more than with his mom and brother in town. Some day he hoped he would have a ranch of his own. Until then he would work for Hank and save his money.

He drove Beth to Shiloh Bend in one of Hank's trucks. The radio was playing some country music. He had it turned down low. She was looking out the window at the landscape as they traveled down the road. He asked her where she wanted to go first.

"Let's go to the apple orchard first. Then I think we should go to the bakery. The last stop will be the Davis farm. Does that sound good to you?"

"That sounds fine to me. I'm just your driver and

helper for the day."

They arrived at the apple orchard and walked into the barn where the apples were stored that were already picked. She found some apples that she wanted. She asked if they had some good cooking apples that were a little on the tart side. The owner had just the apples that she was looking for but didn't have any picked at the time. He told them that he would show them where the trees were if they wanted to pick some.

They followed the owner out to the orchard. He showed them where the trees were. He gave them a crate to put the apples in. Beth started picking the apples and putting them in the crate. Every time she put the apples into the crate she was showing Jake her backside. He was taking a good look and didn't look away fast enough when he heard, "Jake are you looking at my butt?"

"You caught me. You have a mighty nice butt."

"Thank you Jake, but there is more to me besides my nice butt."

"Yes, there is a lot more to you. I'm just trying to say that the view is nice to look at. After all I'm a guy and I enjoy looking at beautiful girls."

"I'm going to take that as a compliment. Now throw me down some apples so that we can get this crate filled."

They filled the crate with apples and Jake carried it to the barn where they had set the other crates of apples that they were getting. The owner had asked them what they were going to do with all apples.

Beth explained that she was going to be doing a lot of baking for the fall festival at the Rocking R Ranch. They are inviting the town to come and enjoy the festival. The town had some storm damage and they were hoping it would be a good thing for the town.

The owner told them to hold on a minute. He walked into the barn and came out with a wagon with two more crates of apples on it and loaded them into the back of the truck. He told them that they were doing a good thing for their town. He sold them all of the apples for a small fee.

The next stop was the bakery. Jake found a place to park right out front. He followed Beth into the store. The bakery smelled like fresh baked bread and something sweet. He thought it smelled so good.

Beth walked up to the counter where a man stood. She told him who she was and the owner was expecting her. The man went through the doorway that led to the back of the bakery. A woman came through the doorway and said "Hi, I'm Ronnie and you must be Beth."

"Yes, it is so nice to meet you. This is my friend Jake that is with me."

"Follow me to the back of the bakery and I will show you were your order is. Let me finish putting icing on these cupcakes before my icing gets too stiff. It will just take me a minute.

Ronnie walked over to the table and picked up the icing bag. She went to work putting the icing on the cupcakes. As she was working Beth asked her some questions. She wanted to know how long she could keep pizza dough in the refrigerator before the yeast would no longer work in the dough.

 Beth told her that she had everything planned out as to when to make everything. She was planning on putting some of it in the freezer until it was ready to be baked. She asked Ronnie if she knew of a place where she could purchase a couple of large cookie sheets. Ronnie told her she had couple that she would give her. As they were talking Jake found a stool to sit down on at the end of the table. As he was listening to them talk he was thinking how he was falling more in love with Beth every time that they were together. He was thinking about her more and more all the time. He knew he was going to be hurt when school was out and she moved on with her life. He knew that she was planning on moving to a city somewhere to pursue her dream of cooking. She would never be happy staying in a farm town like Cedar Creek. He also knew he would never hold her back from going after her dream.

"Jake follow me and I will show you where her order is."

He followed Ronnie to a small room in the back. He noticed the big mixers as they walked by and the shelves on carts that had baking trays on them. He also noticed the big ovens in the back. She pointed to Beth's order. She told him that he could park out back and it would be easier for him to load up.

He went and moved the truck to the back of the store. He loaded it up while Beth paid for the order. She told Ronnie that she hoped that she would come to the festival. She told her that she would put it on her calendar.

Jake drove down the street to a gas station and asked Beth if she wanted something to drink. He was going to get something to drink and use the restroom. She told him to go ahead and when he got back that she would use the restroom.

The last stop was the Davis farm. The back of the truck was full of apples, flour and sugar. Beth was quiet on the way back to the farm. He looked over to her and asked "Is there something wrong? You are so quiet."

"No, I was just thinking. Jake would you do one

more thing for me today?"

"Sure, what would you like for me to do?"

She took a deep breath and said slowly "I want you to kiss me on the lips like you would a girlfriend."

"Why do you want me to kiss you?"

"It would be a nice ending to a nice day."

"I guess one kiss wouldn't hurt."

After picking up the eggs and butter at the Davis farm they headed back to the Rocking R Ranch. "I want to thank you for doing this for me today. It has been a very exciting day for me. I also learned that there are people that really do care about other people, even if they don't live in their own community. The generosity of the people that we saw today has really amazed me, and all they hope is that someday that we will play a good deed forward."

As he parked the truck by the back door he turned to her and said "You are the most amazing and caring person that I have ever met. I hope that you will never change."

"I'm sure that as the years go by, you will think of me differently as we grow older and wiser. I just hope that we will always be friends."

He said to her as he opened the truck door, "I

guess time will tell. It is one of those things that we will have to wait and see." *She has touched my heart in a way that is hard to explain. I will always try to be there for her, if she will let me.*

She told him where she wanted everything. She unloaded everything from inside the truck while Jake took care of the sugar and flour for her. When he was done she walked up to him and put her arms around his neck. She stood on her tip toes so that she could kiss him. "Is that how you would kiss your girlfriend?"

"No, this is how I would kiss her." He placed his lips over hers and run his tongue over the seam of her lips until she opened her mouth. He kissed her until a moan came from her mouth when he sucked on her lower lip before he ended the kiss. He had placed his hands on her sides and started to move them upward before he caught himself.

He looked down into her eyes and noticed that they had turned to a deeper blue in color. He asked her if she was ok. All she could do was nod her head up and down. No words came out of her mouth. He turned and walked out the back door and went to the barn to let Hank know that they made it back.

That was stupid, stupid, stupid to kiss her like that. What in the world was I thinking. I wasn't thinking that is what the problem was. I can't ever do that again. But, that sure was one sweet kiss. It is one that I won't forget for a while. I hope that she enjoyed it as much as I did.

He found Hank in a small corral by the second barn working with one of the horses that he was training. Hank told him that all the chores were done and if he wanted he could take Black Jack out for a ride. He told him that Black Jack needed the exercise.

He saddled up Black Jack and rode him to the stream. He dismounted and let Black Jack get a drink. He was thinking about the kiss that he had with Beth. Oh, how sweet she tasted. How was he ever going to get that out of his mind. He couldn't get mixed up with someone who was going to leave in nine months. Beth had plans to go to cooking school and he was staying here. There was no sense in making things any more complicated than they already were.

In a few days, they would be picking the pumpkins that they had planted. He would make sure that he kept his distance from Beth. He liked her too much but, he also had to think about himself. He just needed to keep their relationship friendly and nothing more. It couldn't be anything more or they would both be hurting when she left town.

He mounted Black Jack and rode back to the barn knowing what he had to do about Beth. He cared about her too much to hurt her. He would never keep her from going after her dream. His dream was here and he knew that she would never stay. They could never be more than friends.

Hank was standing at the corral fence looking at the new colts. They still needed to name the new addition that they just got. He was lost in thought when he heard his great grandfather's voice beside him. "Those kids are doing a great thing by inviting the town out here for the fall festival. The town needs this to remind them that you are all part of the town. The town may be small but the people here have big hearts."

"I'm afraid that it is going to take more than just one day of bring the town together to put the town back together.

"You are right, it is going to take more than one day. The time is getting close for you to make Ella your woman. You have chosen a good person to be your partner in life. She will make a beautiful bride."

"I love her very much. We will work things out. I have faith in us."

"Her mind is playing with her emotions. She needs to still the voice of doubt in her mind. She has nothing to fear but the fear that she has in her mind. You will need to put her mind to rest and let her trust her true feelings."

"I know that she loves me. I guess it is time to give her a little push in the right direction."

"Things will work out. I think you will be married within a year."

"I hope so. Have any suggestions as to a name for the new foal?"

"Yes, I do have a name for her. You should call her Ginger. It will suit her well."

"I like that. Ginger it is then."

He stood there by the corral for a few more minutes thanking his lucky stars that Sandy adopted Ginger. He was happy that his ranch had turned into something more than he expected when he first returned to the Rocking R Ranch. It had taken a lot of hard work and he still had a lot of hard work yet to do to make it a place that he wanted it to be.

CHAPTER 32

On Friday Beth and Jake went into town late in the afternoon. They had a meeting with Seth and Brett. She also had a few things that she wanted to do before they returned to the ranch. They took the posters for the fall festival with them to put in the grocery and the feed store.

They dropped off the flyers at the B&B that Zara Graves owned in town. They talked with Zara a few minutes and told her to make sure that she told her guests about the festival and that they hoped to see her there.

They met with Seth and Brett. They discussed the things that they were doing and the progress on everything. They saw the painted cut outs that Brett painted. One was of a black spider with a hole cut out for the face. The other cut out was of three pumpkins of different sizes with hole cut out for the faces.

She turned to Brett "These are so good! I never knew that you had this kind of talent."

"I had a lot of fun painting them. All of you get behind the pumpkin one so that I can take your picture. I will post it on my computer."

Ella had been cleaning the house when Hank walked in later that afternoon. He went in to ask her what she wanted to do about supper. When he walked into the kitchen he didn't see her or hear her. He called out her name and she didn't answer him.

He walked through the house looking into every room until he found her in his bathroom cleaning out the sink and vanity top. He noticed that she had earphones in and that is why she didn't hear him. She saw his reflection in the mirror. She also noticed how quickly his facial expression had changed when he saw her.

He walked up behind her and slid his arms around her waist. He pulled one of the earphones from her ear as he started kissing her neck. "You are so beautiful."

She leaned back against him as he kissed her. She turned around so that they were facing each other so that she could kiss him. Her arms went up around his neck as their mouths met. She knew he would smell like horses, hay and his own manly scent. She ran her finger thru his hair at the back of his head. He deepened the kiss as if he couldn't get enough of her.

He ended the kiss so that he could return to kissing her neck. He slowly raised her tee shirt so that his hands could feel her soft heated skin. He released a groan from his throat. "I want to make love to you so much."

She unbuttoned his shirt and slipped it off his shoulders. She let it fall to the floor at their feet. She grabbed the bottom of her own shirt to pull it over her head. He began kissing her neck again before moving down toward her breasts.

"I love you Ella." He pulled her bra down so that her breasts were exposed. He bent his head to capture her breast in his mouth. Her nipples were already hard. He sucked the nipple into his mouth and ran his tongue around the peak a few times before he flicked the nipple with the end of his tongue.

She was guiding his face to her other breast. A groan had come from her mouth as she pushed his face closer to her body. He repeated the same thing to her other breast before he went back to kissing her mouth again.

She was leaning into him as if she couldn't get enough of him. She grabbed his belt buckle to undo it and then reached for his zipper. He put his hand on her wrist to stop her. "Ella are you sure?"

"Yes, I'm sure."

He took her hand and moved them into his bedroom. He finished undressing her kissing her body as he went along. He asked her to lay on the bed. He watched her to make sure that she was alright. He unbuckled the belt on his jeans before he laid down next to her.

He started kissing her again. He noticed that as soon as he touched her, her body started to tense up. "Ella look at me." She moved her head so that she could look at his face. In a gentle and loving voice "I love you and I will never hurt you. If you want me to stop just say so. If it is too much for you tell me and I will stop. Do you understand what I'm saying? Tell me you understand."

"Yes, I understand."

"I'm going to make love to you. I'm going to make you mine. Tell me you want to be mine."

"I want to be yours."

He kissed her again and deepened the kiss until he

heard her breathing change. "Close your eyes Ella and just feel my touch on your body. I love you Ella. Your body is more beautiful than I ever expected."

She closed her eyes and felt him touch her breast. She felt his mouth capture her breast while his hand fondled her other breast. The heat inside her body was spreading to her core. He moved his mouth to her rib cage. He continued to kiss her while his hands fondled her breasts. He could hear her breathing speed up. He took his time as he continued down her body. He kissed around her belly button and nipped at her skin a little with his teeth.

He moved his mouth lower to kiss her just above her hairline. He heard her suck in her breath. "Breathe for me baby. You are doing really good. I love you baby." He kissed the top of her hip and started kissing down her leg. He moved further down the bed and placed his hands on her stomach. "I will be kissing every inch of your body that you will allow because I love you baby. I want to know every inch of your body. I want to know what you like and what you don't like. I want you to know and feel that you are loved."

He placed his hand over her sex and could feel how wet she was. He removed his jeans and leaned over her to kiss her mouth again. He grabbed a foil packet from his night stand drawer. "Not yet Hank I want to touch you too." She placed her hands on his chest and could feel how fast his heart was beating. She turned on her side so that they faced each other. She moved her hands across his chest until her fingers touched his hardened nipples. She placed her mouth over one of his nipples. She bit down on it with her teeth and then licked it with her tongue.

She rolled him over on to his back. She moved her hands down his abs that were now tight to her touch. She kissed his belly button like he did hers. He had his hands in her hair moving it out of her way. Her hair always felt like silk going thru his fingers. He loved touching her hair.

Her hand had moved to his hard shaft. A moan came from his mouth as soon as she touched him. She moved her fingers gently down the entire length of him. She saw the moisture coming out of the tip. She put her mouth over the end of his shaft to lick the moisture. She moved her mouth down until it covered just the head of his shaft. She sucked on it just a little before she removed it from her mouth.

He pulled her body up so that he could kiss her again. "Baby, you keep doing that and I won't be able to last more than two minutes. Your mouth is magical woman. I want to be able to please you." His hand cupped her butt as she straddled him. He could feel her wetness on his abdomen. "Let me put on the condom so that you can ride me."

She lifted her body so that she was sitting on his thighs. She watched him put the condom on his shaft. She leaned forward so that she could kiss him. "I'm all yours Ella. Tell me what to do to please you." She raised up on her knees until her sex was just above his shaft. She slowly lowered herself on him until her body took all of him. She stilled her body until her body adjusted to him. Her body was tight as she slowly started to move up and down on him. She fit him like a glove. He moved his hand to her breast to fondle them. He pinched her tight nipples a little bit. He could feel her sex getting tighter. He knew that she was about to climax. He lowered his hand to her sex and started rubbing his thumb across her sex.

"Now Hank now!" He saw her throw her head back as her climax hit her. She continued to ride him until she heard him groan with his release. She fell forward and rested her head on his chest until their breathing returned to normal. Hank kissed the top of her head. "I love you baby. Are you ok?"

"I love you too. Thank you for being so patient with me."

He wrapped his arms around her. One arm held her tight while his other hand was moving up and down her side while his fingers moved thru her silky hair. They stayed that way until he knew he had to get up. Let me go into the bathroom and get rid of this condom. When he returned to the bed he had a warm cloth in his hand. He bent over her and cleaned her sex area then kissed her again. "I need to take a shower and I want you to join me."

He took her hand and lead her to the bathroom. He turned on the water then pulled her into the shower with him. He took the bath sponge with soap on it and washed her body before he washed his own. He washed his hair and then washed her hair. When they were done he wrapped a towel around her body. He dried his body off and placed the towel on the vanity. He got another towel and started working on drying her hair. He found the hair dryer and dried her hair. He brushed out her hair until it fell like a curtain down her back and felt like silk to the touch.

He walked into the bedroom to his dresser. He got her one of his tee- shirts to wear as he handed it to her he said. "You can go upstairs and get dressed or use my bathroom. I 'll clean up in here. What would you like to do about supper? Do you want to go into town or stay here and eat? We will do whatever you feel like doing."

"Let me think about it while I get dressed." She walked out of the room and left him to clean up. He noticed that she hadn't said anything since they got up from the bed. I hope that I didn't scare her. I will see how she acts when she comes back downstairs.

She got dressed and put part of her hair up. *I can't*

believe that I acted like wanton woman. I really enjoyed making love with him. He is going to be a fantastic lover. I hope that next time we have more time to be together I know that the kids are due back any minute.

She took one last glance in the mirror to see if she looked different because she felt different. She went downstairs to see if he got everything taken care of.

When he looked at her he noticed that she looked different her skin had a slight glow to it and she carried herself different when she walked. As always, she took his breath away, her beauty was more than skin deep.

He walked over to her and placed his hand on each side of her face and asked her if she was okay. She nodded her head up and down. Ella please tell me you are okay. "I'm fine thank you for asking me."

"I love you baby and I want to make sure that you are okay with what happened between us."

"I'm fine with what happened between us."

He let out a breath that he didn't realize that he was holding waiting for her response. He looked into her eyes before he lowered his mouth and covered hers with a kiss. When the kiss ended, he bent his head down so that his forehead touched hers. "Hank, we are going to have to do it just one more time just so I know that we have this right."

He looked at her and said "Any time you want to come to my bed. I will never tell you no. I will be more than willing to make love with you."

"Do you think we can find something in the refrigerator to eat?"

"If we can't find anything good we can always go into town."

She moved out of his arms to look for something for them to eat. She found some leftovers in there to serve with a couple of hamburgers. Just as they sat down to eat Beth and Jake walked in the back door. Beth started telling them about some of the things that they had planned for the fall festival.

The four of them sat at the kitchen table talking. The guys excused themselves to do the last check on the barn. They weren't gone long and when they returned Beth had just finished making cookie dough to put in the freezer. The kitchen was all cleaned up. The girls were still talking so Hank went into the den to get some work done while Jake went into the game room to watch a little tv.

When Hank turned on his computer the pictures of him and Ella at Cupid Falls showed up on his screen. They put a smile on his face. *I love her so much. How am I going to be able to keep her in this house? I want her in my bed every night and I want to wake up to her by my side. I'm not going to be able to stand being away from her for any length of time. How am I going to survive until I can marry her?*

He was looking at some spread sheets on his computer when Ella walked in. He looked up at her then pushed away from the desk enough so that she could come and sit on his lap. As soon as she got settled on his lap he kissed her. "Are you ready to go to bed?"

"Yes, I was coming to say good night to you. I have to go into the clinic in the morning. Doc has a surgery scheduled and I will be assisting him. I'm hoping that sometime over this weekend we will be able to spend some time together."

"Right now, my weekend is clear. Maybe we can take a quick ride. I've got some place that I would like to show you."

"That sounds good. I have the rest of this weekend off. I should be back before noon."

He kissed her good night. She walked out of the den to go upstairs. He shut down his computer and turned off the light. *I don't know how I'm going to be able to sleep tonight without thinking about her.*

CHAPTER 33

Saturday afternoon Hank and Ella had a chance to go for the ride. He had saddled up Star and Brownie. They headed toward the canyon so that he could check on the wild mustangs. It had been over a month since he had been to check on them. They stopped at the top of the canyon. They dismounted and took in the view of the mustangs. The herd is getting big again. The black stallion had been busy mating with the mares. He spotted a few new colts in the herd. Hank was telling Ella, "I don't know how he does it, but by spring he will have added more mares to his herd. He may also gather a couple of stallions to help with mating to make the herd bigger. I don't know where he finds them. I try to come up here every month to check on them. This is the first time Star has seen the herd in about a year. She is watching them. I think we should leave before Star decides to join the herd again. She has a much better life now."

They mounted the horses and went back the way they came. When they reached The Rocking R Ranch property line he dismounted Brownie. She dismounted Star and stood beside her. "Is something wrong with Brownie?"

"No, there is nothing wrong with Brownie, but I can't wait any longer to kiss you. Ella, you drive me crazy. I can't get enough of you. I can't wait to make love to you again. Now that I have had you once that is all I crave."

She put her arms around his neck, turned her faced toward his so that she could kiss him. "Hank, you talk too much. Just kiss me." She could feel how much he wanted her. His arms wrapped around her and his hands were sliding down toward her butt to cup her butt cheeks to pull her closer to him.

He deepened the kiss until he was afraid he would lose control. He broke the kiss. He looked into her glazed eyes. He heard the sound of his zipper being undone and felt Ella's hand reach inside his jeans. She grabbed his manhood and started stroking him. With her other hand she unbuckled his belt and unbuttoned his jeans to make more room for her hand to work some magic on him. "Love, what are you doing?"

"I'm just going to relieve some pressure down there for you so you won't be so uncomfortable riding back to the ranch. "

"You don't have to do that."

"I'm taking care of my man. I'm also hoping that it will be enough to satisfy you until we can make love again. Sure, we could do it here in the middle of God's country but, I like privacy."

"I will keep that in my mind, my Love. Can I return the favor for you?"

"If you like you can unbutton and unzip my jeans so that you can feel how much I want you."

"You my Love can be a naughty woman and I'm glad that you are all mine."

"Just kiss me, please."

With satisfied smiles on their faces they mounted their horses and headed toward to the ranch. After a few minutes she asked him, "How well did you know my Uncle Joe?"

"I was wondering when you were going to ask questions about him. Joe bought the place next door about twenty years ago. He didn't have much to do with people. He was a loner. I never heard of him dating anyone. He worked in a factory over in Shiloh Bend for a while. Most of the time he just worked around his place. He was nice enough guy. He would ask me if I needed help around here. Sometimes he would do some odd jobs around here and I would give him some money. I just figured he could use the extra money."

"Do you know anyone named Annalise?"

"The only Annalise I know is Sadie Ballinger's daughter. Why do you ask?"

She explained to him about the letters that she found that were written to her Uncle Joe that were from someone named Annalise. She told him that Uncle Joe visited with her and her family before he went into the Army. She got the impression that they were friends because the letters were all from her.

She also told him that her father never talked about his parents or his brother. She read in one of the letters that their parents were drinkers and abusive. Uncle Joe got into an argument with his parents before he left to go into the Army.

She asked Hank about his funeral and where he was buried. He told her the funeral expenses were all paid for. "He had a grave side service when they buried him. He didn't want people to fuss over him. He died from cancer. He didn't even get any treatment because he didn't want anyone to have to take care of him. "

"Was he alone when he died?" asked Ella

"No, this last time when he got sick, he called me and I took him to the hospital. I stayed with him right up to the time he died. He told me who to contact and that is what I did."

"I'm glad that you stayed with him. Sometime you will have to take me to the cemetery so that I will know where it is. I don't understand why he stayed out here and didn't have any friends that you know of."

When they reached the barn and dismounted Jake came out of the barn to meet them. He asked if they wanted him to take care of the horses. Hank told him that he would take care of them and Jake returned to the barn.

Ella talked to Hank for a few more minutes before she kissed him one more time. She walked to the house to see if she could help Beth with anything. She found her in the kitchen making apple pies. She told her that she would take a quick shower. "I 'll be back to help you in any way that I can."

When Hank and Jake came into the house for supper it smelled like apples and cinnamon. They made a comment on how nice the house smelled. Hank asked if they could sample one of the pies. Beth told him, "There's one in the oven baking. It will be done by the time we sit down to eat supper."

They discussed about picking some of the pumpkins tomorrow. They could put them outside on the lawn until Beth needed them. They planned on picking the rest of the pumpkins a few days before the festival. Seth and Brett were coming out after school to help set up everything for the festival. The festival would be here before they knew it.

Ella called Libby to see if she made any decision about moving there and working for "The Widows Club". She told her about the storm that had destroyed part of the town. Libby asked if anyone was doing anything about rebuilding the businesses that were damaged. She told her that the owner of the Dusty Spur Saloon was having a new roof and windows put in. It also had some interior damage done so it would be a month before it would be all fixed up. The community was helping to get the new roof put on the elementary school so that they could get the school reopened. One of the churches in town told the principal that they could use their building to hold classes in until the roof was repaired.

She also told her that the empty businesses now had boards over the windows. The town was in bad shape, it was going to take some time for it to recover. There wasn't much there to start with. The town was dying a slow death.

Libby told her that she got a phone call from Sadie that morning wanting to know if she had made a decision. She told Ella that she would let Sadie know in a couple of days. Ella understood why she wouldn't want to come to a small town out in the country that had just a few stores, a beauty shop, post office, feed store and one saloon? Ella knew that Libby was going to tell Sadie no to moving here.

CHAPTER 34

The day before the festival Beth had stayed home from school to finish baking some items. It was mid-morning when she heard a knock on the back door. She went to the door and saw Sheriff Gomez standing on the porch. He asked her where Hank was. She told him that he was out in the barn working. She got her phone out and called him. She told him that the Sheriff was there.

Hank walked out of the barn toward the house. He stopped when he got on the porch to talk to Sheriff Gomez. "What can I do for Al? Let's go into the house and get something to drink."

"That's okay, I just came by to tell you that we have arrested all the people that were involved in the drug problem over at Ella's place. She can go back home now if she hasn't already."

"Who was all involved in that ordeal?"

"It seems that Dan Lawson got mixed up with some drug dealer up north of here. He was the one that planted the marijuana plants on Ella's property. He had his buddies come over to cut the stuff down and bring it to him. The dealer got mad at Dan over something and set fire to his barn.

I have an idea that they were behind the things that happened to Ella trying to scare her enough so that she would leave the property, so that they would never get caught."

"What is going to happen to Dan Lawson?"

"We have got enough charges on him that he will be spending a lot of time in jail. He is praying that his brother will find a way to get him out of this mess. The sad part of this whole mess is that Dan did it all just so that he could buy a new tractor."

"I will tell Ella that you stopped by. I hope that you have time to come by here tomorrow and enjoy the festivities that will be going on."

"I'll try and do that just to make sure everyone is having a good time."

He watched Sheriff Gomez drive down the driveway. *How in the world am I going to keep Ella and Beth in my house? I'm not going to be able to handle only seeing her a couple times a week when I'm used to seeing her every day. I want them to stay at my house.*

That night at supper Hank told Ella, Beth and Jake what the Sheriff Gomez told him. He never said a word about Ella and Beth being able to go back to her place. He was still trying to figure out how to keep them there.

After supper Brett and Seth came out to the ranch. They went over the final plans as to where everything was to be placed. They had finished picking the pumpkins that afternoon. The yard was full of pumpkins.

Beth was so excited that she couldn't sleep that night. She was up early the next morning making breakfast and baking the last of the pies. After breakfast, she planned on making the pizzas.

She heard Sam Walker come in the yard. "Where do you want me to park this wagon young lady?"

She told him where to park the wagon. Brett and Seth had arrived and starting working on putting up the cut outs that Brett made. Jake had come out of the barn to help them. Beth walked back into the house to get the pies out of the oven. She already had breakfast made.

Jake came into the house and told her that they had all the tables set up. She was to let him know when she was ready to take her baked goods out so that he could help her. She had a big pot of coffee made and some hot chocolate for the kids.

They had put bales of hay all around the area for people to sit on. They put some benches around a fire pit and started a fire. One of Brett's friends was there with a wagon filled with bales of hay ready to give people rides around the property.

A band had set up on the dance floor that someone had made. A group of Brett's friends had put a band together and played some country music. Later in the afternoon another band played so that people could square dance.

When Beth got a few minutes, she went over to talk to Sam Walker at his chuck wagon. He sold out of the chili that he made and was making another batch of corn bread. "Did you save me any chili?" she asked Sam

"Yes, pretty lady I did save you some. I put the bowl right over here. I promised you a bowl and I never break my word." He walked over to the back of the wagon to get her the chili that he had set aside for her.

"Did you get a lot of people asking about doing future outings for them?"

"Yes, I did. Did you know that there are people

from all over the surrounding areas attending this? I even talked to a couple from out of the state wanting to know where they could go to learn how to cook on an open fire like this. This little festival has turned into something that you can be proud of. I can't believe that four kids put this all together."

"I'm so glad that you did this. Maybe you will get a chance to do more group rides and cook for them. I just hope you get more business from this."

After talking to Sam, she made her way to the dance floor. She walked up to one of the band members. She asked if she could make a small announcement. When they finished playing the song she walked up to the microphone.

"I want to thank everyone for coming here today. I want to give a special thanks to Hank Robinson for allowing us to do this. I want all the kids here to take home a free pumpkin. Please enjoy your time here and thanks again."

The crowd started to dwindle down as the afternoon went by. The band was getting ready to play the last song. Jake went up to Beth and asked her to dance with him. Hank was there dancing with Ella. When the song ended people were walking off the dance floor but, Hank stood there with Ella's hand in his.

"Ella, will you make me the happiest man here today and every day?" He got down on one knee in front of her. He asked her to marry him. He took the ring out of the box while waiting for her reply.

She looked at him with tears in her eyes. She said yes. Behind her Libby said "It is about time you said yes!" Everyone that was around them clapped their hands.

He stood up and put the ring on her finger. He moved his arms around her and kissed her to let her know and everyone else that she belonged to him.

Libby walked up to them and hugged them both. She was so happy for them.

Ella asked Libby, "When did you get here? How long are you staying?"

Libby let out a chuckle then said "I got here last night. I have been here for about an hour. I came here with Sadie. She has been introducing me to people. To answer your last question, I'm going to be here for at least a year. We have a wedding to plan."

Beth and Jake stood next to each other talking about how things went that day. They couldn't believe how many people came to the festival. They still had so much to do before they could call an end to the day. Jake put his arms around Beth. He looked down into her eyes as if looking into her soul. He lowered his mouth to hers and kissed her like she was his girlfriend. Knowing he couldn't keep her.

About the Author

S.L. McPherson lives in middle Tennessee with her family close by. Her son and two daughters encourage her in everything that she does. She attended schools in New York and put her knowledge to work at a printing company where she has been employed for several years. When she is not writing or creating a new character, she enjoys traveling, reading and several hobbies.

You can contact her by email slmcpherson2018@gmail.com she would like to hear from you.

Made in the USA
Lexington, KY
27 July 2019